Special thanks to my son, LA County Sheriff Detective Clay Pritchard, my law enforcement consultant.

And all my friends and family who continue to support my literary efforts, especially my critique buddies. You know who you are.

ONE

Los Angeles–Late Evening

Ohmigod, he was coming toward her! No matter how hard she tried, Sara couldn't stop her heart from pounding. He was the most gorgeous looking man she'd ever seen. A Greek God. Tall, thick dark wavy hair, muscles ripped across a wide bronze chest. A wide smile with glistening white teeth. Eyes dark and mysterious, suggesting he knew the way to please a woman until her toes curled and she screamed for mercy. Only a few more steps across the hot white sandy beach, and he'd be in front of her, laughing, drawing her into his seductive...

The sharp ring of the telephone propelled Sara out of Greece and into her apartment in Sherman Oaks.

"Damn." She'd dozed off after a long day...four private patients, three hours at the clinic and an emergency call from the Psychological Evaluation Team...a possible teen suicide. She was exhausted when she crawled into bed, what seemed like only a few moments before. For a moment she clung to the dream. God, she must be really horny. How long had it been since she'd had a date, never mind sex?

Ring! Ring! Again, the telephone thwarted her desire to sleep. Groaning, she reached across the queen-size bed, fumbled for the phone and cleared her throat.

"This is Dr. Bradley." She tried as best she could to sound more like the professional she was than the dreamer she'd been.

"Hey, Bradley, I need you."

"Is this the infamous Detective Sergeant Joe Hatch?" Sara managed a tired smile. "What's up? You calling to tell me you're finally going to retire after threatening to this past year?"

She rolled over onto her side, looked at the clock on the nightstand; nine forty-five. She groaned and snuggled back into the warm bedding.

"I was just dreaming about a sexy Greek God. Can't this wait until morning?"

"Why is a gorgeous woman like you dreaming instead of enjoying the real thing? Sounds like you should see a shrink."

"Very funny, Joe. What's going on?"

"Sorry to spoil your romantic evening at home, Doc, but I'm at a murder scene in beautiful uptown Los Feliz. I've got a five-year old in shock who may be my only witness, so I naturally thought of you, my favorite shrink. Now get that cute little bottom of yours out of the sack and over here ASAP before I send a squad car after you."

"How do you know what my bottom looks like?" With eyes closed, she smiled.

"Guess I've been looking at too many of my kid's *Playboy* magazines. My imagination's getting out of hand. Seriously, Sara, I need you. How soon can you be here?"

"Where's 'here'?"

"Seventeen Hundred Los Feliz."

"Give me an hour."

"You've got thirty minutes. You shouldn't hit any traffic this time of night. Make it snappy." He hung up.

She fell back against the pillows and struggled to fully wake up. She couldn't help but wonder what she was in for. Not that she wasn't used to getting calls from Joe Hatch at all hours of the day and night, and not that she minded one bit. In fact, her psychological consulting job with the LAPD usually proved to be the most challenging and stimulating part of her practice. Initially she responded to his calls with a sense of resentment at their intrusion into her fairly routine daily schedule. The truth was she really loved the excitement and human drama which always enfolded following his calls.

Now fully awake, she threw back the covers, swung her legs out of bed and went into the bathroom. She splashed cool water on her face and ran the toothbrush over her teeth. The quick comb job did little to tame her shoulder-length thick blond hair. She took a pair of jeans and a sweater from the bedroom closet and pulled them on. Grabbing her large black purse off the dresser, she made her way out of the apartment and down to the garage.

Tension built. She slid onto the front seat of her white Audi and headed out of the garage toward the 101 Freeway. As her hands gripped the steering wheel, she hoped the night wouldn't end up like so many others lately, her head split apart by a crushing migraine and her stomach threatening to spew out her daily food ration.

Twenty-five minutes later, she turned into the driveway of the address. The black-topped road wound through dense hillside foliage and ended at the edge of a half-acre clearing, in the middle of which stood an imposing Tudor home. The house, nestled in the shelter of the Los Feliz/Griffith Park hills, was surrounded by, but obscured from, other homes in the exclusive neighborhood. Nearly all the front room lights were on. They flooded the circular driveway with such intense brightness she almost heard the brooding darkness of the surrounding hillside moan.

Ahead, flashing red lights atop police and emergency vehicles signaled she was at the right place.

She pulled up behind an ambulance, got out of the car and flashed her ID to the first cop. "I'm Dr. Bradley. Where I can find Sergeant Hatch?"

"I believe he's in the house, ma'am. Second floor." He handed her a pair of booties. She bent and pulled them on over her shoes.

"Thanks." She made her way through the front entrance.

After identifying herself several times along the way, she followed Joe Hatch's voice. "Tell the social worker to wait until the shrink's had a chance to talk to the kid. Make sure the booking papers are in order and then turn her over to Children's Services when Dr. Bradley's finished."

He turned to her. "Sara. Finally. Okay, Butler, get back to work." The patrolman turned and hurried down the stairs.

The middle-aged, rotund detective had a swarthy face lined by years of visiting murder scenes and seeing the results of a society plagued with violence.

"What happened here, Joe?"

He grabbed her elbow and hurried her down the hallway. She stepped over blood stains on the white carpet. Her stomach clenched.

"A neighbor came to pick up the kid for a pajama party and found her crying over her mother's body. We think the victim was attacked in the master bedroom and then crawled out here into the hallway before she died. Looks like she was beaten to death."

He shook his head. "This is a nasty one. The dead woman is Felicia Griswold, wife of Judge Julius Griswold, one of the shining stars of LA's judiciary."

Sara couldn't help but notice the cynical tone in his voice when he mentioned Judge Griswold.

"The kid's his stepdaughter, Carly Perez. We called Griswold's service, and they said he's in Santa Barbara for the weekend. We've got a call out to him. Meantime, the Department of Children and Family Services sent a social worker to take her into protective custody for the night until we're able to reach Griswold. The kid's in there with the neighbor, Helene Kessler."

"Has anyone questioned the child yet?"

Hatch shook his head. "She's in pretty bad shape. The social worker couldn't get a word out of her. We don't know what happened or what the kid saw, if anything. I'm hoping you can find out what went on here. I don't know if you can reach her tonight, but I called you to the scene so you can get a sense of her condition and advise me how to proceed with her. She may be my only witness."

"Sarg, we need you here a minute." Hatch turned his head.

Hatch turned back to Sara. "I'll get back with you in a second." He left her standing at the entrance to a bedroom.

A woman, probably the neighbor, Ms. Kessler, sat on the edge of a twin-size bed rocking a small child. The child stared at the ceiling. A wave of nausea rolled through Sara's stomach, leaving her momentarily weak. When it passed as quickly as it came, she pulled her attention off herself and walked over to the woman and child. She sat on the bed beside them.

"Ms. Kessler, my name is Sara Bradley. I'm a psychologist. Sergeant Hatch asked me to see if there's anything I can do to help Carly."

Ms. Kessler looked at Sara through teary eyes. "God only knows what this poor child's been through tonight. She finally stopped crying but hasn't said a word to anyone. I haven't let go of her since I found her."

"I'm glad she has a familiar person with her right now."

Sara knelt down in front of the child, trying to get her attention, but the girl continued staring at the ceiling, closing her eyes from time to time, apparently unwilling to surrender herself to sleep.

"Carly," she said softly. "My name is Sara. You've had a very scary time tonight, haven't you? I want to help make the scary things go away so you can feel safe again. Maybe when you're feeling better I can come and visit you."

The child remained unresponsive. Sara gently brushed her hand across the child's cheek and stood up.

Ms. Kessler's eyes filled with tears again. "Such an awful thing for a child to go through! God only knows what will become of her now. She was so attached to her mother."

Sara touched the woman's shoulder lightly. "Did anyone explain the procedures involved in cases where the police find children without parents present?"

The woman sniffed back some tears. "The social worker gave me her card. She said Carly would be taken to a temporary shelter home until the judge returned."

"That's right. She'll be safe tonight. I'll meet with her regularly to help her through this."

"Thank you, Doctor. Please tell Judge Griswold to call if he needs any help with Carly. We love her dearly."

"I will." Sara hoped to see something which would indicate Carly was coming out of shock, but she continued to stare dead-eyed at the ceiling.

After another brief touch on Carly's cheek, Sara left the room in search of Hatch. He was on the first floor.

"Well, what do you think?"

"She's definitely traumatized, totally unresponsive. She seems afraid to let herself fall asleep. I'd say we've got a long road ahead of us as far as she's concerned. I'm worried about her safety, too. If she saw the murderer, and he finds out she may be able to identify him..."

"Yeah, I know. We're keeping the fact she was here hidden. It won't be in any reports. She'll just be another poor kid who lost her mother to violence. If and when she's able to tell us anything significant, we'll deal with that at the time. I'm counting on you to find out if she's in danger." Joe paused and shook his head. "God, I'm not looking forward to talking to Griswold. He's such a prick. The heat will be on as soon as he returns from Santa Barbara. Just what I need before my retirement, a run-in with a ball-breaker judge."

Sara rolled her eyes. "Your retirement. I'll call Judge Griswold as soon as he's back and make myself available to see Carly every day for the next week at least. The sooner I build up a bond between us, the sooner she'll tell me what happened tonight."

"Good. As I told you, she may be my only witness. I need a statement from her, any kind of statement, as soon as possible. I don't know how long I can keep her involvement a secret. You know how things tend to leak out, no matter how tight a hold we put on them. Right now, she's all I've got. You can imagine the pressure Griswold's going to put on the department."

"I hear you. I'll do what I can, but I'm afraid this could take a long time. I have to go very slow with her. If she saw her mother murdered, well, you can imagine…"

He shook his head. "The ball's in your court, Doc. Thanks for coming down so fast. Sorry for messing up your romantic evening. By the way, how is your love life, anyway?"

Sara laughed. "Fat chance I have a love life with you calling all hours of the day and night."

As she turned to leave, Hatch called to her, "By the way, you going to the Koosman shindig Sunday? I'll bet our illustrious deputy district attorney would love to have a good-looking woman like you to show off to his pals."

She turned back to him and laughed. "Gosh, Joe, I can't decide if that's an insult or a compliment. Yes, I'm going to the Koosman's. See you there." She turned and waved good-bye.

Slowly, she made her way past uniformed police, forensic specialists, plain clothes detectives and walked to her car. Once she'd settled into the comfortable seat, she glanced at her watch. Midnight. She took a deep breath to release the tension built up since Hatch's summons. Poor child had enormous damage inflicted upon her innocence tonight. Sara's mind drifted forward into the future and envisioned the years of therapy, pain and loss Carly would have to experience in order to be free of the trauma. Sara took another deep breath.

Sharp pain shot through her stomach. Damn! Not again. She rested her head back against the seat, closed her eyes and hugged her stomach. After the pain subsided, the throbbing at the back of her neck began like clockwork.

Again she cursed under her breath. The nausea, the stomach pain and then the headache. The cycle was all-too-familiar. With much self-analysis, she managed to pinpoint the start of these physical symptoms to a few months before, after she spent many long hours nurturing a suicidal patient into accepting life rather than death. She'd hoped with time they'd stop, but they occurred more and more frequently and increased in strength and duration.

Her heart pounded. Something was going on of which she had no control, and not being in control triggered all her defenses.

As she sat in her car, the full-blown migraine took hold. She took a deep breath in an effort to relax before driving home. She needed a good night's sleep or a vacation. That was it. She needed a break. Maybe a trip up north to see Mom and Dad would help. Refusing to give in to the pain, she pulled herself together and sat up. She put the key in the ignition and started the engine.

Glancing out the side window to be assured of a safe path, she pulled out past the municipal vehicles, drove down the driveway and eventually onto a major street. She turned into the Friday late-night traffic and headed toward the freeway.

As she drove, she played mental checkers with her appointment book. She needed to free up a few days for a trip north. She knew her parents would be glad to see her. Since their retirement from teaching the year before, they had a lot of free time and enjoyed spending as much of it with Sara, depending on her busy schedule. Yes, she could arrange for a long weekend at the end of the month, that was, if this new case...

Her head pounded. Damn. She'd have to wait and see what happened with the case before making plans. If tonight was any indication, it might be a long time before she could get away.

The headache worsened. Finally, she pulled the car into the garage and walked quickly to her apartment. All she wanted now was the comfort of a hot cup of black tea, a couple of extra-strength Tylenol and her warm bed. Perhaps after a good night's sleep she'd find the answers to questions which nagged her recently. What was her body trying to tell her? Why did she react so violently to certain situations? Most importantly, what could she do to make them stop?

*   *   *

New York City–Late Evening

On the Campus of New York University School of Law in Greenwich Village, a small, white-haired elderly man stood behind the podium of the huge auditorium and raised his tired voice.

"In conclusion, ladies and gentlemen, I want to thank you for your presence these last few days. I'm sure there have been times during this seminar when even dedicated professionals like you had to fight off waves of boredom and tediousness while we speakers droned on. However, I have most sincerely felt your attentiveness and your commitment to the educational renewal aspects of this seminar. I am personally moved by your acknowledgement of my retirement from New York University School of Law. Your presence here allowed me the freedom to express myself as completely as possible and thus will usher me off with a sense of deep satisfaction for the many years I have spent at this hallowed place of learning."

The man stopped to wipe his brow with a handkerchief. "When I look out into this prestigious audience, I feel I have gotten my job done over the last fifty years. I am truly inspired by the level of professionalism and integrity I have heard and observed this week, and am satisfied that I leave the law profession in solid, capable hands. Thank you and good evening."

Michael Grey stood with the rest of the audience and applauded loudly for Professor Leonard Eisen. His old mentor backed away from the podium, bowed with great dignity and walked slowly off the stage, his slightly drooping shoulders belying his proud and almost-regal bearing. He was indeed a legend at NYU Law, a long standing symbol of that eminent institution, steeped in honor and tradition.

As the clapping continued, Professor Eisen returned to his audience for one final recognition. At center stage, he bowed and exited the stage for the final time. The applause subsided. Hundreds of men and women left their seats and filed out of the auditorium.

Michael took a deep breath and followed the crowd into the atrium. He recognized former classmates from his years at the University, and colleagues he knew while working in the Public Defender's office in Manhattan. Several times he nodded his head or spoke a few curt words of acknowledgement. His chest was tighter than a snare drum, and the noise was giving him a headache. He longed for the peace and quiet of his hotel room. Thank God the week was over. How he hated New York and all the memories it brought back. He only hoped he'd be able to get off campus without any more meaningless encounters with people he hadn't seen in years and didn't give a damn if he ever saw again.

No sooner had that thought entered his consciousness than he heard a familiar voice. He turned in its direction.

"Grey! Grey! Over here."

Michael recognized Ron Crestfield, Sid Bloom and Jack Kelly waving to him from about thirty feet away. He shook his head in resignation, cursed under his breath and approached his old law school housemates.

Like the rest of them, Crestfield was in his mid-thirties. Unlike the rest of them, he came from a wealthy family and breezed through law school without a care and with a grin and a gag for all occasions. "We've been waiting for you. Thought tonight would be a good time to tie one on, the four of us, for old times' sake. Probably the last time we'll all be together for a long time, what with your busy schedule sunbathing and chasing the babes out in LA. How about the Irish pub down the street?"

Michael smiled in spite of himself. "How long's it been, Crestfield? Twelve, thirteen years since our glory days at NYU? Haven't you given any thought to growing up yet?"

Crestfield slapped Michael on the arm. "Not if I can help it, my man." He shook his head, exasperated. "Same old Grey. Dull and boring as ever. You most definitely need to unwind tonight."

He grabbed Michael's arm and pulled him out the door. Bloom and Kelly followed, laughing and exchanging wisecracks.

They led Michael down West Fourth Street toward the neighborhood college hangout where they'd spent a lot of time years ago. He pulled his raincoat tighter when the cold, damp April winds whipped through the narrow streets. Maybe he could stand a few hours of relaxation and bullshit with the guys. It wouldn't hurt. Maybe the booze would help dull the ache in his head and loosen the steel bands which gripped his chest.

The pub was crowded. The room was noisy and smoky and the stereo equipment blasted some old Beatles music reminiscent of days gone by, probably in respect to the many alumnae present that night.

The quartet shuffled through the crowd to the back, and as luck would have it, they grabbed a booth being vacated by three young men and one woman dressed in jeans and denim jackets. The seasoned attorneys sat down talking among themselves and laughing at shared moments from long ago. It was difficult for Michael to hear his friends over the din of the pub. A waitress came and took their orders.

"You'll never guess who I ran into last week."

As far as Michael knew, Bloom was still with the Manhattan Public Defender's office. "Larry Harnett. Still ambulance chasing in the Village trying to get a practice going, so he tells me. Christ, remember the time we caught him and that girl fucking their brains out on Eisen's couch? I'll never forget the expression on his face when he thought Eisen had come in and found them. What was her name again? Cindy? Mindy?"

Crestfield remembered. "Lindsay, I think. Lindsay Green. I wonder what happened to her. She was a law student at St. John's at the time, wasn't she?"

"Think so." True to Kelly's Irish ancestry, he'd been the first to party at night and then run ashamedly to confession the next morning to seek absolution.

"Good old St. John's. Remember the Moot Court competition with them in our final year? God, Mike. You were incredible. I still get goose bumps on the back of my neck when I remember your closing arguments to the jury: 'Ladies and gentlemen. Your job here is not to judge this man for what he said or how he said it but rather to proclaim loud and clear without exception his Constitutional right to say it'."

The drinks came. Michael smiled slowly, reached for his scotch on the rocks and took a long drink. "I would hope you'd have something more memorable to recall from our illustrious past than that high-minded philosophical bullshit, Kelly."

"Nix on that, my friend. Whenever I think of Mike Grey, I always think of high-minded philosophical bullshit." He laughed.

The conversation turned away from Michael and continued down memory lane. Occasionally it strayed toward more serious matters, but then one of them, usually Crestfield, would recall the stated purpose of the evening aloud. At that point, it only took the retelling of one of their more outrageous escapades to get the conversation back on course.

Michael sat silently watching his companions, nursing his scotch. He listened more to his own thoughts. He'd never been comfortable in groups, felt like a loner, an outsider. Yet those guys had always been patient and understanding with him in their own unobtrusive way. They only questioned him once about home and family and after his curt response, they never intruded again. For reasons unknown to Michael, they accepted him, respected his privacy...mysterious past and brooding silences notwithstanding...and still included him in their close-knit circle of law school compadres. It was almost as if their shared love of the law was enough to bind them together, perhaps even for life. And that had meant a lot to Michael.

He took a deep breath and gulped the scotch. Eight years. Eight years since he'd left town, vowing to bury all memories of New York deep inside whatever psychological coffin his mind could create. Most of the time he was pretty confident he'd succeeded, but then there were those rare occasions when he had to go back to New York for business. During those times the pressure built up, and hidden memories reached out demanding to be acknowledged. Four or five days were all he could stand before he had to leave the city and retreat once again to the tranquil, passive life he created in Los Angeles. La La Land for some. Nirvana for him.

The next slug of scotch drained his glass. He signaled the waitress for another round. What the hell. Maybe getting plastered with those guys on his last night in New York was a fitting way of saying good-bye to the past once again. He sure as hell didn't plan on coming back in a long time. Never, if he could help it.

As soon as the second round came, Michael reached for his glass and downed it quickly.

TWO

Los Angeles–Saturday Morning

Detective Joe Hatch eyed the man seated across from him. "You always stay past seven when working at the Griswold place?"

Warren Dills sneered. "I told you. I was babysitting a sick filly. You can check that out with Doc Simons. He was at the stable earlier in the afternoon."

"Yeah, I'll be sure to do that. You see anyone else at the house that night?"

Dills was thirty-four, yet he appeared at least ten years older. There was nothing outstanding about Warren Dills. He fit the profile of the streetwise urban drug user perfectly. Except today, the stableman held the dubious distinction of being Hatch's only possible suspect in the Griswold murder. However, rather than bathing in the notoriety, Dills appeared pissed off at having to spend Saturday morning at the police station.

"What's the matter, Hatch, old age affectin' your hearin', or somethin'? I told you, I didn't see no one except that ritzy dame in the Mercedes, and that was only for a second. The headlights from that fuckin' boat she drives blinded me. I don't know what her name is, but I've seen her 'round the house before."

"You hear any noise? Screams? Banging around?"

"Just some high-brow music. Louder than usual, maybe. I don't know. Like I said, I wasn't payin' no attention to the house. I had to check on the sick filly before I left."

"Too bad for you the horse can't talk. What time did you leave the grounds?"

"A few minutes after that car pulled up, I went straight home."

"When was the last time you saw Mrs. Griswold?"

"Earlier in the afternoon, maybe one or two. Looked like she was headin' out to play tennis."

"When did you see the judge last?"

"I don't remember."

Hatch glanced at his partner, Blake, standing against the wall, and then leaned forward in his seat. He scanned the file on the table again. It was difficult to concentrate. Instead of seeing the rap sheet, Hatch imagined him and his wife standing on the bow of a crisp white cruise ship while it cut sharply through the cool blue waters of the South Pacific. The ship headed toward Tahiti. He almost felt the hot sun burning his bare shoulders, the salty sea breeze misting his face.

He sighed and shook his head to clear away the tropical fantasy. Get a grip. One thing at a time. He cleared his throat.

"You know, Dills, you've got a pretty impressive rap sheet running back twelve, fifteen years. Everything under the sun, including several convictions for assault and battery, theft, drug possession, dealing...totaling ten years' time served. Neither me nor any court would think twice before believing you added murder to your list of accomplishments, model citizen that you are."

Hatch slammed the file closed. "Come on, Dills. With this history, you expect me to believe you were playing nursemaid to a sick horse last night? Looks to me, unless you can come up with an alibi, we've got pretty good cause to book you. We've got a witness who places you at the scene, your fingerprints all over the place, and we have a damn solid motive."

Dills sat straight back against the chair, his hands folded lightly on his lap. His voice was low and quiet. The bridled tension and anger Dills seemed to keep tightly under wraps was like a bomb waiting to explode. "Yeah, what motive? You ain't no fuckin' magician, Hatch. You can't put me some place I never was. You can talk to me from now to next Christmas, conjure up any motive you damn well want, but there

ain't no fuckin' way you're goin' to pin this one on me.
I never went into that fuckin' house last night, and I
didn't do Griswold's old lady."

Hatch got up and walked around the table to
stretch his legs, his hands jammed into his pockets.
Dills was too smart to be intimidated by a lot of empty
threats. He'd been around. He knew the system. Still,
Hatch had to try.

"I see you've got a wife and kids. Too bad they
have to get involved in all this shit, 'cause it's going to
hit the fan, you know. You might want to get yourself
a lawyer."

Dills glared at him. "I don't need no lawyer."

Hatch took a deep breath and gave up. He bent
his head in the direction of the door, indicating the
interview was over. "You stay close to home. I want to
be able to find you when I need you."

Dills pushed back the chair and walked toward
the door. As he strolled out of the room, his sarcastic
tone grated on Hatch's thin skin. "I'll be waitin' for
your call, Sarg."

Hatch took a deep breath, closed the file on the
table in front of him and picked it up before he and
Blake left the room.

The halls LAPD's Hollywood Division were
crowded with police officers, both in uniforms and
street clothes. "What's your take on this asshole,
Blake?" Hatch nodded to colleagues while he and his
partner walked down the hall.

"The guy's hardcore. Knows the ropes. Don't think there was anything else you could've said that would've broken him."

"Yeah, my thoughts exactly."

Hatch's cell phone rang.

"Joe, Frank Koosman. I just got the Griswold file thrown on my desk. I didn't even have a chance to look it over before the judge called wanting to know who we've booked and when the grand jury hearing would be called. Can you believe it? Help me out. What'd you have?"

Hatch had known Deputy District Attorney Frank Koosman for over twenty years. During that time, their relationship cooled somewhat when it became more and more obvious Koosman's need to suck up to the political machine which ran Los Angeles tended to be a lot greater than Hatch's. Koosman was considering running for district attorney next year. Well, the city could do worse. This case might be the catalyst to put Koosman's face on the front page before the voters. Joe imagined the enormous pressure he must be under right now.

"I've got nothing at the moment. We, uh, we may have a witness."

"I didn't see anything in your report about a possible witness."

"When patrol answered the nine-one-one call, they were told by the woman who made the call Griswold's stepdaughter was in the house at the time of the murder."

"That's fantastic. What's the problem? Did she give you a statement?"

"She's five years old. As soon as I got there and saw the condition she was in, I called Sara Bradley to come to the scene and assess the kid. Apparently she was in shock, wasn't talking. Sara couldn't get anything from her. She'll stay on top of her and hopefully we'll get something we can work with. In the meantime, we're continuing our investigation, waiting for forensics, canvassing the neighbors. You know, the usual. I'll give Sara a call and see if she's come up with anything. Maybe the kid's in better shape now since she's back home. But last I spoke to Sara, she wasn't too hopeful about getting anything from the girl for a while. I'm not counting on it."

When they reached Hatch's office, Blake shut the door behind them. Hatch continued his conversation with Koosman.

"Otherwise, at the moment, I've got one possible suspect, Griswold's stableman, but nothing concrete ties him to the murder, except a long rap sheet and the fact he was on the property just before the body was discovered."

"And as you can imagine," Koosman added, "Griswold isn't going to let up. Aside from being the grieving husband, his ego is definitely working overtime. I'm counting on you and Bradley to build this case for me. Griswold can be a real pain in the ass, if you know what I mean."

Hatch could almost see Koosman grimace into the phone. "I sure as hell do. I've had the pleasure of running up against His Honor a few times. As far as I'm concerned, the guy's a real prick."

"My feelings exactly. I'm wasting a lot of energy mustering up appropriate sympathy for the grieving widower, but prick or no prick, the man's wife was murdered. We need to put this thing to bed fast, Joe. Keep me informed so I don't look too incompetent every time he calls."

Hatch laughed. "Sure thing. I'll let you know everything I'm doing before I do it. Hang in there."

"Always. See you tomorrow at my house."

Hatch hung up, shaking his head, cursing his bad luck at having gotten assigned this case.

"Why don't you write up the Dills' interview?" He nodded at Blake indicating the door. After Blake left, Hatch went to his desk and sat down. Suddenly, Carly Perez's tiny face flashed through his mind. Damn. What kind of God let kids suffer like that? Just getting by day after day was tough enough. He thought of his five kids, and his paternal instincts went out to her. While it might be difficult to grieve for Griswold, it sure was easy, too easy, to feel for the kid.

He pushed papers around the top of the desk. Those were the times he hated the job the most, when he actually looked forward to retirement. Retirement. Once again the warm gentle breezes of the South Pacific floated into his mind. He better check with Pam to see if she got the brochures he requested. You never knew when they might come in handy.

Suddenly, his office door swung open. Judge Julius Griswold strode toward him. Hatch stood and reached out his hand. The judge ignored the gesture.

"I've just come from Koosman's office. I understand you're in charge of the investigation of my wife's murder. Since he didn't have too many details, I decided to get the pertinent information directly from you."

"Of course, Judge. Please, have a seat." Hatch motioned toward a chair in front of his large metal desk. "My condolences for your loss, sir."

The judge stared at him with small pale gray eyes which reminded Hatch of a bird of prey's, darting around as if surveying its environment for any threats, real or imagined. Hatch wasn't the least bit intimidated by the man's expensive Italian silk suit, shirt and tie. Instead, standing on his slight frame, legs apart, chin raised and arms behind his back. The man had a definite Napoleon complex. It was difficult for Hatch to feel any sympathy for the arrogant little man.

The judge's voice was harsh. "What's happening with the case? Koosman assured me you were a man of action, that you were the best detective in the county. I hope I won't be disappointed with your performance." Griswold glared at him.

"I can assure you, Judge, we have our best investigators on this one. We're working day and night."

"I don't understand why you haven't arrested Warren Dills yet. He's the most logical suspect. The man has a questionable past. What's this about a witness?"

The man showed no sign of grief over his wife's death or concern for his traumatized stepdaughter. Hatch clenched his teeth. "Unfortunately, Judge, we don't have any hard evidence to link him to the murder. We don't have a motive. As far as a witness, apparently your stepdaughter was in the house at the time of the murder, but we have no idea what she saw, if anything. As you know, she's still in a state of shock. I've enlisted the assistance of one of our best psychologists to work with her, hoping to facilitate her recovery so she'll be able to give us some leads. I understand Dr. Bradley feels your stepdaughter's present condition could go on indefinitely. In the meantime, to protect her, we're keeping her name out of our reports and the papers as anything other than the grieving daughter."

He took a breath. "My men are following up on every possible lead, hoping to find something to break this case wide open. I know it's hard to be patient at a time like this, but–"

The judge leaned over and slammed his fist hard on the desk, his thin voice rasping. "Patient? What kind of bullshit are you trying to hand me? Clearly, Warren Dills is guilty of murdering my wife. What do you mean no motive? If you'd ever met my wife, you'd have no doubt as to the motive. Ask anyone. She was a very beautiful young woman. She was alone in the house. Dills saw an opportunity to take his vengeance on the judicial system through her."

He stood straight, his face twisted with anger. "He must have been planning this from the moment he was hired. A sad day for me and my family when I allowed myself to be talked into hiring an ex-con by that son of a bitch liberal-minded golf buddy of mine. Motive, you say? My wife's beauty was the only motive Dills needed."

Hatch rankled. So it began. The little bastard was doing his thing, throwing his weight around, stampeding his way through the system, creating havoc in his wake. It was more and more difficult to conceal his real thoughts and feelings behind a solicitous façade. He managed to square his jaw and release the tension building in his body.

"I attended the autopsy, and there were no signs of sexual penetration or semen in or on your wife. I'll forward a copy of the report as soon as I get it."

The judge's bony face turned bright red during his impassioned speech. His chest rose and fell quickly, but he seemed to settle down. "I don't mean to tell you how to do your job, Detective. Just want you to know I'm here if you need any help."

"I appreciate that, Judge."

Griswold stuck out his hand, and Hatch shook it. The judge turned and left the office.

Hatch stared at the closed door for a long while before turning back to the papers on his desk. What was it about that guy that stuck in his gut like a bull's horn? The hell with him. He could handle him. He'd hand Griswold a case so tight nothing could prevent a conviction. The question was…when?

*　　*　　*

New York City–Saturday Morning

Michael inched his way forward through the belly of the huge 747 toward business class. His head pounded from the booze and lack of sleep. The bright glare of the cabin lights narrowed the pupils of his dark eyes, giving him even more reasons to regret the excesses of the past night.

When he arrived at his assigned seat, he stuffed his travel bag and brown leather jacket in the overhead compartment and slid into the window seat. He fastened his seat belt, ran his hands through his hair and took a deep breath. He needed to psych himself for the long five-hour cross-country flight to Los Angeles. He glanced out the small window and up at the thick gray clouds which threatened the New York skyline. He took a deep breath, and his head throbbed a relentless reminder of the previous night.

He settled back into the seat. Little by little, the tensions drained from his tired body, tensions which had started to build on the flight to New York five days before.

He thought back on last night, the farewell seminar, Professor Eisen in all his hallowed glory, his buddies, the pub. He'd stopped counting after four scotches, and although he wasn't crazy about the taste of liquor, at first it seemed to mellow him out. After a while he was laughing and joking along with the others. It felt good, that renewed sense of freedom, lightheartedness, playfulness. But then, soaked by the alcohol, his mind relaxed too much, and his thick wall of defense began to crumble.

It started with some ridiculous argument with Ron Crestfield over the morality of mandatory spaying and neutering of domestic animals, for God's sake. It had finally collapsed like a brick building in a 9.3 earthquake with the mention of Diane. Diane. The self-centered art student who, after four years, decided her career was more important to her than their relationship. All at once the past rose up and hit him in the gut like a charging bull, blasting him into full awareness for the first time in years. Memories flooded in, almost drowning him, tearing his stomach apart with burning heat and rage. It was all he could do to get out of the pub and away from his friends before he became violently ill.

He'd barely gotten back to the hotel room and thrown himself down on the bed before the memories overwhelmed him like dust in a tornado. If he could just focus on one of them, maybe they would all disappear. Instead, the illusive images flew out of his mind's grasp just when he thought he had hold of one. It was the alcohol that made it so difficult to function cognitively. Suddenly, one image became clear, that of his drunken father. The comparison hit him like a ton of bricks. So that was how the old man spent most of his days, in a ghostly nightmare, out of control, powerless to gain a rational foothold on his mind. Well, fuck'm. The old bastard deserved every bit of misery he'd had.

Lying on top of the bedspread, his arm thrown across his forehead, Michael thought about his father for the first time in years. He conjured up scenes from the past like frames of film passing through his brain...the old farmhouse in upstate New York, the death of his mother when he was six, the cruel, distorted face of his old man, venting the loss of his wife on the young son who was still alive. It all came back last night, the ugly pictures of his father ranting and raving around the house then grabbing the leather horse reins. He'd flail them about until they struck Michael time and time again, leaving his arms, legs, back, even his face covered with bloody cuts and lashes.

At those times, his only reprieve came from his father's limited physical strength when. Exhausted from the amount of energy he needed to beat his son, the man would collapse unconscious on the floor. Michael recalled the shame he'd felt at school each time he explained away the bruises and the black eyes.

Michael eased as far back into the seat of the jet liner as possible. If he could just sleep for the next few hours, he'd have made it through another horrendous homecoming. Homecoming. That was a laugh. Hell coming was more like it. The last time. No more trips to New York.

Fuck New York, fuck New York, fuck New York.

The sound of the huge jet engines revving up shook Michael out of his morbid memories. The roar of the powerful engines brought him a moment of comfort. Soon the bulky liner was racing down the runway. It rose, arching upward, piercing through the dark storm clouds which blanketed the city.

Michael loosened his seat belt the moment the sign flashed, relaxed even deeper into the seat and closed his eyes. As the invincible city shrank beneath him, it seemed to lose its power over him. The droning engines further relaxed him. He was glad to be leaving New York and the memories it held. Or maybe he was just kidding himself into thinking he'd ever be rid of the memories. Maybe there wasn't a place deep enough inside the human mind to hide memories like his forever. Surely, if there was, he would have found it by now. Obviously there wasn't, not when five short days back in the city could bring it all up so easily, so painfully as though all these years of forgetting hadn't happened. Maybe he deserved to feel the pain once in a while. Maybe this was his punishment for having left in the first place, for running out on...

There was nothing he could have done to change things. So he'd left. Maybe he should've stayed. Maybe…

He shook his head in an effort to change the direction his mind was headed. "Maybe" was an infinite dark alleyway to nowhere. It served no purpose and resulted only in frustration and bitterness, and he'd had enough of that. What he needed now was to feel the warm sun on his body and soak up the comforting solitude his life in Los Angeles had become, the healing, soothing retreat from the nightmare that had once been New York.

Thoughts of the calm blue Pacific, clean white sand and cool ocean breezes settled down upon him with a tranquilizing effect. Recalling the peace and order of his life those past eight years lulled him into a dreamlike sleep and the next two hours passed quickly.

"Excuse me, sir. Would you like to see this morning's edition of the *New York Times*?"

The pleasant perky voice of the flight attendant brought him back to consciousness. She stood over him, smiling a bit too sweetly. He stared at her intensely for a short moment, blinking a few times before he recalled where he was and where he was going.

"Sure." He cleared his husky voice. "Thanks. Oh, miss. Could I have a cup of black coffee?"

She smiled politely and handed him the paper. "Of course." She turned and headed back toward the galley of the huge aircraft.

Michael rested the paper on his lap, waiting to return fully to the land of the living before attempting to look at it. After a few moments, he picked it up and browsed through it. His coffee arrived. A few sips of the hot liquid seemed to do the trick. He settled into reading the morning edition.

A small article on page four got his attention.

NINTH DISTRICT COURT JUDGE'S WIFE FOUND MURDERED

The headline glared at him. He read the article thoroughly. So, Napoleon has his name in lights again. This time it wasn't the result of one of his ego-building grandstanding courtroom decisions, the bastard's usual way of gaining notoriety. Michael wouldn't be surprised, though, if the judge wasn't lapping it up anyway.

He'd run into Judge Julius Griswold several times in court and had been disgusted by his prejudicial statements and severe sentences. While Michael empathized with the wife's pain and suffering, it was difficult to find any sympathy for Griswold.

Reading further he caught the name of the deputy district attorney who'd be handling the case. Michael had known Frank Koosman for nearly eight years, ever since coming to LA and worked together in the Public Defender's office. They'd maintained a limited social connection over the years, even after

Frank had gone into the DA's office and Michael had left to start his own law practice. He knew Frank was campaigning for the DA spot in the coming election. Maybe the Griswold case would sew it up for him.

He finished with the paper about the same time he drank the last slug of cool coffee. He tossed the paper on the empty seat beside him and turned to look out the window. Most of the dark clouds had disappeared. The airplane sped westward through gentler, more welcoming skies. He closed his eyes. Rather than keep him awake, the shot of caffeine he'd ingested seemed to have a tranquilizing effect on him. One more hour, and he'd be back in LA, back to his routine and sterile existence. Though it was filled only with work, his life was satisfying and most definitely manageable.

THREE

Los Angeles–Sunday

Sara reached for the latch which separated her from Deputy District Attorney Frank Koosman's backyard. Then she stopped. Although her meeting that morning with Carly Perez had been depressing, the sounds of happy children playing and splashing in a swimming pool on the other side of the tall wooden gate made her smile. She pushed open the gate and walked into the yard.

She looked forward to relaxing for a few hours. She'd eagerly accepted Frank Koosman's invitation, although was a bit surprised by it. She'd only met him and his wife socially a few times, mostly at Joe Hatch's home, and didn't consider herself one of his close friends. But she needed a break, so she decided to accept the invitation, particularly since Joe and Pam Hatch would be there.

The last couple days had been tough. After seeing Carly Perez at the Children's Shelter Saturday morning before she was picked up and taken home by the Judge, Sara had managed to see a few of her private practice patients. Her stomach gave her little respite from discomfort, often acting up at the most inauspicious moments. It was becoming a definite problem. Maybe it was time to see a doctor. She adjusted her sunglasses and took a deep breath.

Twenty or thirty adults milled in small groups around the black-bottom oval swimming pool. Drinks and food trays rested in their hands or on their laps. As many, if not more, children of all ages ran here and there, splashing in the pool and climbing like monkeys on the playground equipment.

Frank and Lily Koosman waved her over. "About time you got here. I'm ready for a private session with you." Lily smiled. "These kids are driving me crazy. I'm getting too old for all this commotion."

Sara laughed, pulled off her sunglasses and kissed Lily on the cheek. She was a stylishly attractive woman in her late forties, the mother of four.

"Thanks for inviting me. How'd you know I was due for a change of scenery?"

"I'm not surprised. Frank tells me the county keeps you very busy. I'm glad you were free to help us celebrate our baby's birthday."

Frank snickered. "Baby? Huh!"

"How old is the birthday girl today?"

"She's only five, but I swear there's an adult living inside her. Some of the things she comes out with..." Lily shook her head. "I suppose that's what happens when there are three college-aged siblings in the house. You look adorable, Sara. Thanks for coming."

Sara handed a brightly wrapped gift to Lily. "Give this to Ellen, will you? I hope it's appropriate. I guessed at her age."

"Why, thank you. I'll put it with the others. Make yourself at home, dear. Now, Frank, you leave this young lady alone and let her relax today. No shoptalk." She kissed him on the cheek and left them.

Frank took Sara's elbow and led her toward the buffet table. His salt and pepper hair reminded Sara of a man confident in his ability to get the job done fairly. "Anything new on the Griswold case?"

He laughed. "Shush. Don't let Lily hear you. She'll have my head. You heard the ultimatum."

Sara chuckled. "Sorry. Bad habit. Guess I'm as much a workaholic as the next."

"An awful disease, isn't it? That's one of the reasons for this get-together. I thought of the hardest working people I knew in county service, past and present, and called you all in for a day of relaxation. I thought you, in particular, would appreciate my commitment to the well-being of us tired, underpaid public servants."

"I definitely do, but I managed to schedule a quick visit with Carly this morning. I guess my mind's still on the case."

"How's she doing?"

At the buffet table, Sara filled a plate with garden salad, saffron rice, bar-b-cued chicken and fresh fruit. Frank poured her a glass of mineral water.

"She's still traumatized, unresponsive. I'm planning on seeing her every day for a while until she feels safe enough to talk to me." She took a bite of food. "I can't push her. She's got to come around at her own pace. Don't forget, we're dealing with a very young, fragile ego. With the trauma she's been through, it wouldn't take much to push her over the edge." She sipped the mineral water. "I'm really glad you and Hatch are keeping her presence at the house that night quiet. If she saw something, she's at risk. I hope you find the person who did this quickly."

She turned and leaned back against the table. Her attention was drawn to the other side of the patio. A man with thick dark hair stared at her. He stood off to the side of a small group of people, a glass in his hand. He was tall and muscular and wore beige slacks and a green and white cotton short-sleeved shirt, open at the neck.

Yes, he was definitely staring at her. Their eyes met, and her breath stopped. She frowned, surprised by the quickness and intensity of the physical reaction she felt in that brief moment. At once she was reminded of a similar feeling. This man was the attorney she'd been so attracted to in court a couple of weeks before.

She'd been there supporting a rape victim who was on the stand. After completing her testimony, the young girl thanked Sara for her help and turned to leave the courtroom when a tall, good-looking man in a dark blue suit carrying several legal folders under his arm and a briefcase in his hand, bumped into the girl.

"Excuse me." His hand reached out to offer support. She pulled away and continued out of the courtroom. He turned and walked forward to the defense attorney's table.

There was something so familiar about him Sara couldn't help but stare. She'd never met him before, so she stayed hoping something he said or did would jog her memory and explain the *déjà vu* which held her riveted.

There was some whispering and moving about between the court clerk and the court reporter. The man turned slowly and looked around the room, as if sensing being watched. In that moment, their eyes met and, for a few seconds, they faced each other. Then the judge's voice caught the man's attention, and he turned back to the matter at hand.

"Your Honor, I wish to present a Motion of Postponement in the Matter of the Los Angeles County Zoo versus Jankowsky. My client is in the hospital and unable to be present in court tomorrow as ordered. We ask for a postponement until next Monday, at which time Mr. Jankowsky will have regained his health and be in attendance."

The judge looked over the file in front of him. "I see this is the second postponement you've asked for, Counselor. Do you think we'll get to hear this case before the end of the year?"

The judge's sarcasm wasn't lost on Sara.

"My client will be ready next Monday, your Honor, and apologizes for this unforeseen delay. I assure the Court he's very anxious to settle the matter."

"I should hope so. I'll grant the postponement, but you'd better be prepared to finish this case Monday. Is that clear, Mr. Grey?"

"Absolutely. Thank you, Your Honor." Grey closed his file, gathered his papers, turned and walked through the courtroom and out the door.

Now, recalling that brief encounter, Sara was suddenly embarrassed. She turned away and walked toward the pool. Frank followed, apparently unaware of what had caused Sara's attention to wander.

"If I want to stay in the good graces of my wife, I'd better stop discussing business. Why don't you take it easy for the rest of the day? I promise I won't bother you. I trust you, Sara. You'll get through to Carly. Sit. Eat. Enjoy. I'm going to greet some guests who've just arrived. See you later." He walked away.

She slid onto an empty lounge chair at the edge of the pool and dug into her chicken and salad. Her mind fixated on trying to understand what happened when she recognized the stranger. Occasionally, other guests came over and sat in the lounge chair next to her and attempted to engage her in casual conversation. However, they must have sensed her lack of focus on their conversations, because they soon moved on. During those brief exchanges, it was difficult to concentrate on anything except the man and her strange reaction to him. Finally, she gave up trying to figure it out and put it out of her mind.

She turned her attention to the group of children playing volleyball in the pool. She put her plate down, got up, and sat on the edge of the pool. She kicked off her sandals and dangled her feet in the cool water, watching the game, cheering each player on and getting caught up in the fervor of the competition.

From the deeper end of the pool, a woman screamed.

"Kathy! Kathy! Someone please help my daughter. She's fallen in the pool. I can't swim."

Sara was on her feet. Since she was the closest to the drowning child, she dove into the pool. The moment before she hit the water, a splash sounded from the other side.

They reached the little girl at the same time. The child was several feet below the surface, struggling with panic and fear written on her face. Sara reached for one flailing arm, a man grabbed the other. Together they kicked to the surface, pulling the child up with them. Sara surrendered her to him. He drew the frightened girl into his arms, swam to the edge of the pool and lifted her out of the water and into the waiting arms of her panic-stricken mother.

"She seems okay." His voice was deep and calm. The child choked a few times and began to cry. "Just frightened." He hoisted himself out of the pool.

"Thank God! Thank you both so much." The mother took the child into the house.

Sara remained in the water.

The man shook off loose water running down his face. His deep voice broke into her trance. "You plan on staying in the pool?" He smiled.

The guests were drifting back to their interrupted conversations. The children resumed the volleyball game. The man staring at her was the one who'd so mysteriously attracted her in court. He squatted at the edge of the pool in front of her. The sun shone directly behind him, and she squinted to look at him.

His arm reached out. "Want a lift?"

Without a word, she reached for his hand. It was large and strong. In a moment, she stood next to him. He had to be several inches over six feet. Her five-six statue seemed miniscule next to him. The cool air hit her body and chills peppered her arms. She was vividly aware of his handsome face, the square chin and dark wavy hair. His eyes were deep blue, like the pool of a sheltered lagoon. Mostly it was the thin jagged scar running down his right cheek three or four inches which got her attention. Although barely visible beneath his LA tan, the brutality of it struck her. She shook herself back to the present, hugging her chest. Damn! Embarrassment heated her cheeks. Her soaked clothes clung tightly to her.

"You're cold. Why don't you come into the house? I'll see if I can find you something else to put on. A dry towel at least." He held her hand and led the way through the kitchen and into a small bathroom.

She still hadn't spoken. She followed like a child. The feeling was strange, yet familiar, and left her speechless, unwilling to break the spell. He pulled out a large towel from a cabinet and wrapped it around her shoulders. Then he grabbed another to dry himself. They moved into the kitchen.

"Thanks." She hugged the soft cotton towel closely around her body.

"How about a cup of hot coffee? Or would you prefer tea?"

He rubbed his hair until the water stopped dripping onto his face, staring at her through those amazing dark blue eyes. Silently, in a gentle, almost intimate gesture, he took the hand towel and wiped her face dry, then the edges of her hair.

They stood there, quietly looking at each other. Two women's voices coming into the kitchen disturbed the tranquility of the moment and brought Sara to her senses.

"Here they are, the heroes. Nice job, you two." Each woman gave a thumbs-up and walked through to the patio.

Sara shook her head and stepped back from him. His hand, which held the towel, was left stranded in midair.

Snap out of it! She was acting like a damned teenager. Instinctively, she straightened her back and reached her hand out to him. As she did so, the towel slipped down over her right breast, exposing its fullness beneath the clinging shirt. His eyes were quick to notice.

"I'm Sara Bradley. I work for the county as a psychological consultant from time to time."

He held her hand a moment longer than an introductory handshake required.

She pulled it easily from his grasp and wrapped the towel around her body again.

"Michael Grey. I used to work with Frank in the public defender's' office a few years ago."

"I see. Another fellow workaholic Frank seems intent on saving."

Michael tilted his head a bit and squinted. "I beg your pardon?"

She laughed, more from nervousness at being near him than from the failed humor. "Not important. I believe we've met before, unofficially, that is. Judge Edwards' courtroom a couple weeks ago."

She took a chance bringing that up. What if he didn't remember? She was probably making a fool of herself, but then she never was one to hold back. She thrived on taking risks.

Michael nodded. "Of course. I remember. You were standing next to a woman I accidentally bumped into. A friend of yours?"

"A patient."

He wrinkled his brow. "I came into the courtroom at the end of her testimony. A rape case, I gathered. I remember thinking what an excellent job she did on the stand, considering the circumstances. You did a good job with her."

His voice was mellow and soothing.

This is ridiculous. They were dripping wet, making small talk in the kitchen. This stranger seemed to have a strong hold on her senses.

"Well, I, ah, I think the party's over for me. I enjoyed swimming with you, Mr. Grey. Say good-bye to Frank and Lily for me, will you? Tell them I'll return the towel the next time I see them." Again, she reached for his hand.

He held it for a long moment. "It's Michael. I hope we met again soon."

Her stomach quivered. She let go of his hand and left the kitchen. She had to get out of there. Without extending thanks and good-byes to the Koosmans, she retrieved her sandals from the pool area, swept quickly out of the backyard and almost ran to her car. The thought of home calmed her shaking body but did little to ease the confusion in her mind. She'd never been so embarrassed in her life. Why did she act like that with him? God, she hoped she'd never see him again.

FOUR

Even at seven a.m., Michael's drive downtown to his office was slow. He always left his condo as early as possible, but in Los Angeles, traffic was a given no matter what time of day or night. That morning, instead of giving in to frustration, he sat comfortably in the driver's seat of his BMW and reflected on the surprising events of the day before.

He'd reluctantly agreed to attend the Koosmans' party. He wasn't much of a socializer, but after the long and painful week he'd spent in New York, he knew he needed an immediate jolt of LA superficiality to put the past back in the steel coffin he'd built over the years. The party proved to be the perfect drug of choice, until he dove in the pool and came face to face with Sara Bradley.

Never had he felt such an instant charge of electricity course through his body at a woman's touch. Sure, she was gorgeous and her wet clothes didn't hide the fact of her slim curvy body. Over the years, he'd met and dated plenty of beautiful women, but none of them caused his heart to pound and palms to sweat, even after a dip in the cool water of the pool. What the hell was that all about?

After Sara left, he decided to call it a day, too. He'd walked out into the sunshine, enjoying the warm sun on his wet body. Frank headed toward him, waving. He slapped Michael on the shoulder with the other hand when he was in front of him.

"Thanks for your help back there. I thought for a moment we'd be calling nine-one-one. Thank God you and Sara were quick to respond. By the way, where is our lovely heroine?"

"She decided she was too wet to stay any longer. She asked me to tell you she'll return the towel I gave her next time she sees you."

"She needn't worry about the damn towel, but that's a shrink for you, always looking out for the other person. I'll call tomorrow and thank her. Did you two get a chance to formally meet?"

Michael didn't like where this conversation headed. "Briefly."

"Too bad. She's a beauty, isn't she? Bright, successful, great personality. Hard to find that combination these days, I hear. Are you still playing hard to get or have you found the right woman and settled down?"

Michael grimaced. Why was it people always tried to fix him up with every attractive woman they knew? Why couldn't they be content to let him live his own life?

"Don't worry, Frank. When I find the right woman, you'll be the first to know. In the meantime, I've got to get home. I have a lot of work to do before the day's over. Thanks for the invitation. My regards to Lily and the birthday girl. See you in court." Michael gently slugged the older man on his arm before turning and leaving.

The traffic thickened as it usually did at the cutoff for the 110 Freeway. Maybe the universe was trying to tell him something. Maybe he should stop being so stubborn and open his eyes. Sara was definitely an interesting woman, but more telling was his intense reaction to her. He stopped himself. Enough with the obsession. He had no time or energy to date, never mind start a relationship. Relationship? Where had that thought come from?

She certainly triggered his curiosity. Who exactly was Sara Bradley, and why did she have such an effect on him? Would he ever see her again? His gut said he would.

As he unlocked the door and stepped into the office suite he shared with his friend and former law school colleague, Alan Douglas, he relaxed and looked forward to getting back on track. Work was always his salvation and right now he needed a strong dose of it.

He switched on the overhead lights, tossed his suit jacket on a nearby sofa, went to his desk and turned on the computer. Within moments, he was deeply immersed in a motion he had to present in court later that day. He barely heard the arrival of their secretary, Katie Cummings, or the greeting she gave Alan when he made his appearance soon after. Nor was he fully cognizant of the ringing phones, murmuring voices and clicking computer keys outside his office until a knock on his door broke his concentration.

"Come in." Michael's attention was fixated on the computer screen.

"Hey, pal. Welcome back. How about taking some time out for a burger and a synopsis of your week in the Big Apple?" Alan Douglas smiled at his friend.

Michael pulled off his wire-rimmed glasses, pushed back in his chair and wrinkled his forehead. "I don't think so. I have to file a motion this afternoon. Why don't you bring me something back?"

Alan closed the door behind him and slid into the chair opposite Michael, putting one foot on the desk. He tossed a wad of paper from one hand to the other, smiling. Michael couldn't help but grin. Alan had a boyishness about him which greatly contrasted Michael's more serious nature. Opposites attracted. Wasn't that the old saying? They were housemates at NYU Law School and remained friends over the years.

They'd kept in touch when Alan moved to Los Angeles after passing the New York State Bar. With the California Bar under his belt, he opened his practice. When Michael arrived in LA, Alan was the first person he looked up. Years later, when Michael left the public defender's office, they decided to share a suite together. Alan was a few years younger and married with two kids, a fact which made Michael feel much older than his thirty-eight years.

"That motion wouldn't be for the case of the Los Angeles County Zoo versus Jankowsky, would it?" Alan's whimsical smile brightened his face.

Michael grinned. "As a matter of fact, it is. The zoo continues to press its countersuit against my client. I thought the appearance we made in court before I left for New York would be our last, but it wasn't meant to be."

"Ah, yes, a very tricky slip and fall. Let me see if I can get this straight. The polar bear keeper first sued the zoo for failing to provide sufficient food for the bears, the lack of which resulted in his being mauled and bitten when he slipped on a pile of bear excrement and fractured his leg. When the case was dismissed, the county then turned around and sued the bear keeper for failing to keep the polar bear den clean and sanitary. Did I get that right?"

Michael laughed. "Right enough."

Alan shook his head. "Really, Mike, you do get your share of winners."

"What can I say? I'm merely a servant of the people, an interpreter of the law, who, it seems, no matter how educated he gets, how much money he makes and how enlightened he is, always winds up dealing with a lot of shit."

"Why, Mike, my man, that's the first glimpse of your incredibly droll sense of humor I've caught in a long time. That trip to the Fatherland must have done you some good, after all. Could it be Brother Michael abandoned his self-inflicted vow of celibacy and managed to find time for a juicy little sexual encounter between those dull and boring legal seminars?"

Michael gave him a sharp look.

"No, huh? Well, then it must have been Eisen and his semi-seductive, nocturnal get-togethers. How is the old goat, anyway?"

Michael frowned. "Actually, he's slowing down. He was barely able to get through the daily activities at the conference, much less host any evening get-togethers. I didn't get a chance to talk to our old mentor much. That was disappointing. Bullshitting with him is usually the only way I stay sane when I'm in New York."

Alan shook his head. "I don't know. Any other self-respecting, good-looking, eligible bachelor would take advantage of all the Big Apple has to offer and find himself some hot, sexy female companionship for an unencumbered one-week stand. Not you. You'd rather hang around aging lawyers who are so out of touch with the real world they still think governments are run by the people, and it's a sign of disrespect to sue your neighbor. You know, Mike, I'm concerned about you. I can't remember the last time you had a date, or are you holding out on me?"

Michael shook his head. "You know, you really are a pain in the ass. Let me assure you I happen to find my quiet monk-like existence, though Spartan by your standards, relatively satisfying, so please spare yourself any anxiety."

"Relatively satisfying sounds pretty damn boring, if you ask me."

Michael stretched his arms up over his head, becoming bored with the turn of the conversation. "I don't remember asking. Now, get the hell out of here, will you, and let a man get back to work. A California burger with the works is all I need right now, thank you very much."

Alan stood and tossed the wad of paper at his friend. "Okay, Mr. Grey. See if I care if your dick drops off from lack of use."

As Alan walked over to the door, Michael turned his attention once again to his computer. After a few moments, he looked up. Alan stood by the door, this time his smile was gone. He stood quietly, looking at Michael.

"Forget something?"

Alan hesitated a moment, looking as though weighing the pros and cons of continuing the conversation.

He took a deep breath, possibly to fortify himself. "There's something I've been meaning to talk to you about. Maybe this isn't a good time, but I'm going to say it anyway and hope you don't throw me out on my ass. This has been bothering me for a long time, and I want to get it off my chest. You do with it what you will, but I have to have my day in court, so to speak."

Michael leaned back in his chair and glanced at Alan. "Shoot."

Alan still seemed a bit unsure of his ground but continued in an apologetic tone. "I know you're going to tell me it's none of my business, and you're probably right, but we've known each other a long time. We've been through a lot together...law school...Diane...me and Nancy..."

"Alan..."

"All right. All right." He took another deep breath. "You're a good friend, Mike, and a brilliant lawyer. A hell of a lot better than me and most others I know. You always were. From the very beginning you had passion, enthusiasm. God! You were inspiring to listen to in court. Something has gone out of you since you left the public defender's' office. You've changed over the years. Very slowly, very subtly. It seems once you got your practice up and running, and we settled in here together, the fire burned out. The passion's gone."

He walked toward Michael. "You come in here, work only God knows how long and go home to an empty apartment. At least you used to have your love of the law, but I don't even see that any more. Work just seems to be somewhere for you to hide. I'm worried about you. Call it sappy, tell me to mind my own damn business, but I have to tell you, you've slipped into mediocrity. You've become almost an automaton. I'm wondering where it's all heading. You don't have to answer. I just had to get this off my chest."

He took another deep breath, seemingly relieved to have finally said it all.

Michael stared at his friend.

After a long moment of silence, Alan turned to leave the office. At the door, he turned back. "To put it in a nutshell, you've really grown into your name. Grey certainly does suit you." He left the office, closing the door behind him.

Michael gazed at the closed door for a long time, his mind blank. After a while, he pushed back his chair and swiveled it around to face the window. Instead of the panoramic vastness of Los Angeles, he saw nothing except the brutally honest picture Alan painted. His departing comment really hit home. Grey.

Suddenly, Michael saw how perfectly he'd shaped his life to match the name he'd chosen for himself after leaving the farm. Somewhere between his escape from the boondocks of upstate New York, to the streets of Manhattan, he decided what the rest of his life would be like and picked his new name as a reminder. Grey. Uncommitted, unattached, a man who moved about in shadows, always staying emotionally out of reach.

Except for Diane, his one and only attempt at a long-term relationship, he'd lived up to his standards. Hell, everyone was entitled to one mistake. She, the carefree young artist, had chosen Paris over her dark, brooding lover. His only intimate connection after Diane to any person or thing was his love of the law. Somehow his uncanny ability to discern black and white out of the pea soup called life on an objective level brought him some measure of peace and satisfaction. His emersion into work gave him the permission he needed to separate himself from people on an emotional level. He managed to justify these dualities, find some harmony in an all-too-chaotic world.

Yes. Grey suited him well. He repeated the name silently over and over again, allowing it to penetrate deep. He shuddered from a chill not generated by the temperature of the office.

For the first time, he wondered if the name fit too perfectly. Maybe Alan was right. Maybe the emptiness wasn't peace but rather boredom and resignation. Perhaps on some unconscious level he determined that was the most he could expect out of life and decided it was good enough. But was it?

Sara Bradley suddenly flashed before him. He was back at the party, drying her face, listening to her words, drawn to her like a magnet by some unknown force. Strange he'd think about her now. Was the world conspiring against his self-imposed independence? First Koosman's comments, now Alan's, then Sara's beautiful face appearing from nowhere. What the hell was going on?

At the sound of the door opening, he swiveled his chair around again, tense and ready for another assault on his persona. Alan entered, but the expression on his face showed his usual lightheartedness.

Michael relaxed. Alan walked toward the desk, pulled out a chair, sat down and handed him a wrapped burger and large Coke.

"This one's on me." He smiled as though their previous conversation never happened. "Call it a homecoming present." He unwrapped his own burger and took a big bite.

"I see your pal Koosman's in the news again." Alan chewed on his lunch. "This could be his big break. I hear the district attorney's spot will be up for grabs next year."

Michael reached for his lunch and began making headway into the huge, messy burger. "Yeah. Read about it on the plane. Any leads?

"Cops aren't saying, but, of course, Griswold's already giving them and Koosman a hard time. This case might be the one Koosman's been looking for to propel him into the limelight and get elected D.A. next year."

Michael shook his head. "I wonder if the flack he's going to get from Griswold will be worth it."

"You could be right about that. God, that man's a real bastard. Did you hear the one about the newly arrived Mexican illegal who happened to be with his lowlife cousin when he was busted for possession of a controlled substance? Unfortunately, the cousin had a long record of drug running. Instead of calling immigration and throwing the unlucky alien back across the border, Griswold held him for conspiracy and threw the book at him. Geez, that guy's bad news for any hardworking honest litigator on either side of the fence. It's amazing he's still on the bench."

"I hear he's got connections in Sacramento." Michael took a long drink of his Coke.

"Well, it's still a shame about his wife. I hear they have a kid. Now she'll grow up without a mother and only Griswold. Wonder what kind of a father he is, given his incredibly arrogant personality."

"Yeah, a real tough break for the kid."

Michael's thoughts turned ugly. Thoughts of growing up without a mother hit home. He lost his when he was five. He decided to put the brakes on that line of thinking, including everything growing up with only his father had meant.

"I'm sure Frank will come out looking good. Maybe a little bruised, but he can handle it."

Michael finished his burger. "Now, why don't you get the hell out of here and let me get back to work. I have to get to court with this motion."

Alan clicked his tongue, tossed his garbage into a nearby trash can and got up. "Ah, yes. Far be it from me to keep a man from his bears." He got up and walked to the door and turned. *"Ciao."* He left.

The door closed behind him, leaving Michael alone with his thoughts, as well as the work which had piled up in his absence. A sense of uneasiness lingered from the conversation. He looked at his watch. God damn! He didn't have time for any more mental masturbation. He had a job to do.

As he turned back to the computer and continued working, he was aware, for the first time, of the feeling of relief which fell over him when he plunged headfirst into his work. Instead of appreciating the feeling, he wanted to justify it, apologize for it. That made him angry. So what if his work was an escape? So what if he'd become a mediocre human being? He didn't have to answer to anyone for his life except himself. After all, he made his choices along the way, and he was pleased and satisfied with the way things turned out. He was content. At least...at least that was what he believed up to now. But maybe...

FIVE

Sara rang the bell of the Griswold home. A small, plump middle-aged Hispanic woman opened the door.

"Hi, I'm Sara Bradley. You must be Juana. I spoke with you earlier this morning."

The housekeeper smiled. "*Si, claro.* Come een." She opened the door wide, and Sara stepped into the light, airy foyer.

"Please. Follow me into de study. You may wait here. I will tell de judge you have come."

"Thank you, Juana."

Despite the semi-closed dark wooden shutters, the bright warm afternoon sun managed to filter through, casting luminous rays across the study. The hardwood oak floors were polished to a bright sheen. A thick Persian carpet lay in the center of the room. A heavy carved oak desk with a leather chair sat behind it. Two high-backed armchairs upholstered in soft, dark brown leather faced the desk. Bookshelves lined two walls of the room. On the wall across from the desk, a painting of a ship floundering on raging green seas brought some life into the dreary room.

The study door opened. Sara turned and Judge Julius Griswold stepped inside. He was dressed in a navy pinstriped suit, white dress shirt and gray and blue striped tie. He held a briefcase in one hand. A sudden queasiness of her stomach attested to her immediate sense of distrust. Her uneasiness instantly reminded her of Joe Hatch's recent uncomplimentary remarks about the judge. Strange, she felt the same way about the man before they were even introduced. She made a conscious effort to remain objective in her interactions with him.

He extended a hand to her as soon as he was within reach. "Hello, Dr. Bradley." The arrogant tone of his voice only added to her initial repugnant reaction.

They shook hands. "I made a point of working at home this morning so I could meet with you. However, I'm afraid I have to rush to court in a few moments. Please." He waved toward one of the armchairs. "Have a seat."

The judge seated himself in the chair across from her. "Deputy District Attorney Koosman told me how helpful you were with Carly the other night. I'm grateful for your assistance. Can't imagine what she went through." He attempted a smile, but it never reached his eyes.

"I don't know how helpful I was. Carly was totally unresponsive and your neighbor, Ms. Kessler, did a good job of comforting her. We really don't know what she saw, if anything. We just know she's in shock. I saw her briefly at the children's shelter before you brought her home. At that time her condition hadn't changed."

She moved slightly in the chair, his piercing eyes unnerving her. "However, I did get some general information about her from the social worker at the shelter. I was hoping perhaps you could fill me in on her usual daily routine and behaviors."

"Of course. I'll do whatever I can to help. What is it you'd like to know?"

His smile seemed plastic, but in an effort to grant him an excuse for his insincerity, she attributed it to the strain he must be under.

"I understand you and Mrs. Griswold were married for only three years, and you've not yet legally adopted Carly."

"That's correct. The adoption proceedings are in the works and should be completed within the next few months. Carly's normally a happy, sweet child. She and her mother were very close. She seemed to respond quite easily to her new life with me, and our relationship is growing each day. I'm very concerned about her welfare. I only hope she'll snap out of this melancholia quickly so we can get back to our normal routine, except, of course, sadly, without her mother." Again, the artificial smile.

"I'm afraid I can't be more specific as to when that might happen. She may come around at any moment or it could take months or even years. I'd like to see her every day, if possible, but certainly every other day. Should I work out a schedule with you or the person who will be doing the caretaking while you're at work?"

"For the time being, Juana will be assuming the child care responsibilities. She and Carly get along splendidly. I understand she has several nieces and nephews and seems to have a way with children. You can speak with her to arrange a schedule before you leave. Now, I'm afraid I must be heading downtown."

"Of course, Judge. May I see Carly before I leave?"

"Certainly."

The judge stood and walked toward the door. He opened it for her, once in the foyer, called for Juana. She came in a moment.

Sara thought his next words dribbled in condescension. "Juana, please take Dr. Bradley to see Carly. Also, I'd like you to make arrangements with her to visit with Carly as often as she wishes."

His pompous attitude came across as pretentious, but Sara smiled at him nonetheless.

"Thank you, Judge."

He reached out for her hand. "A pleasure meeting you, Doctor. If I can be of any further assistance, please let me know. I care deeply for Carly. She has become like my own child, and I want only the best for her. Good day."

They shook hands again. His was cool and damp. He turned and in a moment the front door closed.

"Come dees way, Dr. Bradley. Carly ees in her room."

She followed Juana up the winding stairs. Chills rushed over her when she recalled the deep dark bloodstain which previously marred the carpet in the hallway. Juana stopped in front of an open doorway and motioned for her to go in.

"Thank you."

The housekeeper left them alone.

The room was large and bright, with gentle pastel wall coverings and a Little Mermaid bedspread. Toys were neatly set on shelves and on the white carpet everywhere about the room. They sat silently, as if patiently waiting to be taken from their dormant places and brought to life through the vivid imagination of a child.

But no child played there that day.

Carly sat on top of the comforter, her back against the headboard, a doll lying absently in her lap. Her small fingers randomly stroked the doll. Her eyes were vacant, as if not really seeing what she looked at.

Sara's stomach flipped and nausea took hold. Soon the headache began. She pushed it from her mind and walked slowly toward Carly.

"Hi, Carly, it's Sara. I'm glad to see you again."

She sat down on the edge of the bed, careful not to move too close, to intrude too soon into the protective space the child had built up around her.

"I see you have a lot of toys. So many stuffed animals...books...and dolls. This doll is very pretty. Does she have a name?"

The child hugged her doll to her small chest.

"Another time, perhaps we could play a game, and I can try to guess her name. Would you like that?"

Silence.

"Her hair is beautiful and long, just like yours."

At last the child responded. "This baby is much prettier than me. I'm ugly."

"That must make you feel sad."

"No. Just bad. I'm bad and ugly."

Sara's heart went out to the child from the pain in her voice and in her dark brown eyes.

"Sometimes when bad things happen we think it's because we're bad, like when we have a bad dream or a nightmare. That doesn't mean we're bad."

Carly shook her small head slowly and her long dark hair swayed back and forth. "Everything is bad. My mommy is gone, and she isn't coming home." She rocked back and forth with her eyes closed. She lay down on the bed, curled up on her side and soon fell asleep, the doll clutched tightly in her arms.

Sara watched her for a moment. She pushed a lock of hair off the child's forehead and left the room, closing the door behind her. As she made her way down the stairs, Juana came into the foyer, a dish towel over her shoulder.

"Has Carly always been this quiet?"

Juana looked at her with sad eyes. "Oh, no, Doctor, just since Mrs. Griswold died. The little one ees very sad now. And frightened. I think she ees very frightened. Can you help her? She used to be such a happy, playful child. It ees so sad to see her this way." The woman's eyes filled with tears.

"I know, Juana. I'll come around every day and spend some time with her. Perhaps after she has built up some trust she'll be able to talk about that awful night. Talking will help free her from the horrors of it."

She patted the older woman's shoulder. "In the meantime, I'm glad she has you to love her. That's all anyone can do for her now. I'll come by tomorrow around ten."

Juana led her to the door. She stood on the porch and glanced up into the bright spring sky. The warmth of the sun's rays failed to dispel the chill which invaded her the moment she entered the house. Particularly, when she'd entered Carly's room. She folded her arms around her waist to warm up, vaguely aware of the nausea.

Standing there in the sun, she was lost in random thoughts for a while until she remembered her mid-afternoon appointment at the Criminal Court building. That realization propelled her to action. If she didn't hurry, she'd be late. She went to her car and headed southeast toward downtown.

SIX

"Joe! Joe Hatch."

The insistent call brought Hatch out of his reverie and back to the present. He strolled through the wardroom of the LAPD Hollywood Division, the room humming with activity. He breathed in the scene while he strolled toward his office. A microcosm of Angelinos filled the large rectangular room almost to capacity. Male and female police officers, local citizens and suspected lawbreakers were all engaged in the fine art of information exchange. They spoke to each other in different languages. Police reports were filled out on computers. Occasionally a four-letter word sounded above the din when someone's impatience with the system got the better of him. A few individuals planned ahead and brought lunch. Greasy burgers, garlic, jalapenos and other assorted local flavors floated through the large airless room, intoxicating the nostrils of the less far-sighted with the scents of many different ethnic delicacies. A sense of community hit him, and he realized how much at home he was there.

"Hatch." There it was again. Frank Koosman waved across the room. Hatch walked toward the deputy district attorney.

"Frank? What the hell're you doing here? Don't they keep you busy enough in your end of town?"

The two men shook hands. "Actually, I have a meeting here with the chief. Thought I'd see if you've come up with anything new on our favorite case."

Hatch walked out of the squad room and down the hallway, Koosman following at his heels. When they were inside his small, messy office, Hatch shut the door behind them. "I see our friend has recently filed a police report regarding some stolen jewelry. Did you know about that?"

"As a matter of fact, I got a call from Griswold just this morning. He finally got the chance to take an inventory at the house. He's discovered some jewelry missing, about twenty thousand dollars' worth, I think it was. Correct me if I'm wrong. A couple of rings and a necklace."

Hatch sat down on the edge of his desk facing Koosman. "That's about right. Makes our job easier. At least now we may have a motive to work with."

"What's the latest on Dills?" Koosman sat in the chair Hatch indicated while the detective walked around his desk and sat down heavily in the chair behind it.

"He's got a history of armed robbery, a great need for extra cash, what with the drug habit he's supporting. However, when I ran him through our narco boys, they told me he's been off the streets for a while. But you know how it is with mainliners, the smallest stressor, and they're back on the juice. I still need some hard evidence to link him. So far nothing's turned up."

"Is there any possibility of getting a search warrant for his place?"

"I suppose we could find a cooperative judge, what with all the pressure Griswold's putting on this. I'll get on it ASAP."

"What's the latest from Bradley? Any news from the kid?"

"Nothing yet. Sara's concerned about pushing her too hard, so I guess we can't count on anything from her. I'll be honest, Frank. I don't have a good feeling about this. Two weeks now and we're no closer to making an arrest than we were when the call came in."

His phone rang. "Hatch here."

Hatch continued to eye Koosman while he spoke into the phone. "What do you have? I don't make a habit of drinking during working hours."

He paused a moment. "Okay. I'll meet you." He hung up.

"Well, Frank, I think the break we've been waiting for is about to happen. That was Dills. Says he's got some info for me. Want to tag along?"

"I better not. Just call me when you get back." He walked toward the door, then turned to face Hatch. "You know, Joe, I've been thinking about retirement more and more lately. I'm getting sick and tired of all this shit."

Hatch smiled. "That'll be the day. You and I are lifers, and you know it. No fishing, sunbathing or girlie chasing for us. Too boring. Just scumbags, deviants and crazies from now until we croak. Besides, what would the good people of Los Angeles do without us?"

Koosman nodded. "I'm sold. I'll be sure to have you write my campaign speech next year. With a job description like that, I bet I'll get the sympathy vote, if nothing else." He left the office with a wave of his arm.

Hatch looked after Koosman for a moment before grabbing his jacket, adjusting the weapon nestling in his shoulder holster and calling out to his partner, Blake. "Hey, kid, leave that gorgeous young police officer alone. We've got a date waiting for us at the Paradise Club."

How he hated training rookies. He much preferred being on his own. Unfortunately, that's what happened when you had seniority and knew your stuff. Some vulture was always picking your brain. Well, they could pick away. Pretty soon there'd be nothing left, and he could go off to that island paradise which continued to invade his dreams at night. That would serve them right, the bastards

* * *

Very little mid-afternoon sunlight filtered through the greasy windows of the small, dirty bar. Hatch had trouble adjusting coming in from the bright daylight. A few of the patrons might have been regulars, with washed out complexions and shabby clothes. Some sat at tables; two were seated at the bar.

Hatch and Blake approached the dark wooden bar. Silently, they sat down next to Warren Dills, one on each side of him. Dills looked hard at Blake and then at Hatch.

"I didn't tell you to bring an audience."

"This is my partner, Detective Blake. Anything you have to say to me, you can say to him."

Dills grabbed his beer and brought it to his mouth. "I don't think so." He took a long drink.

Hatch stared at Dills, then spoke to his partner. "Detective Blake, why don't you meander over to the jukebox and see if they have any Charlie Daniels' tunes. I could sure use some good old hillbilly music about now."

Blake rolled his eyes and ambled over to the jukebox, pretending to browse through the menu.

"Are you happy now? So, what do you have that's so important you had to drag me away from the station on this lovely afternoon?"

Dills seemed more agitated than when Hatch first questioned him. His gnarly hands moved nervously around his beer mug. The muscles in his cheeks flexed when he tightened his jaw, relaxed it and tightened it again. Despite the moderate temperature in the room, Dills sweated at the hairline. His voice, although hard and angry, betrayed a hint of the anxiety he appeared to be experiencing.

Hatch waited.

Dills took another long slug of his beer. "What kind of a deal do you think the guy who did the Griswold woman will get?"

"He'll get the book thrown at him. You can count on it. I hear Judge Griswold doesn't think too kindly of macho types that get their kicks beating defenseless women to death, particularly when we're talking about his wife."

Dills stared down into his mug. "What kind of time are we looking at?"

"You've been around. You know the way the game is played. There's Murder One and Murder Two. We're looking at anything from twenty to life. You finished playing twenty questions or you got something for me?"

Dills drank again. His hands continuously turned the mug while he stared down into his beer. "It's gettin' harder and harder to make ends meet out here, you know. The wife's naggin' at me all the time, the kids want this and that, doctor bills. Anyway, it was only a matter of time before you put two and two together, big dick that you are. Only a matter of time."

"Cut the bullshit. I've still got a long day ahead of me. Shit or get off the pot. I see my partner's getting antsy over there. Mustn't be any Charlie Daniels in the box."

Dills stared ahead. In a low, barely audible voice he said, "I did the Griswold dame. I went after the jewelry, she caught me. I beat the shit out of her. I didn't mean to kill her. I, ah, kinda liked her. She was decent, treated me with respect, you know, not like some other broads in her position might have. She would've nailed me, though, so I had no choice." His voice cracked a little, and he took another long drink.

Hatch stared at him for a long moment, allowing the shock to settle in. When was the last time it had been this easy? "You ready to put that in writing?"

Slowly, Dills nodded.

"Blake, come on over here. Looks like we got ourselves a real live mother fucker. Get up and spread 'em." Hatch proceeded to do the customary pat down while Blake Mirandized the prisoner.

"I'd say that little episode will wind up costing you money instead of eliminating those bills. I guess you'll be needing a lawyer. Cuff him, Blake."

Hatch's actions got little attention from the other bar patrons. That sort of thing must happen regularly around there.

They walked out into the sunlight to the waiting car. Hatch slowly shook his head as, once again, he was overwhelmed by the incredible mess the world was in, at least LA, his world.

SEVEN

"I can't believe you said that, Dana. I am *not* a wuss."

Sara positioned her feet apart and her arms held high over her shoulder with the bat gripped tightly in her hands, waiting for the ball. When it reached the plate, she swung with all her might, and the softball went sailing into center field.

"Good shot. Let me rephrase the statement. Since when have you become such an emotional beanbag? There. Is that better?" Her best friend, Dana Ingraham, crouched behind the plate to catch any ball Sara missed.

Keeping an eye on the pitcher and the ball, Sara shook her head, rolled her eyes and smiled. "Well, when you put it that way…"

She swung and hit the next ball to right field. Normally she loved batting practice with her teammates on the local Boys and Girls softball team, but today Dana was giving her a hard time after Sara told her about the events at the pool party.

"Seriously, we've known each other since freshman year at UCLA, and not once have I seen you so confused over your reaction to a man. You've always been Miss Cool, in control of your emotions; always the one to end the relationship. Actually, I've almost felt sorry for some of the guys you've dated."

"Damn, Dana, I'm not *that* much of a bitch." This time Sara missed the fastball which landed solidly in Dana's glove.

"Did I say you were a bitch? No, you just like to string the guys along, play it cool, calm, never let your hair down, never get too close."

"So maybe you can understand why my lightning reaction to Michael Grey has me so flummoxed." Sara swung and missed. "Damn! I can't concentrate. Sorry I even told you about him." When she missed the next ball, she held up her hand and traded Dana the bat for the glove.

Dana smashed the next ball to the shortstop who tossed the ball back to the pitcher for another round.

"All right. We'll continue this later. We both need to practice. If our team doesn't beat Sammy's Sluggers on Saturday, we'll be sent to Little League!" Dana hit a slow curveball over the fence in right field.

"That's more like it!" Sara said.

Fifteen minutes later, she and Dana sat on the bench and watched their other teammates take turns at the plate.

"So what's up with this guy Grey?"

Sara took a long slug of cold water from a plastic bottle. "Damned if I can figure it out. It was the second time I've seen him, and both times I had this strange but familiar feeling I'd known him in a past life. Each time my body reacted like a love-sick teenager. Crazy, huh?"

"Maybe. Maybe not. I've read about things like that happening all the time. In fact, one of my colleagues at the paper did an expose on groups that tout reincarnation, channeling and other alternative theories to life and death."

Sara snickered. "Just because one investigative reporter digs up dirt on this type of phenomenon doesn't mean it's true."

Dana drank from her water bottle. "I know. I know. I'm just saying..."

"Anyway, forget about me. Tell me what's happening with Greg. Still giving you a hard time?"

The look on Dana's face caused Sara to wrinkle her eyebrows.

"I'll tell you, Sara, he's starting to piss me off. Ever since I broke up with him, he calls at all hours day and night, sends me flowers at home and at the paper, leaves pleading messages on my phone to take him back. The guy's driving me nuts."

Sara gave her a worried look. "Really, Dana, you should call the police and make a stalking report. I know they won't do very much at this point, but at least you'll be on record. If Greg continues, or his behavior escalates, you might be able to get a TRO on him."

"What good's a temporary restraining order going to do? You know as well as I do they don't stop anyone from getting to someone if they've a mind to. No, I'll just keep ignoring him and hope he'll go away." She sighed.

They watched softball practice in silence for a while.

"So, what new and interesting story are you working on now?" Sara asked.

Dana smiled. "Thought you'd never ask. I've been visiting underground nightclubs for a couple of weeks. It's amazing how many there are in the LA area. They run the gamut on themes and activities. Some are pretty harmless, just the usual triple play...dancing, drinking and drugging. I've found a couple which sent the hair on my arms skyward when I entered."

"How so?"

"As an investigative reporter, I've come across a lot of weird and kinky things, but there's one club in particular which I'm going to focus on, it's so icky."

Sara laughed. "Icky. Is that a new professional term used by twenty-first century reporters?"

"Well, it's the most accurate way I can describe this place."

"Pray explain."

"Okay. First and foremost, all the patrons or guests are in costume. Immediately begs the question who are these people, and why do they need to be anonymous?"

"Ah. I can see right away why your investigative juices started flowing."

"You betcha. The costumes themselves were unorthodox, very colorful, very expensive and detailed."

"Such as?"

"I saw a medieval knight dressed in white tights and tails with a metal helmet covering his entire face except for small slits for the eyes, nose and mouth; a dragon with a green scaly coat and a long six-foot tail he slung over his arm; Jack-the-Ripper guy with a mask a Hollywood special effects movie makeup artist might envy; a six-foot man dressed as Little Bo Peep tugging a live sheep behind him. And the *piece de resistance*, someone dressed like a Catholic Pope, trailing a five-foot wooden cross behind him."

Sara raised her eyebrows. "I see what you mean. What was going on, the triple play?"

"More like a double play. Drinking and drugs. No dancing. The patrons milled around the room, sat at the bar and at tables and appeared to be engaged in furtive conversations with one another. There was music playing, but not dance music. Baroque organ music, low and thunderous. I tell you, Sara, the place gave me the creeps."

"How'd you get the lead? Did you go in costume? Were they all men?"

Dana laughed. "I got an anonymous tip about it and yeah, I wore a costume. Believe me, I was totally underdressed compared to the others. As far as their sex, honestly, it was hard to tell. I think there were a few women hiding inside some of the smaller costumes."

"So now what?"

"I intend to go back a few more times. Hopefully I'll get someone willing to give me an interview. Next time I plan on wearing something a bit more appropriate like, maybe, a dominatrix."

Sara glanced at her friend's small pixie face and short curly dark hair and laughed. "You, a dominatrix? You have to tell me the next time you go. This I've got to see."

They spent the next hour hanging out at the softball field. Occasionally, Sara glanced over at Dana. Although she was all smiles and friendly conversation, Sara sensed an underlying tension. They left, waving good-bye to their teammates and strolled toward their cars.

"I'm worried about you. I don't like this business with Greg. You sure you don't want to file a report with the police? I have a contact at the LAPD. I know he'd do what he could to help you."

"No, I'm fine. Greg might be a jerk and a two-timer, but he doesn't have a vicious bone in his body. He's too much of a weakling."

They arrived at their cars. "I hope you're right, but please, let me know if I can do anything to help. I don't want anything to happen to you. Whose shoulder would I cry on when my crazies rear their ugly heads?"

Dana smiled and gave Sara a hug. "Don't worry about me." She squinted at Sara. "I think what you need is a long night of hot sexy passion with some gorgeous hunk. Why don't you call this guy Michael Grey and see what he has to offer?"

Sara laughed. "You're awful. Never mind my sex life. You watch out for yours." She kissed Dana on the cheek. "Take care. See you at the Boys and Girls game. Love ya." She got in her car and waved at Dana when she drove away.

It was true she'd been thinking about Michael since the party. His face would pop up at the most unexpected times and along with it a rehash of the emotions that confused her. It wasn't a future with him which triggered her imagination but the past, for some unknown reason. She shook her head. Enough. She had more important things to consider than a man in her life right now.

At that moment, Carly Perez's tiny face flashed by. What was going on with her? What had she seen at her home the night her mother died? When would she open up and invite Sara into her world?

EIGHT

Hatch, Blake and two uniformed officers stood on the porch of a small, dilapidated house on Normandy Avenue. Hatch rang the bell and knocked. After a few moments, a young woman opened the door, dressed in shabby jeans and an old white sweatshirt. A young boy, perhaps three or four years old, stood next to her, his thumb in his mouth, holding a stuffed toy in his free hand.

"Mrs. Dills? I'm Detective Sergeant Hatch. I'm sorry to trouble you, ma'am. May we come in?"

"What for? You've already got my Warren. What else do you want?"

"We have a search warrant to look through your place. Won't bother you any. Just a routine search. May we come in?"

The woman eyed him suspiciously. She looked back and forth from the warrant to him. "Well, I guess I got no choice, do I? Don't make no noise. I just put the baby down for a nap."

"We'll be quiet as we can, ma'am. This won't take very long."

Hatch ushered his team into the house. With hands gloved in latex, they began to search the small rooms crowded with old furniture. Children's toys were scattered about the room. The woman sat on the sofa clutching the child on her lap. She appeared nervous while the officers walked around opening drawers, peering behind books, moving the furniture and replacing it.

Suddenly, from one of the back rooms, someone called out. Hatch followed the sound of the voice. Blake stood inside the closet of a tiny room, an open shoe box in his hand.

"Look what we got here, Sarg. Matches the description of the items taken from the Griswold house. Should I keep looking?"

Hatch carefully took the box from Blake. Several necklaces and rings lay inside. He closed the box and slipped it into a heavy, clear plastic bag.

"Yeah. See what else you can come up with we could use. The more we get on him, the tighter the case. We don't want this one to slip away."

"Right." Blake continued searching through the room.

Hatch took the plastic bag and went into the living room. He walked over to where Mrs. Dills sat. "You ever see this shoe box before?"

The woman inspected the box carefully with her eyes. "Can't say's I have. Where'd you find it?"

"In the rear left room. You sure you don't recognize this?"

"I've never seen it before. That's my husband's workroom. He fixes things for the neighbors for extra money. He works in that room late at night sometimes. I don't ever go in it."

"I'll have to take it downtown. If it's not what I think it is, it'll be returned to you shortly."

Blake and the other cops completed their search of the premises. He shook his head. "Nothing else, Sarg."

"Okay, then. Sorry to have troubled you, Mrs. Dills. Thanks for your cooperation. I'm glad I didn't have to make this any harder on you than it already is."

They left the house and walked down the front steps. The uniformed officers got into their patrol car. Hatch and Blake slid into the unmarked Crown Vic. Hatch looked back. Mrs. Dills stood behind the screen door, her face lined with concern, her arm grabbing her son around his shoulders. Hatch shook his head. Kids. Always the innocent victims. Growing up these days was hard enough without the added burden of fucked-up parents. He thanked God again his kids were grown and seemed to all be headed toward productive, happy lives.

He sat in the passenger seat while Blake drove toward the station, the plastic bag resting in his lap. The contents of the shoe box jingled with each pothole.

NINE

"I don't know about you, Carly, but I'm awfully hot and thirsty. I think an ice cream cone would really hit the spot right now. What do you say?"

Carly just shrugged her tiny shoulders in silence. Sara gently pushed the child's hair back from her eyes. "Come on. Let's get two big chocolate cones."

She took hold of the child's hand. They walked to the nearest concession booth. She inhaled the warm spring air. The sky was clear. She'd decided a trip to the LA Zoo and a change of scenery might be good for Carly, who continued to be sullen, lethargic and uncommunicative much of the time. Occasionally, Sara caught glimpses of the happy, trusting child Carly must have been before her mother's tragic death, but then she'd slip back into her new persona. Perhaps she drew comfort there. Sara's only strategy was to continue seeing her, being caring and affirming and watching for clues as to what was going on unconsciously inside the child. A hint of fear went through Sara whenever she thought about Carly. What would happen when the child began talking and remembering? Would her life be in danger then?

On almost every visit, Sara's emotions seemed to get triggered. Her heart went out to the child in such a personal, unprofessional way she questioned her objectivity. Counter transference, the neo-Freudians called it. Damn uncomfortable and confusing she called it. Rose Goodman's face flashed in her mind. A sharp stab of pain stabbed her belly, reminding her of a promise she'd made to call her mentor.

For now, though, maybe ice cream would help numb the uneasiness in her stomach and make points with Carly. She was willing to try anything to resolve both frustrating problems.

She handed Carly a cone, exchanged money and another cone with the vendor and turned around to continue their exploration of the zoo. She stopped walking when she caught sight of a familiar figure leaning against the railing in front of the polar bear exhibit. He watched the bears and appeared to be making notes on a yellow legal pad. He was dressed in casual dark blue slacks and a white, cotton long-sleeved shirt.

She shook her head in confusion at the now familiar physical reaction she had around him. What was it about that man that caused her to react so strongly? He was just another good-looking guy. She'd dated many of them in the past fifteen years, for God's sake. She needed to stop acting like a teenager. She straightened her shoulders, determined to settle down. She'd take the bull by the horns, if only to prove she was in control of this thing, whatever it was. Leading Carly by her free hand, she walked toward him.

"I would never have expected you to have a fascination with polar bears. Did you learn to swim by watching them?" By keeping her tone light, she hoped to hide her nervousness.

Michael turned and faced her. "Sara."

Hearing her name spoken in his rich, deep voice caused her to suck in a quick breath. Embarrassed by her reaction, she turned quickly to look at the bears, feeling safer and more certain of them than herself.

"They're wonderful, aren't they," she said, "so majestic, so impervious to the world around them. I envy their ability to maintain their dignity in the face of such an unnatural environment."

She felt the intensity of his gaze. It left her with sweaty palms and a queasy stomach.

"Seriously, what brings you to the zoo today?" Her question was more of a diversion from the uncomfortable feelings she experienced rather than from a need to know.

"Business. I'm representing a man who's being sued by the zoo. A nuisance suit really. A favor for one of my bigger clients."

His eyes diverted to the child beside her. "Your daughter?"

Sara smiled and looked down at Carly. "A friend."

He leaned over slightly. "Hi. Are you enjoying the zoo?"

Carly looked at Michael briefly then backed up against Sara's legs and turned her face away.

"She's a bit shy these days and by now probably very tired. We've been here for hours. It's time for us to be going. Nice seeing you again."

When she turned and led the child away, she sensed his eyes on her back.

"Sara. Have dinner with me tonight."

She turned around. It was more of a statement than a question, but she didn't mind the tone. She walked back and looked into his handsome face. Her analytical mind assessed her physical reaction. She knew it was more than just sexual. That would've been familiar and understandable. After all, he was not only good-looking, with thick, dark hair and clear, dark eyes, but he had a strong masculine presence and oozed self-confidence. She took a deep breath. Curious by nature, she was determined to get to the bottom of her uncomfortable attraction to him. She calmed down and regained her self-control.

Reaching into her handbag, she pulled out a pencil and paper, wrote down her address and phone number and handed it to him.

"I'd like that. I could be ready by eight."

"Eight it is. I'll pick you up. Dress casual. I feel a need to walk the beach tonight."

She was drawn into his warm smile. She couldn't help but return one.

"See you later." She turned and led Carly toward the zoo exit, feeling his eyes on her back until they were far away from him.

"I had fun today, Carly. I hope you did, too. Which animal did you like best?" Sara tried to engage the child in conversation. Anything to stop thinking about the meeting with Michael Grey. It'd been a while since she'd been on a date. Just too busy to go on a manhunt, as Dana would put it. She felt both nervous and excited at the possibility of a new relationship. Funny, she had a sense dating Michael Grey would be more than just casual, but where that idea came from she had no clue.

They were nearly at Sara's car when a racing engine grabbed her attention. She looked toward the sound and was surprised to see a black car barreling toward them. What was wrong with the driver? Didn't he see them? Was he drunk? High on something? There was no time to figure it out. The car was almost on them when Sara yanked Carly out of the way. They fell on the pavement, their ice cream cones smashing beside them. The car never stopped, but roared out of the zoo parking lot and out of sight.

Shaken, Sara rose and helped a crying Carly to her feet. Sara shook with rage at the recklessness of the driver, but stuffed her anger and put her arms around Carly.

"It's okay, sweetie. Everything's okay. Are you hurt? Let me look at you. Your knees are scraped a little but they're not bleeding. Oh, look at my elbow. I have a sore, too." She tried to laugh. "We look like twins."

Carly was no longer crying. She pulled Sara's arm toward her and examined the scrape. "We can't be twins. You're too big. Besides, my sores are on my knees and yours is on your arm." She wiped her tears off her cheeks. "I'm thirsty. Can we get a drink?"

Sara smiled. "Good idea. I'll bet we'll feel better after a cold lemonade. How's that sound?"

Sara was relieved to see Carly smile and nod her head.

After stopping at a fast-food drive-thru and slurping down lemonade, the rest of the short ride back to the Griswold home was uneventful. Sara handed the girl over to the housekeeper, Juana, who hugged her and kissed her knees, promising to clean them up and let Carly help her make dinner.

Sara sat in her car for a moment, her mind spinning. What the hell had happened? It sure felt like that was no accident. She was convinced the driver meant to run them down, or at least put a deadly scare into them. Who would want to hurt them? Suddenly another question, even more startling popped into her head. Who was the intended victim? Carly or her?

TEN

Michael purposely kept their conversation on a casual level during the thirty-minute ride from Sherman Oaks to Santa Monica. It would be better to keep his distance, check things out and try to understand what was going on between them.

His invitation earlier was totally unexpected and out of character. He generally only dated woman whom he'd known for years. Career women who weren't interested in long-term relationships or commitments. Something warned him Sara didn't fall into that category. She was different. A red flag waved in front of him, but he ignored it. He decided to take Alan's advice and jump into the unknown. He wanted to find out who Sara Bradley was and why she seemed to have a hold on him.

Was she having the same thoughts? Perhaps her curiosity was piqued as much as his? Maybe she also wanted to play it out and see where it would lead.

Michael pulled his BMW in front of a small restaurant on the beach. The valet opened Sara's door. Her light green skirt hugged her calves as she walked. The matching top that tied in a knot at her waist accentuated her long tan arms, delicate neck and full, round breasts.

As they walked into the restaurant, he held her arm, her skin soft and smooth.

Inside, the atmosphere was quiet, elegant, intimate. The maître d' seated them at a small oval driftwood booth enclosed on three sides. The ocean was framed in a window on the rear wall. The maître d' pulled out a chair for Sara. Michael seated himself across from her.

There were only a few electric lights with low-wattage bulbs scattered on the walls around the room. The bulbs were housed in nautical casings to blend in with the ship and sea motif. Each table had a candle in the middle which flickered its golden mellow light across the faces of the guests. The dim ambiance made menu reading difficult.

Michael ordered a bottle of California's best sparkling white wine and with little conversation, they examined the menu and made their selections. When the wine came, they settled into easy conversation.

"You mentioned you knew Frank Koosman from the public defender's office."

"That's right. When I came to California, I interviewed with him and was hired. Most of my legal experience has been in defense. We worked together for over three years. He eventually switched sides. I think it finally got to him...the hypocrisy of having to defend people who do everything but admit their guilt to you and then wait for you to wave a magic wand and set them free."

"Is that why you left the P.D.'s office?"

"That and the desire to make real money for a change."

Sara returned his smile. "I know what you mean. I certainly can't get rich on what I bill the county. Truthfully, I sometimes wonder if I don't have some deep, dark psychological reason for avoiding wealth."

Her eyes sparkled when she laughed. "So, Frank went into the D.A.'s office and you..."

"I stayed with public defense for a few more years. A glutton for punishment, I guess. Anyway, a few years ago I left and opened a private practice."

"Which includes polar bears, I recently discovered."

"When you work for yourself, you can pick and choose your cases. Believe it or not, polar bears are a step up from some of the people I defended as a P.D. One day I decided I'd had enough and left."

"I can imagine. I've had to deal with some pretty ugly stuff from time to time, particularly with the LAPD. Sometimes I wonder why I chose this line of work."

Her honest smile and admission jolted him. He was suddenly aware of how calm and relaxed he felt.

He actually enjoyed sitting there having a normal conversation with a woman who stirred his emotions without fear and trepidation. That was new, scary and temporarily took his breath away, leaving his heart pounding rapidly. Just as fast as the realization came, it left, leaving him once again calm and wanting to continue wading in the new emotional waters Sara poured around him.

"I was kidding about the money. The only thing money means to me is independence. I guess that's my main priority in life. At least it has been up to now. I went into law purely for personal reasons, not idealistic. It was something I could make a commitment to that would always be there, unchanging, constant. Something I could trust and count on other than myself."

"I think I went into Psychology for very much the same reasons. A search for personal fulfillment, a sense of peace, a need to know more about myself. My earliest memories are of being in an orphanage when I was four years old. I have no idea what went on for the first four years of my life."

Her expression darkened and her voice deepened. "Sometimes, at night, I feel the loneliness and fear which were my only companions during those many long months before I was adopted."

Even in the dimness of the dining room, the shadow of sadness floated across her eyes for a brief moment. The need to reach out to her, hold her and make the sadness go away shook him.

"The Bradleys literally saved my life when they adopted me. They gave me the kind of home every child should have, one with love, care, security, support. I think a part of me wanted to be a psychologist as a kind of payback for all they gave me. Somewhere I got the idea I could alleviate some of the suffering in the world."

She gently tossed her hair back from her cheek. "Of course, now I know how naive I was. Not that I don't love my work. Often I come out of a session feeling truly humbled and inspired by the courage and strength people have. I feel very privileged to be able to work with people on such intimate levels."

She leaned forward, her arms on the table, her eyes shining. "I have this philosophy of life, you see. I don't think we ever really escape our roots. We're all victims of our environment. Life is about learning to adapt and work as best we can with what we were given." She sat back a bit. "Some of us are lucky enough to create a life that makes sense, despite the past."

As the waiter appeared with their main courses, she cleared her throat and took a sip of her wine.

Michael remained silent. Her words could have depicted his early life experiences. He shuddered. Add some violence, rage and then complete emotional withdrawal, and there he was, years later, still battling with his inner demons.

They were relatively quiet during the meal of lobster, baked potato and asparagus, with minor comments about the dinner, the restaurant and their experiences dining in LA. When they left the restaurant, Michael drove toward the Marina and parked in the garage under his condo. He turned to her, resting his arm against the back of the seat.

"How about a walk on the beach? Hopefully we can work off some of those calories we added on at dinner."

"Sounds wonderful."

They left the car, walked fifty yards to the beach, took off their shoes and stepped barefoot onto the cool white sand. They walked toward the ocean. The night was very black. Only a quarter moon and a few stars guided their way toward the Pacific. Lights from the homes behind them faded when they got closer to their destination. After their feet touched the first flood of cold water which splash on them, they turned and walked along the shore.

He kept his hands jammed into the pockets of his slacks. She walked with her arms swinging lightly at her sides. The unevenness of the sand seemed to affect her balance, for she occasionally brushed against him. Whenever her slim body touched his, he pulled away as if a spark jumped out and seared him. They continued walking in silence. Despite his physical reactions, a soothing comfortable mood prevailed. He didn't feel the need to fill the empty space with meaningless words. The ocean breeze floated the faint scent of her clean hair and light perfume his way, making it difficult to keep his mind on causal thoughts.

After a while, the wind picked up, and they headed back. At one point, they slipped on their shoes. He grabbed her hand, and they started to run. By the time they reached his car, they were both out of breath and laughing.

"Are you up for something hot to drink before I drive you home?"

"You couldn't conjure up some hot cocoa, could you?"

He smiled. "I believe I can."

He led the way to his condo. He turned on a lamp near the sofa in front of the fireplace. "Make yourself at home. I'll be right back."

He returned with two steaming cups of hot cocoa and placed them on the glass top table in front of the sofa. He sat down at one end of the sofa, she at the other. He turned sideways to face her. Here, in the intimacy of his home, keeping a distance between them seemed a good idea.

She took a sip of the cocoa. "Hmm, this hits the spot."

What was going on in her mind beside hot cocoa? She suddenly took a deep breath and put her cup down. She walked over to the wall where hundreds of books lined wooden shelves from floor to ceiling. She walked slowly along the wall, often bending her head to read the titles. Would she put two and two together and figure out what he had years before? Each book represented a panel in his coat of armor, a brick in the wall he built around himself over the years, an escape into beauty, poetry and perfection from an ugly, imperfect world. For him, literature was a place where all of life's stories rhymed, had a logical reason for existence and usually ended happily, if not in harmonious completion. Definitely not the real world as he experienced it.

He felt exposed, vulnerable. As she glided around the room, he realized he didn't have to protect himself from her. How he knew this, and why, he had no idea.

"Don't tell me you've read all these."

"Most of them. I've been told I lead a very boring life."

Her hand gently caressed the books while she strolled. "Shakespeare, Faulkner, Byron, Twain, Oliver Wendell Holmes. I wouldn't exactly call these boring. Escapism perhaps. Mine's music. That's where I go to lose myself."

She returned to the sofa, sat back against the cushions and turned to look at him. Silence hung in the air. Again, she seemed to back off, possibly as shaken as he was by the tangible connection between them. She seemed confused. He was caught between wanting to take her into his arms and feel her body against his and a strong sense of danger if he did. He decided to do what any good lawyer would do...wait and see what her next move would be.

She gazed at him through doe-like eyes. "I've really enjoyed this evening, Michael, a pleasant change from most of the dates I've had. You're easy to be with, not pretentious, obnoxious and arrogant like most of the men I meet. I really appreciate that about you."

He didn't respond. Instead, he leaned toward her and pushed a few strands of hair behind her ear and ran his knuckles along her cheek.

She looked away and then back at him. "I guess I'm wondering, where do we go from here? I want us to be friends, maybe more, but something stops me from knowing clearly what's next. I don't understand what that's all about."

"When I get into a place like that, I generally try to sort everything out. I list exactly what my options are, feel them out, go with one of them until I reach a snag and then try another. Eventually, I hit on the right one. This has worked for me in the past."

She smiled. "My decision-making process looks something like that. Something else we have in common."

She took a deep, shaky breath. "Okay. What are our options? Briefly, as I see it, we could shake hands and part company, consider the evening a pleasant experience and close the books on seeing each other again. Under this same option, we could take it all the way and jump into bed and get whatever pleasure we can from this, our one and only night together.

"Option two: we could admit there's something going on between us which we need time to explore. This option leaves us with two choices. A, to say good night for now with the intention of slowly discovering who we are for each other and what that could mean or B, we could throw caution to the wind, take a risk and spend the rest of the night trying to find out."

He was surprised and pleased with her calm straight-forward words. He sipped his cocoa, trying to settle his racing heart. "I believe you've covered all the options I had in mind. What are you leaning toward?"

She seemed a bit put off by his calmness. There was some defensiveness in her voice. "To tell you the truth, the first option doesn't interest me at all, being untrue and not my style. As far as I'm concerned, one-night stands aren't worth the time and energy they require. I guess that leaves us with option two, A and B."

"Those would be my choices, too. What does our learned shrink say about risk taking?"

She looked at her cup. It was as if her mind raced through options, possibilities, choices. "I think you should take me home now."

He was disappointed. Slowly, he put his cup down. "All right,"

They walked to the door. Before opening it, he put his hands on her shoulders and turned her around to face him.

"I respect your decision, Sara, as well as your courage and frankness. They're refreshing. I want you to know I'd like nothing better than to make love to you tonight, but I leave the matter totally in your hands to pursue it whenever you want, however you want. Maybe I'm being a coward, but I sense you're the braver of the two of us. I trust your instincts better than my own at the moment."

He leaned down and gently kissed her forehead. When he looked into her eyes, though, much of his caution faded. He pulled her into his arms. His mouth found hers, and he kissed her slowly, with passion. Her arms went around his neck. She returned the kiss with such abandon he reluctantly pushed her away.

"I think I'd better get you home, before we change our minds and do something we may both regret."

*   *   *

A few hours later, Michael got out of the shower. Was that the doorbell? Who the hell could that be at this hour?

The evening with Sara had left him feeling very dissatisfied, restless. He was angry for not taking the initiative, for giving himself another lonely, empty night. Sometimes he hated the cautious way he'd learned to live, cursed his own cowardliness, his own fears.

The damn bell again. He grabbed a large black bath towel, wrapped it around his waist and went to the door.

She stood there, dressed in a light blue jogging suit, looking as though she just came from a ten-mile run. Her beautiful face was flushed; her chest rose and fell quickly, her eyes bright and almost wild.

"Please." As if to stop him from responding to her surprise return, she held up her right hand. "Don't say anything. Just let me speak before I lose my nerve, wake up, realize what I've done by coming here and die from shame."

She shook her head slightly as if she couldn't believe she stood at his front door. She swept past him into the dimly lighted living room.

He closed the door and leaned against it.

She paced back and forth and spoke quickly and decisively, almost frantically. "You must think I'm crazy coming back here after what we said. I know, I do. Honestly, I don't understand why I'm here. I hardly know you. We've only met twice before tonight. Okay, so maybe there's something...electric...that gets sparked when we're together, but I swear to you, I'm not the kind who usually goes around giving into every romantic notion. I promise I've never done that before."

She continued pacing back and forth, wringing her hands in front of her. "Not that I haven't had my share of lovers. Actually, I started rather young–thirteen or fourteen, I think. Maybe I was looking for the love I missed as a very young child, I don't know." She laughed nervously.

"Believe it or not, I've not had a lot of personal therapy, just enough to get me through college. It's just that it's been a long time since...I mean, I've been putting so much time into my work, I..."

"Sara. You don't have to go into all of this now."

"Yes. Yes, I do. It's important you know where I'm coming from. Besides, something very strange and scary happened after I left you at the zoo. Made me realize that you never know when the next moment could be your last. So even though things are getting cloudy and unsettled with me right now, and I really don't need any more confusion, I don't care. So, why am I here?" She paused and took a breath. "We made a very logical, rational decision to take time to nurture this thing along, see what it is before we jump into bed. I really think that's the wise thing to do. So you can throw me out any time you want, and I won't be mad. In fact, I wish you would. I really wish you would."

She stopped for a moment, sighed and blinked away the tears which filled her eyes. "You see, Michael, I'm scared."

The tears and the look of total vulnerability in her flushed face had him automatically take a couple of steps toward her, but he stopped.

He took a deep breath instead. "I know what you mean. Beginnings are always hard, especially for people like us."

He stood there, his arms at his sides. Sensing his calm strength, she seemed to relax.

A slight smile came over her face. "People like us." She took a deep breath, as though to absorb his verbal acknowledgement of the bond building between them.

"I really am scared to death, Michael. Do you know why?" Her voice was barely a whisper "I sense you could touch places inside me no one has ever touched. What petrifies me most is I want you to."

Something snapped inside him. His reserve, his caution, his logical mind, all disappeared. He was overwhelmed by a great need. Slowly he walked over to her, fully alive for the first time in so many years. Slowly, he put his arms around her and held her so close she could probably hear his heart pounding in his chest. He didn't care. Her warm soft body, childlike, yet fully a woman, momentarily filled the emptiness inside. It was all he needed. He wanted to stand there holding her forever. Surely it would be enough.

But stronger urgings took over. He began to caress her sweet-smelling hair with his lips, moving slowly down toward her ear. He kissed the soft lobe and gently traced his mouth down her neck. Her body arched closer to him, urging him to continue. Her arms reached up and surrounded his neck, her fingers moving against his damp skin. He pulled far enough away and searched her eyes, to be sure before he went further.

Seeing her willingness to join with him, he moved his hand up and caressed her check gently; his thumb moved across her parted lips. Her eyes were misty, full of permission, surrender and passion. His heart pounded in his ears. His need for her cried out in every nerve of his body. He reached down and kissed her mouth with such tenderness she moaned and pulled herself closer to him. He'd never experienced such an overwhelming sense of both vulnerability and power at the same time, of wanting to give and needing to receive in the same moment.

Her hands moved slowly across his bare shoulders, alongside his neck. Her fingers traveled through his hair, all the time her body arched closer and closer to him. Their bodies seemed to fuse into one, in so intimate a movement he resisted pulling away even briefly. He finally did, long enough to pick her up and carry her into his dark bedroom, into the black hole of the unknown.

ELEVEN

The following evening Sara jerked awake and sat up, adjusting her eyes to the darkness of the room. She was safe. This was her bedroom, she repeated over and over to calm herself. She sat back against the headboard and pulled the comforter up to her neck, more for safety than for warmth. Tears started to flow, but she didn't understand why. Stabs of pain jabbed her stomach again, worse than ever before. She wrapped her arms around herself. Even though she was now fully awake, she couldn't keep the frightening pictures out of her mind. Experiencing them awake was even more bone chilling than asleep.

She'd tossed and turned, trying to escape the haunting images. Bright reds, yellows and purples lashed out at her. Clothed faceless figures swirled about in raging silence. From time to time, one huge figure loomed forward. She screamed. It was male, large and dark, glowing inside an ember of fire. The face was blurred, making recognition impossible. The dream more surrealistic and frightening. The dance went on and on. The male figure floated back and forth in the air, lunging at her.

Another figure appeared from time to time, darkly shaded, but not frightening, standing to the side as if watching the huge male figure's whirling performance. Cautious. Quiet. He held a large stick of some kind, and his presence in the dream brought her a veil of peace. A goat whirled by. A cow. A dog. Several kittens. All monstrously out of proportion and resembling caricatures rather than real animals.

The huge male lunged forward, this time with arms outstretched as if reaching for her. The horror of that menacing beckoning figure brought her back to the present. She couldn't stop her heart from racing, couldn't warm her body which was cold and wet from sweat.

After a while, she stopped crying. Her stomach relaxed. She turned to the clock on the nightstand. Twelve forty-three. She got out of bed, walked to the bathroom and, without turning on the harsh lights, rinsed her face with warm water. Back in bed, she lay down, staring at the ceiling, wrapping the comforter around her.

What the hell was that all about? She recalled having that dream, or one similar to it, several times before, but never associated with such irrational fear.

Whatever was bothering her was intensifying, as if her mind needed sleep to release its ghostly secrets.

Her analytical thought processes took over. Yet the fear returned with each new conjecture of possible sources of what was troubling her. However, this time the fear seemed more natural, more authentic. Less supernatural.

Michael's face popped into her head. Her eyes filled with tears. Michael. Thinking of him, his gentleness, his strength, his caring, had her crave an urgent need to feel his arms around her, hear his deep, quiet voice, to be soothed by his strong presence.

She'd never experienced anything like their coming together the other night. She'd always enjoyed sex, had probably been more promiscuous than most of her high school friends. Yet those early encounters were only physical releases. She was often left unsatisfied and wondering what was missing, and if she'd ever find it.

With Michael it was different. They shared an unguarded, deeply profound connection. The way he touched her, kissed her, pleasured her, she wanted to rekindle those moments. She wished he was there next to her. She wanted to feel his gentle touch, be overwhelmed by his body inside hers and know, for certain, she was safe from whatever secrets her unconscious held.

She wanted to call him. Should she? The hour was late, and she really had no right, no permission to do so. Her mind sought relief from the fear, confusion and the interminable loneliness. She reached for the phone and dialed his number.

After a few rings, he answered, his voice heavy from sleep.

"Oh, dear, I woke you. I hoped you'd be awake. I thought ambitious attorneys never slept."

Michael cleared his voice and seemed at once present to the conversation. "I must be having a wet dream. I'm imagining Sara's voice on the phone and strange things are happening to my otherwise always-in-control body."

She smiled, immediately glad she called. "At least your dream sounds pleasant. I just had an awful nightmare."

"And you thought you were calling the local chapter of Ghostbusters? Well, I'm sorry to disappoint, but you've reached the home of LA's most cowardly attorney. However, for a fee and for special clients, I do make house calls."

She laughed "Oh, really? What kind of fee are we talking?"

"I usually wait until after the job is done and charge by the results I produce. As you are probably aware, California is well-known for its contingency litigation."

"Oh, too bad. I don't think I can afford you. The word around town is you produce amazing results. I guess I'll have to call somewhere else."

His voice and their banter helped return her to a normal state of mind. The affect he had on her was mind-boggling.

"Actually, I'm feeling better now. You can go back to sleep, back to those sexual fantasies you were having."

"To tell you the truth, I'd rather experience the real thing. Are you sure you don't want any company?"

She smiled again. "How about tomorrow night, or should I say tonight?"

"Sounds good to me. Are you up for a Lakers' game? I know where I can score some great tickets."

"Perfect. I need to watch some fast competitive physical activity. I seem to have a lot of aggression to release."

"Good. Then, after the game, we'll switch mode from observer to participant."

"I don't know. After this nightmare, I'm not sure if I can contain all my aggressive impulses."

"Then we'll have to get together more often so you can let them all out, maybe even every day if possible. What do you say about that?"

She laughed. "I say, let's take one day at a time, my friend. My patients need me to keep my feet on the ground. That's difficult around you. I'll see you tonight."

She was about to hang up. "Michael?"

"Yeah?"

"Thanks for being there."

She thought she heard a slight smile in his voice. "No problem. See you later."

*   *   *

The warmth and familiarity of her apartment hit him as soon as he walked through the door. Beige carpeting, pale blue and white striped upholstered sofa and chairs and light oak tables filled the room. Dimly lit white pottery lamps and green plants of every shape and size dotted the edges of the room and hung in front of the sliding glass doors leading to the patio.

He followed her into the kitchen and sat on a barstool.

She pulled cheese and wine from the refrigerator and crackers from the cupboards. She pushed her long wavy hair back from her face while she cut up an apple and tore apart an orange, arranging everything onto a large platter.

"I don't know about you, but watching the Lakers always makes me hungry." She poured the wine. "And thirsty." She handed him a chilled glass.

He took it, staring into her dark eyes. "So, tell me, any more bad dreams?"

"No." She reached out for her glass. Her face flushed. She avoided his stare and then returned it. "Let's make a toast…to the end of nightmares and all things scary…to life and the freedom to live it to its fullest."

Their glasses touched; they sipped their wine. "I had fun tonight. It's been a long time since I jumped up and down, yelled and screamed and clapped like a kid." She grinned. "Except, of course, when I play softball."

"Softball?"

"Yeah. My best friend, Dana, and I volunteer at the Valley Boys and Girls Club. We're on their softball team. It's a lot of fun. You'll have to come and watch our next game. We're playing our rivals, Sammy's Sluggers. They've beat us the last five times. Our reputation is now on the line." She laughed.

Her face glowed. God, she was beautiful! So alive and vital, so full of life. Sometimes he was jealous of her ability to be so carefree, so apparently unencumbered from the burdens of the past. So unlike himself.

The sudden wave of emotion which rushed through him left him feeling exposed, vulnerable. His first reaction was to reign in his emotions, but then he felt brave enough to go with the flow. "Count me there."

Her eyes softened. She leaned over and kissed him lightly on the mouth, brief, spontaneous, unrehearsed. It surprised him, and apparently her, because she pulled away, her cheeks flushed. She cleared her throat. "Why don't you carry the wine bottle and glasses to the coffee table? I'll bring the platter."

She followed him into the living room. "I'm driving to Sacramento this weekend to see my folks. It may be the last time I can get away for a while. Do you have any family in California?"

His brow wrinkled. "Not that I know of. In fact, as far as I know, I'm the last survivor of my clan, not that there's anyone who'd be sorry to see the line die out for good."

He slid back into the thick cushions and took another sip from his glass. He rested his head on the back of the sofa.

"You sound cynical. Do you ever miss the idea of having a family you can trust and count on when you need them, who would be there for you?"

He tried to tone down his bitterness. "It's hard to miss something you never had. I don't remember my mother. She died when I was five or six. My father was an alcoholic. A mean, brutal man who took out his anger on anyone near him. For years after my mother died, it was me. Then it was a new wife and then...anyway, I left when I was thirteen. I never looked back. I have no regrets about leaving, except, I admit, sometimes I wonder..."

Stop it. He hardly knew this woman. It wasn't safe to reveal so much. He closed his eyes briefly, but it was hard not to open up to her. Was it because she was such a good listener or because he suddenly had a great need to unburden himself? Either way it was too soon. He took a long drink, emptying his glass.

"Sorry, kiddo. By the look on your face, I'd say I've put a damper on the wonderful evening you were having. I have a bad habit of pulling everyone into my morose reveries. I think maybe Alan is right. He claims I'm no fun to have around." He smiled. "All I do is work like a fool and make a lot of money. Depressing, isn't it."

"Who's Alan?"

"An old friend of mine. We share office space."

"Well, you know what they say about all work and no play."

He put his empty glass on the table, sat back against the cushions once again and reached out and touched her long silky hair. Her gentle eyes and her soft hair against his fingers seemed to melt the bitterness away. "You're all I want right now, Sara, and I admit I'm embarrassed to say that."

"Embarrassed?"

"Needing someone is new for me. I'm not sure what it means or what to do about it or even if it's a good idea for us to get too involved." When had he suddenly developed this ability for intimate conversation?

"Is this a new concern or the old one I thought we settled the other night?"

"The old one, with a new twist."

"What twist is that?"

"I've been alone most of my life. I've learned how to take care of myself, to protect myself, and I've done a good job of it. The walls around me are thick. Nobody gets in anymore. Now, here you are, and I feel the armor beginning to crack. Instead of worrying about myself, I wonder what's behind the walls. Do I have anything to give? I want to be there for you, but I don't know if I can."

She took a deep breath. Her hand came up and pressed against his while he continued caressing her hair. She turned her face and kissed the palm of his hand. Then she turned back to him.

"So far, I have no complaints. Should any arise, I promise to let you know. I trust you to deal with them at that time. In the meantime, we both know there are no guarantees. All we have is the moment in front of us. So far, for me, those moments with you have been perfect."

He pulled her into his arms and held her for a while before pulling away. He kissed her gently on her cheek, then her eyes and finally her parted lips.

After a few moments, she pulled just far enough away to look at him. "Something tells me I shouldn't have cut up all this cheese and fruit."

He kissed her again. "Don't worry. We'll have it for breakfast."

"Hmm." She groaned when his hand moved along her side and found her breast. He pulled her down on top of him.

"Great idea."

TWELVE

The jury slowly parade into the court room. None of their twelve stoic faces betrayed any clue as to the decision they'd reached. Seven women and five men selected by Michael and the opposing attorney during the *voir dire* portion of the trial. They ranged between the ages of twenty and fifty-five, of varying races and colors, indicative of the integrated society that was Los Angeles.

As they sat down in the jury box, he was fascinated, intrigued, by this minuscule moment in time which held great import for the man seated beside him. Those twelve people held the fate of his client in their hands, and at this moment, only they knew what his client's life would look like in the immediate future. Would incarceration be waiting for him, jail time for innocently defending his property against some crack-head punk who'd been intent on robbing him? Perhaps the next few moments would herald in another win for the little guy against the system, one citizen who had the courage to stand up for himself at the risk of criminal prosecution for carrying a concealed weapon.

Michael always found this part of every trial the most compelling. Not the possibility of winning or losing another case. He was too good a lawyer, too self-assured to let himself get caught up in the ego trips many of his fellow attorneys were on. He thrived on the suspense while he waited to see where the dice would fall, how fate would intervene in someone's life and dictate future events.

As he looked at the jurors, he equated that moment to psychic energy pulling people toward their destinies. Those strangers now held the power over his client's life and somewhere deep inside, Michael was both enraged and seduced by that thought.

The judge's interrogative broke through his thoughts. "Has the jury reached a verdict?"

One male juror on the end of the first row stood. "We have, Your Honor."

"Would you please tell the Court your verdict?"

"On Count One, assault with a deadly weapon, we find the defendant not guilty."

"Thank you, jurors. The Court wishes to thank you all for the time and effort you have exerted in carrying out your civic duties during this trial. You are dismissed. Defendant is free to go. Court is adjourned."

As the jury and the observers slowly shuffled out of the courtroom, Michael's client grabbed his hand and pumped it up and down. His small round face was radiant with happiness. "Thank you, Mr. Grey! Thank you very much. I don't know what I would've done if I'd been sent to jail, or what my family would've done without me to support them. We owe you so much."

"My pleasure, Mr. Martinez. We were lucky to have a sympathetic jury. I'm glad everything turned out well for you. Be sure to speak with the clerk. There are papers you must sign before you can leave."

Martinez tugged heartily once again on Michael's hand. The man's wife and several teenaged children rushed to him, their faces lit with joy and relief.

Michael shuffled his papers, tossed them into his briefcase, closed it and made his way out of the courtroom. The hallway was busy with people coming and going in and out of courtrooms, elevators, restrooms. Some were probably heading for lunch either inside the building or somewhere outside in the warm spring sunshine. As he walked into the first floor lobby heading for the parking lot, a hand pulled on his arm at the same time a voice broke into his pensive thoughts.

"Mike! Mike. Hold on a minute. God, you're a hard man to get a hold of, what with these crowds and your long legs."

Michael turned. A colleague from the public defender's office was at his side.

"Howard Weiss. Long time no see."

"A very long time. What's the matter, you too busy raking in the bucks to take time out to come and visit your old buddies? I saw you posted for Department One Twenty-Seven this morning, and I decided it would be as good a place as any to catch you. How about lunch? Or do you have a hot date with a polar bear?"

"Very funny. I see you haven't lost your sharp wit. I guess they aren't working you hard enough in the P.D.'s office."

The two left the building and walked down Temple, heading toward Olvera Street, the site of the first settlement in Los Angeles hundreds of years before. The street contained old Mexican style buildings, now converted into restaurants and shops. An aged Spanish mission stood majestically at the edge of the square. Open booths filled the middle of the street where Hispanic merchants sold leather goods, ponchos, rugs, pottery, cactus and whatever else they could offer to souvenir-hungry visitors and bargain-seeking locals.

Old town was a nice divergence for the hundreds of professionals who worked nearby. The pueblo was an escape from the madness of modern day living. It offered the charm and serenity of an era long gone but not forgotten by the continuing flow of immigrants that steadily came into California.

The two attorneys made their way into one of the cantinas on the street and settled into a booth near a window. Michael leaned back and relaxed against the cushions. He automatically ran his fingers through his hair briefly. He was pleased with the outcome of the case; glad the Martinez family could get back to their regular life and put the horror of the last few months behind them. In fact, he was generally satisfied with the world lately, ever since Sara came into his life.

"Yo! Counselor. Where are you? I've been going on for the last ten minutes, and you haven't said 'boo.' What's going on inside that deep well you call a mind?"

"Sorry, Howard, just relaxing and enjoying the moment, if you will."

"Ah, yes, the thrill of victory. I know it well. So, what've you been up to lately besides polar bears?"

"God, I'll bet you guys in P.D. must have split a gut when you heard about that case. No other newsworthy activities going on?" He smiled. "Same old stuff. What about you, anything interesting in the works?"

The waitress came, and they ordered iced tea, chicken burritos and ensaladas.

Weiss leaned back against the booth, his right hand in his belt, his left arm on the table. "As a matter of fact, that's why I wanted to see you. Remember the Griswold murder? I was assigned the case after the stableman, Warren Dills, called Joe Hatch and confessed. The guy has a long rap sheet, mostly drug convictions and petty theft. You know the type. Because of Griswold, they want to throw the book at him. I've been postponing taking the deal to Dills because I just don't feel right about the whole thing."

"What'd you mean?"

Weiss shrugged his shoulders sheepishly. "We worked together long enough for you to know the kind of lawyer I am. I care about my clients and work hard for them. I've put in over twenty years and will probably retire from county service. Sometimes the routine of the job gets to me but, in fact, I'm satisfied with myself and my work ethic."

Michael was surprised by Weiss' honest admissions and didn't know how to respond.

Weiss continued with an embarrassed look on his face. "Any way, my new case got me thinking. There's no question in my mind Dills is capable of murdering someone. He has a long rap sheet and a drug abuse history. A career criminal. However, when I met him, his attitude took me by surprise. I've had to start thinking about the case rather than reacting from rote."

Michael's interest sparked. "How was his attitude different from your other clients?"

"You know how they usually strut around, arrogant, mouthing off, maintaining their innocence? Not Dills. He sat in the interview room leaning back in his chair, bored, listless, resigned. Had no interest in talking to me, didn't care about discussing a plea bargain I presented. Just wanted to get it over with so he could be left alone to do his time. His words."

"Interesting, but not that unusual. Something else bothering you about this case?"

"Yeah. After meeting with Dills, I ran into Joe Hatch. He was rushing, so I made a comment about him running to catch the lunch wagon. He parlayed with the familiar quip about me being a Weiss guy, you know how that goes. Anyway, when I told him he had a weak case, his feathers got ruffled. He warned me to back off, let it alone, don't pull any tricks to mess up the conviction. I can't imagine the pressure they're all under with Griswold breathing down their necks. His reaction forced me to read between the lines of the case file, and I tell you, Mike, something stinks here."

Michael took a bite of his burrito. "What are they offering?"

"I finally got them to take the death sentence off the table. We're down to twenty-five to life, no parole."

"So what does this have to do with me?"

"Damn it, Mike, it's just too neat and tidy. The police really don't have anything except the confession and some stolen jewelry found in Dills' place. I've found several holes in the case, which could blow it wide open and be good for reasonable doubt. I wanted to plead him innocent and go to trial, but Dills insisted on pleading guilty. 'Leave it alone,' he says, 'I'll do the time.' He should be fighting this but he doesn't seem to have the stomach for it. To be honest with you, neither do I."

Weiss took a long slug of his iced tea. "I don't have the time or the inclination to buck Griswold. Hell. I've got to work with the bastard for the next few years. But I'll tell you, I don't feel right sandbagging Dills, junky punk that he is. I just don't like the feel of the whole thing. I want you to take the case."

Michael frowned. "I left the P.D.'s office so I wouldn't have to get lowlifes like Dills off on technicalities anymore. I put in my time defending the Constitution and putting scum like Dills back on the street. I'm not interested in doing it again. I like the way I've been sleeping at night these past few years."

"Thing is, Mike, I'm not talking technicalities. My gut tells me the guy's innocent."

"What about the confession?"

"That's the only hitch, and I'll admit it's a big one, particularly with a client who gets hostile when I bring up the possibility of changing his plea. He's totally uncooperative."

"What do you want from me?"

"Look at the file. Talk to him. See what you think. If you feel the same way I do, then take the case. Some pro bono work might come in handy at income tax time."

The waitress refilled their iced tea glasses. They continued eating in silence, Michael churning over Weiss' words.

After several minutes, Weiss asked, "Well? What'd you say? Are you ready for a challenge? At least come and talk to the guy before you make a decision."

Michael looked up from his plate. "Where's he being held?"

"With County so overcrowded, they just transferred him to Wayside awaiting acceptance of the deal and then sentencing. He's in Maximum. I'm going out there on Wednesday. I could pick you up at home, and we could drive there first thing."

Michael looked at Weiss, but his mind was racing ahead, anticipating the interview, scanning the files, making a decision. The main question was: did he really want or need to get into something like this?

"I'll be ready at seven. You have my address?"

Weiss' smile seemed to reflect a sense of relief. "Sure do. Remember that night I dropped you off after the get-together at Jackson's a few months ago? Anyway, I'll be there at seven. Thanks Mike. I really think you'll find this one very interesting."

Michael tipped his glass at him before taking another sip. "No promises, Howard. You're not off the hook yet."

"I hear you. Well, if worse comes to worse, at least I'll have company on the ride to Wayside."

*   *   *

Weiss' steel gray SUV pulled into a parking space marked "Visitor." Michael glanced ahead at the entrance to the North County Correctional

Facility at Saugus. The Peter Pitchess Honor Ranch, locally known as Wayside, was located in the northwest corner of Los Angeles County, nestled in a valley which rarely felt the gentle caress of rain, acid or otherwise. Originally, it'd been built to house medium to low security prisoners. As the criminal population in the county increased, however, this once state-of-the-art facility now housed maximum security prisoners, as well as murderers and lifers awaiting trial and eventual deportation to state and federal detention centers.

Michael stared out the window. The terrain was bare and stark. It was blanketed by those hearty desert shrubs which could withstand the intense glare of the relentless sun, the dry desert winds and the lack of water. Only various shades of brown, pale yellow, beige and rust decorated the sparse land. On closer inspection, the blackened remnants of wildfires which constantly threatened the area were evident.

Even before Michael stepped out of the car, he sensed a return of the old feelings of fear, isolation and incredible loneliness initially spawned as a child. These were triggered each time he interviewed a client in one of these places. As a public defender, he'd spent a lot of time in the jails of LA County, and even though it'd been a few years since he'd been to the Wayside facility, old ghostly memories washed over him like a wave of warm mist.

He got out and stood for a moment, looking up at the concrete walls. While Weiss fumbled with the car keys, Michael tried to shake off eerie feelings. By the time the two entered the building and got their visitors passes, he was mentally back on track.

"Did you get a chance to look through the files?" Weiss questioned him while they walked toward the reception area.

"I went over them last night for a couple of hours. I have to agree with you. On the surface it looks like a neat little package, but there are a lot of unanswered questions I think our friend Mr. Koosman and his cronies have been unwilling to look at. Several loose ends. When I finished reading, I had more questions than answers. I also saw where you stopped in your investigation. I can't say I blame you for not wanting to dig any deeper. I'm not so sure I want to either. To tell you the truth, Howard, I don't like being here or having anything to do with defending murderers or even accused murderers."

He stopped talking. He was trying to justify his being there to himself rather than to Weiss. Why was he there? Why was he even considering getting involved in a murder case after his dramatic exodus from the P.D.'s office five years before? Was some unknown force taking control and leading him into places he didn't really want to go but felt compelled to follow?

They requested a private visitation room. A table and four chairs occupied the middle of the small room. Nothing adorned the cold concrete white-washed walls. The door, with a small window in the top half, opened, and a deputy sheriff ushered in a man, handcuffed him to the table and said, "I'll be right outside if you need me." He left the room.

Michael absently noticed him standing in the hallway, leaning against the door.

He gave Warren Dills the once-over. The prisoner sat slouched in a chair across from the two attorneys, decked out in the orange jumpsuit. His face was expressionless. He stared across at the two men. His long hair was pulled back in a ponytail. A small hole in his right ear showed the absence of an earring. His dark eyes were vacant, portraying a sense of emptiness. Michael was hard-pressed to find any sign of life or feeling in the man.

"Dills, I want you to meet a colleague of mine, Michael Grey. I've asked him to come and talk to you about your case. I wanted to see if he could find anything I'd missed that might be helpful in your plea bargain. Just tying up loose ends."

Dills' voice was very low and monotone when he spoke, still devoid of feeling. "Why're you bangin' your head against the wall, man? I killed the bitch. That's all there is to it. Don't do me no favors. Let's get this thing over with so I can get on with serving my time. I don't feel like goin' over the whole thing again with another fucking suit."

"I've never met a man so eager to do time before. What's happened? You found Jesus or something," Weiss asked.

"Yeah, you might say that. I done the dirty deed. Now I'm willin' to pay the price. Refreshin' ain't it." Dills snickered.

Michael stared at him. What most interested him was the lack of feeling and expression in the man's face. Michael's gaze turned to the notes in front of him. "So, Dills, let me get this straight. You were working at the Griswold house for a few months, doing your job, staying out of trouble. Suddenly you realized you had yourself a pretty little setup. These people had money, and they were beginning to trust you. You knew their comings and goings. It was easy for you to pick a night when no one would be around and then grab as much as you could from the house and get out before anyone saw you. But something went wrong. Mrs. Griswold came in unexpected and caught you in the act. You struggled with her, beating her unconscious, grabbed as much jewelry as you could and left the house. As best I can put it together, that's about it. Did I leave anything out?" Michael looked up at Dills curiously.

"Nope, you got it. That's it in a nutshell."

"I see. So, let's take it from there. You went home. Stashed the jewelry in a shoe box in a bedroom closet and went about your business as though nothing had happened. When Sergeant Hatch questioned you, you denied being in the house, said you hadn't done anything wrong. So he lets you go. You're home free and clear. A woman dies and you're in the clear. No witnesses, no one to put you in the house, nothing.

Then unexpectedly a week later you call Hatch and confess to the murder. I tell you, I'm sure as hell curious what went on with you that week."

Dills looked at Michael through empty eyes. "Well, like your pal there said, I seen the light. Praise the Lord and all that shit. You know what I mean? Thought it was best to come clean and pay my dues. What can I tell you? That's the kinda guy I am."

Michael decided to push a few buttons to see what would open up. "You know, I think you're full of shit."

Dills stirred in his chair uncomfortably, showing signs of emotion for the first time. He looked over at Weiss. "Why the hell did you bring this asshole here, huh? I don't know what you want from me. I told you I killed the bitch. End of story. Why don't you get off my back and leave me alone?"

Michael looked down at the file again. "Says here you have a wife and two small children. You give any mind to them when you went on your alleged robbery and killing spree?"

This time Dills' anger bubbled up to the surface and spread over his face. "You leave my family out of this, man."

"What's going to happen to them now you're off the grid? Does your wife work outside the home? How's she going to feed the kids? Guess we'll have another family living off welfare. Too bad she had to go and pick such a lousy provider for a husband and father of her children."

Dills sat forward, slammed his hands on the table, staring at Michael, eyes burning with anger. "My family is none of your fuckin' business, you bastard." Slowly, Dills regained his self-control and slinked back into his chair again, his eyes calm and vacant. "You don't have to worry about 'em. I'm taking care of 'em." He turned to Weiss. "Get this mother fucker out of here and don't bring him back. Guard!"

Michael mentally reviewed what just happened. The anger and frustration he'd expected, but there was something else. Bitterness, resentfulness, perhaps a trace of fear. Not fear at being convicted. Something Michael couldn't put his finger on. Dills seemed more concerned about his family than the fact he was looking at life in prison.

Michael was hooked. He was compelled to find out exactly what was going on, even though Dills wouldn't be a very cooperative client.

"I think I've heard enough. I'll be seeing you, Dills."

Weiss stood and knocked at the door for the deputy. After Dills and the deputy left, he returned to his seat. Michael quietly pushed the papers back into the file, stuffed it into his briefcase and stood.

"Well, Mike. What do you think? Does it seem as fishy to you as it does to me?"

"I've never heard a convict refuse help from his attorney before. When I was a P.D., my clients were constantly calling and demanding attention, like whiney needy babies."

"Exactly. This guy is one for the books. So, what do you say?"

"What makes you think I'll have more success in getting the truth out of him than you? I can't say we hit it off too well."

Weiss smiled. "I have every faith in your powers of persuasion. Don't worry about the change of representation. I'll handle it with Dills and Judge Longmire. Thanks, Mike. I know you'll do right by him. The poor bastard won't know what's hit him when he finds himself back on the street."

Weiss slapped Michael on the back. They headed out of the room, down the hallway, turned in their passes and stepped out into the hot, dry air. As they got into the car and pulled away from the facility, Michael shook his head. Well, Alan told him to start taking risks again. First Sara and now Dills. Alan would be as happy as a pig in shit when he told him.

Weiss drove away from the facility and onto the Five Freeway South to LA. Michael settled into the comfortable seat. As the tires gripped the hot concrete roadway clocking the miles to the city, he remained silent, staring at the road, questioning his motives for accepting the case and wondering what the hell he got himself into.

THIRTEEN

Sara closed her apartment door behind her with one foot, tying not to topple the groceries stuffed haphazardly into the two brown bags she carried. She made her way to the kitchen and deposited the bags on the counter. Her eyes caught sight of the flashing numbers on the answering machine. As she unpacked the groceries, she reached over and pushed the playback button.

"Hi, Doc. Sorry to call at the last minute, but it looks like I'll be working till midnight on a new case. I have to skip dinner with you tonight. Don't forget, if you get another one of those nasty nightmares, who you gonna call...?" Michael hung up at that point.

Sara laughed out loud, her heart thumping immediately to the sound of his deep, mellow voice. A second later another voice called out from the machine.

"Hello, Dr. Bradley. My name is Mrs. Glazer. I'm Carly Perez' teacher at the Trencher School. I have some concerns about her I'd like to discuss with you. My number is two one three, five five five, seven two one nine. Thank you."

Sara stopped unpacking and quickly played back the last message, writing down the phone number.

Carly had been back in school for a while. Although she was still somber and quiet, rarely speaking, Sara felt getting back to her normal activities such as school might help her feel safe enough to open up. She saw her three times a week, sometimes in her office, sometimes at school, yet not much progress had been made. The child was unable or unwilling to talk about the night her mother was murdered. Whenever Sara approached the subject, she turned away, grabbed her doll and hugged it to her chest. From that point on, Sara lost whatever connection she'd made with her and the session ended in frustration.

She glanced up at the clock. Four twenty. As soon as she finished putting the groceries away, she dialed Mrs. Glazer. A receptionist answered and called the teacher to the phone.

"Mrs. Glazer? This is Sara Bradley. You left a message on my machine regarding Carly Perez."

"Oh, yes, Dr. Bradley. Thank you for calling back so soon. I was told by Carly's nanny, Juana, you are working with Carly. She gave me your number. I hope you don't mind my calling."

"Of course not. Anything you can tell me about Carly will be helpful."

"Well, I'm not sure how significant this is, but she's constantly getting into fistfights with little boys in her class, particularly, two or three who play together. I've noticed it's been happening more and more since...since she lost her mother. I know that night must have been very traumatic for her, but she was always such a sweet little girl. I can't understand the drastic change of behavior since she's come back to school."

She paused. "She sits in class, staring out the window, paying little attention to the lesson being taught. However, in the school yard her demeanor changes radically. She's become a bully, picking on some of the smaller children, taking their toys, pushing them out of line for the playground equipment, pulling hair, biting. She's never done those things before. She used to be the best behaved child in my class. Now she's becoming a real discipline problem. When I mentioned this to Juana, she got very upset and suggested I speak with you. I don't think it's fair that poor woman is left with the burden of disciplining Carly. I wonder just how available Judge Griswold is for her, with his busy schedule and all."

"I can understand your concern, Mrs. Glazer. I'm sure you're caught between your sympathy for Carly and your need to manage your class. I thank you for letting me know what's been happening. I've not seen that part of Carly, and my knowing how she's acting out that way is helpful. Do you think I could come by tomorrow and watch her at the playground?"

"Of course. Anytime. Just ask for me at the office."

"I'll check my calendar and let you know what time I can come by. I really appreciate your call."

"I'm very glad to have your help, Dr. Bradley. As I've said, this isn't like Carly. I don't want to see this situation go unresolved. That would only lead to more problems throughout her school years."

"I understand. She's lucky to have you in her life right now. Good-bye, Mrs. Glazer."

Sara wasn't surprised. She knew it was only a matter of time before Carly acted out the hostility and aggression she must be feeling since her mother's brutal death. That was actually a sign of progress. She looked forward to visiting the school.

*   *   *

The following afternoon, Sara leaned against the white-washed stucco wall of the hacienda-style school building, her arms folded across her chest. From time to time, she put her hand up to shade her eyes from the warm May sun. The glare was strong enough to penetrate her sunglasses, sting her eyes and make her wish she was back in the air conditioned Audi.

She watched the small group of kindergartners while they played in the school yard. Particularly, she watched Carly Perez.

The child sat alone on a bench watching the other children run back and forth, in and out of large hollow red, green and yellow cylinders which lay like mammoth prehistoric creatures in a sandy corner of the playground.

Her attention shifted to a bald, paunchy man who stood on the sidewalk with his hands in his pockets staring at the children through the cyclone fence. There was something about the man which caused a chill to run though her. Her skin began to crawl. Was he one of those predators who preferred victimizing children rather than adults? Darn. He was staring at Carly. Why was he so focused on her? Did he know her? Sara's continuing concern for Carly's safety sprang into her mind. Could that man be a threat?

Her attention was jerked back to the school yard. She pulled her body away from the wall and tensed. For no apparent reason, Carly pushed a little boy. He wouldn't be bullied, especially by a girl, so he pushed back. Carly then struck out in full fury, her little arms flailing about, her fists clenched shut. She screamed at the top of her lungs, frightening the other children who stood away from her to avoid being hit. At first the boy accepted the blows, a look of surprise on his face. Then he hit back.

The playground monitor came running over to the children. She pulled Carly away from the boy, and shouted at him to stop. When he realized Carly was encircled within the restraining arms of the woman and powerless to hit him anymore, he stopped fighting. The woman told the other children to go back to their play and turned away with Carly, kicking and trying to free herself. The two of them headed toward the school and disappeared into the building.

Sara followed them. By the time she entered the school, Carly and the woman were out of sight. Another woman, probably mid-forties, short dark hair and a round pleasant face, approached Sara.

"Dr. Bradley." She reached out and shook Sara's hand. "I'm Edith Glazer. I'm glad you were here just now. That is the kind of behavior that's been happening for the last week, totally out of character for Carly. She's been with us for over two years, and this is the first time she's ever been a problem."

"I see what you mean. May I go and speak with her now?"

"Of course. Go right in. She's in the playroom around the corner."

Sara followed Mrs. Glazer's direction. Carly sat at a small desk, alone in the room, a crayon in her hand. Her head leaned over a large piece of paper on which she was drawing. Sara walked over to the desk, pulled up another small seat and sat down in front of her. The child had yet to acknowledge Sara's presence. Sara remained quiet, respecting the child's apparent need for quiet.

After several minutes, Carly spoke, her eyes glued to the picture she drew. "Yesterday Juana took me to the zoo, and we saw the bears again. They didn't look very happy. The mommy bear kept yawning and making funny noises when the baby bear wanted to play. Sometimes she pushed him away and then went to sleep."

"Did the baby bear try to play with anyone else?"

"No. She only wanted to play with her mommy, but she was sleeping."

"I'll bet the baby bear felt very angry about that."

Carly was silent. She continued to stare down at her picture. Sara studied the paper. She cleared her mind of any outside thoughts in an effort to become open to ideas and interpretations which the drawings might inspire. That technique had been useful in the past, but while she watched the child's little hand slowly continue to mark the paper, nothing seemed to be clicking.

Carly used a black crayon. Straight lines scattered haphazardly across the page in no obvious pattern, making no concrete impression on Sara's trained mind. Yet the child continued to mark the paper in a purposeful way, guided by some invisible force.

"I think at night time when all the people go home, the mommy and daddy animals wake up and do bad things no one can see. They have a secret." Tears ran down Carly's cheeks.

Sara jumped into the opening. "What kind of secrets, sweetie?"

Carly didn't answer.

Sara felt herself being drawn to the child, almost pulled into her. Her thoughts turned to images of her standing in a barn, where rays of light shone through the loose boards. She smelled the sweet fragrance of dry hay and almost felt its brittleness beneath her feet. The image was so strong, so real, she was sure Carly heard her heart pounding in her chest. Her hands were cold and sweaty.

The scene disappeared. She came back to the reality of the classroom and the child sitting in front of her with such a force, she jerked to her feet, knocking the chair out from under her. She shook herself free of the image.

The sound of the wooden chair hitting the hard surface broke the spell.

Carly looked up at Sara curiously. "Hi, Sara, did you come to take me home from school today?"

Sara grabbed her shoulder bag tightly and smiled at Carly, hopefully appearing more relaxed and composed than she felt.

"I sure did, sweetie. We can wait until you've finished drawing. That looks like the beginning of an interesting picture. Are those lines going to be people?"

The child giggled. "No, silly! They don't have faces, do they?"

Sara smiled and wrinkled her brow. "I guess you're right. Is this a picture of rain?"

Again Carly laughed and shook her head. "It's a puzzle, like in Mommy's crossword book. With lots of lines. Someday I'll make boxes and then words, and then everyone will know the puzzle. Will you play this game with me?"

"I'd love to. What should I do?"

Carly handed the paper to Sara. "You keep this. Next time I'll draw some more and then maybe you can guess. Can we go home now? I'm tired."

"I'm ready if you are."

When Carly nodded her little head, her dark hair shook.

"Good. Let's say good-bye to Mrs. Glazer before we go. Then what do you say we stop at the bakery on the way to your house and pick up some fresh cookies."

"Can we bring some home for Juana?"

"Definitely" Sara reached out and took her outstretched hand. "I think we all deserve a treat today. Let's go."

No sooner had Sara left Carly with Juana and gotten back into her car when a wave of dizziness washed over her. She gripped the edge of the steering wheel until the black spots disappeared. Pains stabbed her stomach. Another migraine pounded her head.

"Damn." She banged the steering wheel. "Enough of this."

She retrieved her iPhone from the bottom of her purse and clicked on the number. A gentle voice answered, every syllable sending shooting stabs of pain through her throbbing head.

"Rose? This is Sara, Sara Bradley."

"Sara? It's wonderful to hear from you. You sound distressed. How may I help you?"

Sara smiled. That was just like Rose, so willing to be there when she needed her. "Actually, I was wondering if you could see me tonight. I, I need help with a problem. I, I don't seem to be making much headway dealing with it myself."

"You shouldn't have to deal with it by yourself, and shame on you for trying to do so. My last appointment for the evening just canceled. Can you make it here around eight? Or would you like me to come to your place?"

"Oh, no, I feel bad enough bothering you as it is. I'll come to your office at eight."

"Why don't you come to the house? We'll be more comfortable."

"Okay. Thanks, Rose. I'll see you at eight."

Sara barely got home before collapsing on her bed. She lay down and pulled the covers around her. Here, safe in bed, wrapped in the warm comforter, her tense body relaxed. With that came tears of shame and fear. Shame for not being strong enough to deal with whatever was bothering her in a more positive way; fear of finding out what was apparently hidden so deep within, her body was forced to cry out for relief in such a painful way.

She turned onto her side, hugging her arms about her chest, and let the sobs come until there was nothing left but exhaustion. She longed for the peace of sleep, but it didn't come. As her mind fought for rest, eerie memories of the bald, fat man at the school yard floated in and out. In a dream-like state, he chased her and Carly. Sara's heart pounded in fear, both for herself and the child. She tossed and turned until finally she drifted into a restless sleep.

*   *   *

When she awoke from her uneasy nap, her first thought was of Carly Perez. Was the child in danger? Sara had to know for sure, and realized who could help her find out the truth.

Before driving to Rose's home, she dialed Joe Hatch.

He picked up after three rings. "Hatch."

"Joe, its Sara."

"Hey, Bradley. How've you been? I bet you miss my late night calls. How's it going with the kid?"

"That's why I'm calling. Something's come up that has me worried about her safety."

"What?" There was a shift in Hatch's demeanor. He was all business now.

"I took her to the zoo recently and when we were leaving, a car nearly ran us over in the parking lot."

"Jeez. You okay?"

"Yes, we're fine, but I'm sure it wasn't an accident. Someone deliberately headed right for us. We barely got out of the way."

"Now why would someone want to hurt you? Upset any of your patients recently?"

"I'm not so sure the driver was aiming for me. I think he meant to hurt Carly."

"Carly? What makes you say that?"

"I don't know. Instinct maybe. And then today, at her school, a fat, bald man stared at her from behind the school yard fence. He was so creepy I got a chill just looking at him. Joe, are you sure you have the murderer behind bars? He didn't make bail, did he?"

"No. He's tucked nice and safe at Wayside. You're probably over-reacting. Go home, take a long hot bubble bath, do your nails or whatever you do to relax. I'm sure it was just some asshole either drunk or high on something."

"Don't humor me, Joe." Now she was angry. "I think Carly may be at risk. I'm afraid for her."

He was silent for a moment. "I don't know what to tell you, Sara. I can't justify putting a detail on her when we have the perp locked up. Just tell the nanny to be on the lookout for any signs of trouble. Maybe you can voice your concerns to the judge. He might be willing to hire a bodyguard."

"I doubt that, not when you're all convinced you have the right man in jail." She sighed. They were silent for a few moments. Then Sara got an idea.

"What if I show her a photo of the man you're so certain is the murderer?"

"Why now? When I asked you to do that before, you refused, saying it wouldn't be good for her."

"She's much stronger now, and she trusts me. She may recognize him since he worked on the estate. I'll know by her response if she shows any fear or anxiety when she looks at him. Please, Joe."

"I don't know. Koosman's convinced we've got the right man. For God's sake, Sara, he confessed."

"Yes, but the case against him would be a lot stronger if we knew for certain he was the one Carly saw that night. That would eliminate any reasonable doubt and strengthen your case. There'd be no room for a good defense attorney to try to plead down his sentence. You'd be sure to get the maximum allowable sentence for him."

"Damn it, Sara. Don't tell me how to do my job."

"Then let me do mine. I need to know that my patient is safe."

It took a while for Hatch to respond. "All right. Come by the station tomorrow, and I'll give you some mug shots."

She smiled into the phone. "Thanks, Joe. This way we'll both be sure we're doing the right thing."

"Yeah, well, we'll see, won't we?" He hung up.

Sara breathed a sigh of relief. One problem solved, at least for the immediate future. Onto the next one.

*   *   *

A short drive later, Sara stood at the door to Rose Goodman's home. Finally, after much hesitation, she knocked. Rose answered immediately. The older woman's face registered surprise. Sara hadn't taken much time to get ready before leaving her apartment. She hadn't even tried to cover up the dark circles under her eyes. She'd barely brushed her long wavy hair and hastily pulled on a baggy black sweater which hung down to the middle of her thighs over faded jeans.

"Come in, my dear." Dr. Goodman closed the door, and gave Sara a warm, gentle hug. "I'm so glad to see you. It's been a while. I've got some hot tea waiting."

Sara followed Dr. Goodman into the living room. A couple of aspirins and a two-hour nap had helped to relieve most of the headache and all of the stomach pains, but the suddenness and intensity of the attack left her shaken. She allowed herself the luxury of accepting the caring concern from her long-time mentor and friend. After slipping off her shoes, she sank down into the deep cushions of the sofa and pulled her legs up under her.

"Thank you for seeing me right away, Rose. I've been putting this off for some time now, but today I...I..."

Rose handed her a hot cup of black tea and settled down into the sofa beside her.

Sara sipped it. As the warm liquid slid down her throat, her body relaxed.

"You know well enough, one of the benefits of our profession," Rose said, "is the freedom to make our own work schedule and to work until we die if we choose. So, at my age, I see only a few patients. Today was exceptionally light. Besides, you know I would've made arrangements to see you no matter what."

Sara's eyes filled with tears of gratitude. "You've always been there for me. Have I told you how much I appreciate that?"

Rose laughed. "Only every time we get together, which, I might add, has been very infrequent over the years, much too infrequent."

"You know I pride myself at being able to handle things alone. Call it my stubbornness, my inflexibility, even my neurosis, if you will, it's important for my self-esteem." Sara sighed. "But tonight, I feel as though I've hit the wall, and I'll be damned if I know what it's all about. It's very frightening for me not to understand everything. I feel so out of control."

Rose smiled. "I'm sure it is. But you, of all people, should know each of us reaches a place sometime in our lives, often many times, when we're unable to cope with what's happening. That's when we should reach out for help. There's no shame in that."

"I know, I know. I tell my patients this every day. It's easy for me to see beyond their words to what's really bothering them, but I don't seem to be able to do that for myself. I, I don't know what's bothering me."

"What are your symptoms?"

"I've been getting stomach pains, nausea and migraines. An occasional nightmare. Everything started a while back, maybe four or five months, and it's getting worse, which surprises me, actually."

"Why's that?"

Sara smiled. "I've been seeing a man this past month, pretty steadily. He's very special. Different from any man I've ever gone out with, very caring and supportive. We have a lot of fun when we're together."

"Good for you. You deserve to have someone special in your life. I've always been concerned about your intense preoccupation with work. I'm surprised you haven't had those physical symptoms sooner. Too much work and not enough play are very unhealthy, particularly in our field."

"You're right, but then why aren't these symptoms disappearing instead of escalating?"

"When was the last time you felt this way?"

"Today, just before I called you. I felt as though I'd been hit by a truck I hadn't seen coming."

"Do you recall what you were doing just before they appeared?"

"I was in the middle of a session with a young patient when it started. By the time I got into my car, it hit full blast—headache, nausea, dizziness."

"Was the session particularly stressful?"

"Not really. In fact, I'm finally making some progress with the child."

"Do you want to tell me about it?"

"I don't mind, but I don't think it has anything to do with my physical symptoms. They began long before I started working with her."

"You said they've escalated recently. I wonder if this case could have any bearing on that."

Sara stood, crossed her arms about her chest and paced the room. "I don't know. Why should this case affect me differently from any of the others? I've worked with plenty of young children, some in even more distress than Carly, and I didn't have this kind of reaction. I just don't understand."

"I hear some impatience, even anger, in your voice, as though it's not all right with you to not understand yourself at every moment. We've talked about this issue before, haven't we? The strict, rigid rules you have for yourself. Your discomfort with the unknown. Your need to control. I suspect you've reached the limits of your ability to contain your personal ambiguity. Perhaps you're punishing yourself rather harshly with each attack as it occurs, rather than accepting it, learning from it, allowing it to tell you something more about yourself, and moving on."

Sara's eyes filled with tears. "Even if it's the same old pattern, it's never felt this intense." She turned and faced the older woman. "I'm scared. I'm not sure I want to find out what this is all about. Something tells me to run away and leave it be."

"But you can't, my dear. Apparently, you've been doing that for some time, and now your body is protesting. It won't let you run away any more. You must stand and face it, whatever it is."

Sara grimaced. "I was hoping you wouldn't say that."

Rose stood and pulled Sara into her arms. "I'm not able to be this confrontational with many people, my dear, but you have always demonstrated so much courage and resilience. Beneath your conscious fears, I sense a part of you that demands total honesty from me and total integrity from yourself. I've always admired you for that quality."

After Sara disengaged herself from Rose's embrace, Rose continued, "Now, the next thing I'm going to say won't be easy to hear. I want you to take some time to think about it and all the ramifications it entails before you decide to do anything about it."

A chill suddenly ran through Sara. She hugged herself tightly for warmth and support. Her voice sounded like a barely audible whisper. "What is it, Rose?"

"I think it's time you gathered more information on your natural parents. The more you know about them, and the first four years of your life before you woke up in the orphanage, the better off you'll be. Knowing your past may shed some light on what's bothering you now."

Sara took a deep breath. So, the moment she'd avoided for so long was there. She'd always known it was just a matter of time before she had to find out about her biological parents, her roots. Known this and still avoided it. Rose was right. She'd spoken the unspoken that Sara had been pushing out of her mind for a long time.

She turned and walked over to the window. The cool dryness of the early summer evening just beyond the screened window filled her senses.

She took a deep, shaky breath. "I don't need time to decide. I've been preparing myself for this moment for a long time. I'll ask Michael to help me with the legal aspects of getting my adoption files."

"Good. Let's set up some time each week to get together. I'm sure you want to get past all this and get on with your life, especially now you have this new relationship to enjoy."

Sara pulled out a tissue, wiped her eyes, blew her nose and smiled. "I wonder if Michael would still be interested in me if he saw me like this."

"If he's the man you say he is, he'd want to be there to help you through it. If not, he's not for you."

Sara laughed. "I've always been jealous of your children, Rose. It must have been wonderful growing up with a mother like you."

Rose snickered. "Well, I hope you never get to talk with any of them. I'm sure they'd give you enough dirt to change your opinion of me. Now, go home and have a good night's sleep. You look like you've been through the proverbial wringer."

She walked Sara to the door, her arm still about Sara's shoulders. "Good night, my dear. See you next week."

FOURTEEN

Sara opened the door to the office and stepped inside. The first thing she noticed was the deep brown leather sofa and the glass coffee table piled with magazines. They sat in front of a half wall of windows on the left-hand side of the large room. A secretary's desk along with a computer workstation lined the opposite wall. Across from where Sara stood was a closed door.

The door next to the secretarial station was wide open, allowing bright sunlight from the inner office to shine through to the reception area.

A man knelt on the floor, his back to her, so involved in something he didn't hear her enter. A young woman dressed in a sharp red business suit stood next to him watching whatever it was he was doing with equal attention. The long sleeves of his white dress shirt were rolled up past his elbows.

"There. I think I've got it. Now, see this light here? When I push the button it should go on, and the thing should start revving up like a son of a bitch. Back up, Katie. Let's see if we can get this sucker going."

In a moment, a loud piercing whistle blew. Suddenly a two-feet-long red and white fire truck shot out from in front of him and went careening across the room, ramming into the opposite wall.

Sara laughed out loud. Shades of Christmas past flashed in her mind.

The man jumped to his feet, turned and looked at her, a sheepish grin flooding his features. "A present for my kid. He's four today. Can I help you with anything?"

The woman standing next to him seemed barely able to control her laughter. Shaking her head, she went back to her desk and pounded away on the computer keyboard.

Sara cleared the laughter from her voice. "Yes. I'm looking for Michael Grey. I understand this is his office."

He gave her teal blue suit, navy blue heels and matching leather shoulder bag an approving once-over. "You're in the right place. I think Mike's hiding behind the door over there, up to his neck in work as usual."

He walked toward her with his hand outstretched, a huge smile on his face. "I'm Alan Douglas, Mike's buddy and office mate."

She shook his hand. "I'm Sara Bradley. I thought I'd surprise him. I was hoping to tear him away for an early dinner."

Alan laughed and gave her an appraising glance. "Well, if anyone can do that, I'll bet it's you. Come on. I'll lead you into the lion's den." He turned and walked to Michael's office, knocked twice and opened the door.

"Yo, Mike. Take a break. I've got a surprise for you." He ushered Sara into the room.

She spoke in a teasing voice. "What kind of friend are you? Your buddy's out there struggling with his son's toy, and you're in here hiding behind the books."

Michael looked up quickly from the papers he'd been reading. He pulled off his wire-rimmed glasses, his face showing surprise at the interruption, then recognition. A smile lit up his face, but after a brief look at his friend, he toned it down and sat back in his tall leather chair.

"Is that what all the racket was about? I don't know, Douglas. You keep this up, I'll have to move out. A man's got to have peace and quiet while he's working."

His words addressed Alan, but the veiled intimacy in his dark eyes when he looked at her caught her breath.

"What brings you downtown today, Doc, another mission of mercy?"

"Yes, but not for one of my patients. I thought I might rescue you from the heavy burden of your own labors." Her lips curved upward.

Alan must have sensed the electricity between the two because he cleared his throat before speaking. "Well, I better get going. Like I said, we have a birthday party planned at the house tonight. In fact, why don't you two kids stop in for dessert later?"

Sara pulled her gaze away from Michael and smiled at Alan. "Maybe we will. Thanks for the invitation." Again she shook hands with him.

"A pleasure meeting you, Sara. Now I understand why Mike has suddenly and mysteriously become almost bearable to live with lately. Hope to see you later."

He gave Michael the high sign with his thumb before he left the room, closing the door behind him.

She smiled at Michael. "I like him."

He got out of his chair and walked toward her. As usual, a hot rush ran through her body. No longer a surprise, she accepted it as a very special part of her attraction to him. Ditto her growing obsession with thinking about him constantly and wanting to be near him.

Her arms stayed at her sides. She backed up against the door when he approached. His left arm reached up over her head, his palm pressing flat against the door. It trapped her, stopped her from leaving. When his right hand moved under her hair and gently pulled her face up to his, leaving was the last thing on her mind. He bent down and kissed her. Her body went limp. She leaned into him. The only movement in the room was their mouths against each other's, touching, pressing, pulling, sucking, tongues dancing, a uniquely primitive form of communication which transcended language. Somewhere amid the rushing noises in her head, there was the muted sound of a ticking clock. She tried to focus on it in order to stay in touch with reality.

After a while, he pulled far enough away and looked into her eyes. "Well, my dear Dr. Bradley. I declare your mission of mercy a smashing success. You've lifted the burden of my miserable daily existence." He smiled, a teasing lilt in his deep voice. "The problem is, I'm left standing here with nothing but pornographic ideations and fantasies swimming around in my lecherous, tainted mind. Unfortunately, something tells me you didn't come here with the intention of satisfying any of my baser, primal needs at this hour of the day." He kissed her again then pulled back. "So, what can I do for you?"

She smiled. She caught her breath and settled her racing heart. "I have a favor to ask. A legal favor."

Michael's eyebrows rose slightly, and he looked at her curiously. He reached for her hand, led her to a chair in front of the desk and motioned for her to sit down. He sat on the edge of his desk, facing her, his palms resting on the surface. "What do you need?"

Her breath pulled in sharply at his question. She sensed his open, honest willingness to help her. "My adoption records from New York."

Michael watched her silently for a moment. She imagined his mind clicking into legal mode, digging into recesses where his New York law info was stored. She watched him, a bit tense, waiting for his response, a part of her hoping he'd come back with a very apologetic, "Sorry, Sara, but that's impossible."

Instead, he said, "It may take some time, but that shouldn't be a problem."

Just like that. No questions. No prying. Just unconditional support. She took a deep breath, tears threatening to spill out onto her cheeks. "Thank you."

She stood up and moved closer to him. "You're a very special person, Michael Grey. Whoever that woman was in your past who hurt you so deeply, she was a fool to let you go. I guess her loss is my gain."

Apparently, her acknowledgement left him at a loss for words, so instead of responding, he pulled her into his arms and claimed her mouth again.

She pulled back and locked her hands around his neck. She gently touched the scar on his face. "How did you get this?"

He immediately pulled back. Was that a flash of fear or anger on his face? Whatever it was, it disappeared as quickly as it came. He ignored the question and returned to light banter once again. "Now that you have rescued me from my computer, and I've resolved all your legal dilemmas, I'm wondering what's next."

She decided not to push the matter of the scar. Apparently, it was a sore subject, one he didn't want to talk about, so she smiled. "There's always dinner and later dessert at Alan's."

He shook his head slowly, deliberately. "No way. It's been...how long...three days, eight hours and twenty-seven minutes, and I'm not sharing you with anyone tonight. The Douglas' will have to wait. I've waited long enough. Your place or mine?"

"Mine's closer."

"Then off we go to Sherman Oaks."

*   *   *

Sara's shrill scream woke him suddenly from a sound sleep. He turned to her, leaning on his left elbow. His right hand reached for her face to brush away the long hair which had been tossed across it. Her damp skin was hot and sweaty, her eyes closed. She was hyperventilating, gasping for breath and clutching the covers. Suddenly he panicked, fear overwhelming him. He couldn't remember the last time he'd felt that intense fear. Even more amazing, he wasn't afraid for himself. He was afraid for her.

"Sweetheart, what is it? What's wrong? One of your nightmares?"

Slowly she opened her eyes. She focused on his face and her heavy breathing slowed. She bit her lower lip and nodded. Her face wrinkled in pain. "God, it hurts so much!"

"What? What hurts? Where does it hurt?"

"My head and my stomach."

"What can I do to help? Tell me what to do."

She began to sob. Tears streamed down her face.

"Hold me. Just hold me until it goes away."

He gently pulled her into his arms and held her as tight as he dared. Her arm went across his bare chest. She cried uncontrollably for quite some time, deep sobs shaking her body. He tried to stop them by pulling her closer. He whispered to her gently from a place of strength and knowing, a place as unfamiliar to him as the words he whispered. "That's right, honey. Let it out. Don't be afraid. Let it go."

Soon her sobs stopped and her breathing was shallow once again. His hand caressed her damp face. She was nearly asleep from exhaustion. He leaned back into the bed, still holding her tightly, and stared up into the darkness at the ceiling.

When his own body relaxed, he took stock of the broad array of feelings he'd just experienced. His highly trained mind took over and listed them. There was the disabling confusion at not knowing the cause of her pain; incredible frustration at not being able to take it away and especially the overwhelming desire, almost need, to protect her. The last was the most mystifying and strangely satisfying to him. It had been many years since he'd felt such intense compassion for another human being. He'd refused to let himself become drawn into another's pain, to trigger those feelings in him, to touch such a deep place inside.

He took a deep, shaky breath. Drowsiness overcame him. As he began to drift off into sleep, he was at peace, in touch with the most profound experience of loving another human being he'd ever felt.

She stirred. He woke and lay there sensing the deep darkness and empty silence that was predawn. He concluded they must have slept for several hours. She snuggled closer to him. Her hand, still resting on his bare chest moved slowly, brushing across his nipple. She nestled her face into the nook of his neck. Her hand continued its intimate exploration of his body. His hand moved to her thigh and slid past her waist until it found her breast. His thumb caressed her nipple.

This time their usual fierce passionate lovemaking was different, tempered by the intense feelings they both experienced hours before. Their bodies moved slowly against each other. He felt overwhelmingly humbled by his newfound feelings toward her, the incredible vulnerability and trust he sensed in her. She moved her lips up his neck toward his ear.

"I love you, Michael," she whispered.

He turned his face in the darkness until his mouth found hers. Since words were difficult for him, he answered with his body.

*   *   *

Later that morning she was in the kitchen, dressed in a beige and white long skirt and hip-length matching blouse, pulled together at the waist by a gold and white chain belt. She stood in front of the sink humming an old Paul Simon tune, her back to him. He moved up slowly behind her, reached out, put his hands on her shoulders. He bent and kissed her neck. She moved into him slightly at his touch.

"Hmm. Good morning. How about some grapefruit, bagels and cream cheese?"

He moved over to the refrigerator, opened the door and took out a bottle of orange juice. "What? No pancakes, eggs, bacon and sausage?"

She continued to cut the grapefruit. "Sorry, Charlie, for that menu you'll have to try the IHOP down the street. This working woman has a date with a five-year old in less than an hour."

He found two glasses in a cabinet and went to the island, sat down on a stool and poured the juice. She turned, a plate filled with grapefruit in each hand, and sat across from him. The cereal bowls, bagels and cream cheese were already there.

He glanced up and noticed her looking at his shirt.

"I think I'd better start carrying a change of clothes in my car. Showing up at work in the same clothes two days in a row will start tongues wagging."

"I've got a better idea. I'll make some room in my closet. You can leave a few things here."

"Okay." He spread cream cheese on his bagel. "Tell me. What does a shrink do when she continues having nightmares that wake her up screaming in pain?"

Her cheeks turned pink. She took a sip of juice. "Well, the first thing she does is go to a medical doctor to rule out any physical problems."

"And then?"

"Then she makes an appointment with her own shrink and looks for possible unconscious causation."

"So, when is your appointment?"

"As a matter of fact, I'm seeing Rose tonight."

"Good. That's not my field of expertise, you know. I dropped Freudian Dream Analysis 101 for History of American Jurisprudence and never made it up."

She laughed. "Good to know. I'll remember to bring you along next time I have to appear in court to handle a parking ticket."

He smiled. She certainly didn't look any worse for wear after the night before. Her cheeks were blushed a natural soft rosy color; her eyes were clear and bright. God, what an amazing woman.

She took a long drink of coffee. "You might not be up for a serious conversation at breakfast, but I want to say something before I go."

"Shoot." He pushed the hollowed grapefruit shell aside, reached for the warm, cinnamon raisin bagel and took a bite.

"I want you to know I haven't been with anyone else since, since that first night with you. I've never been able to handle more than one relationship at a time. Too complicated, and, and in this case, not necessary. You fill up my life completely. There's no need for anyone else. You don't have to respond. I just wanted you to know where I'm coming from."

There was a long moment of silence.

"I guess that's something else we have in common." He held her gaze then looked away and pulled back a bit. "By the way, I've just taken on a case from a P.D. friend of mine which requires a lot of background work. I'm attempting to have the plea changed and go to trial. I'm nowhere near prepared. I'll be burning the candle at both ends for a while. Just wanted you to know."

She smiled and reached into her pocket and handed him a key. "Then you'll want this. I believe Sherman Oaks is nearer to downtown than the Marina."

He looked at her closely for a few moments. Finally he took the key then pulled her hand to his lips and kissed it gently.

"You'll be sorry you gave me this when I come crawling in at two or three a.m. I'll try to be quiet and not wake you."

Sara smiled lightly. "If you want to keep that key you'd better wake me once in a while." She leaned over and kissed him.

She put the breakfast things away, grabbed her purse and hurried toward the door. With her hand on the knob, she turned and looked at him for a moment. "I'm glad you were here last night, Michael."

She turned, opened the door and closed it behind her.

*   *   *

Armed with the photo of Warren Dills in her purse, Sara went to the Trencher school. At the reception desk, she asked to have a private talk with Carly Perez. The secretary handed a note to one of the children helping out in the office, and in a moment the boy returned with Carly. The secretary showed Sara and Carly into a small room down the hall and closed the door behind them.

They sat. Sara smiled at Carly. The child seemed quiet but relaxed. "I'm sorry to take you out of class."

"It's okay. We were only doing the ABCs and I already know them."

"I know how smart you are. In fact, that's why I wanted to see you today. I found a new game I wanted to play with you. It's called "Guess Who This Is." Would you like to play?"

"I like games." Carly's eyes brightened.

"Good." Sara pulled out photos she knew Carly would recognize and laid them down on the table one at a time.

"Who's this?"

Carly smiled. "You know who that is. It's Juana."

"Right. Now, who's this?"

"That's Mrs. Kessler. She's my friend's mommy."

"Good. What about this picture?"

She laughed. "That's Jingles, my pony. Maybe someday you can take one of our horses and ride with me and Jingles in the park."

"I'd like that. I've always loved horses." Then she put the picture of Warren Dills in front of the child. "Who's this?"

"That's the man who takes care of the horses. I don't know his name." Her expression didn't change one bit. No aversion. No anxiety. Nothing to suggest she had anything to fear from him.

Sara showed her a few more photos before putting them all back in her purse. "You did great. I knew you would. Are you ready to go back to your class now?"

Carly stood. "Okay."

Sara walked her out to the reception area. "All done. See you soon, Carly." She went with another child to her classroom.

Sara thanked the secretary and headed out to her car, anxiety sweeping through her. This time, it wasn't for herself, but for Carly. Sara was now certain the child was in danger. She had to have a conversation with Joe Hatch as soon as possible.

FIFTEEN

Hatch and his partner, Blake, slumped on the front seat of the unmarked Crown Vic. Hatch laid back against the headrest, attempting to use one of those meditation exercises he learned at the department's stress management class. He closed his eyes, took long, deep breaths. The air went in and out of his nostrils. He focused on the rise and fall of his chest. He allowed all the frustration, anger and pent-up feelings to roll upwards through his body–from the toes, past the legs and stomach, through the chest and neck. Then he imagined there was an opening at the top of his head. He let all that stored up crap out of his body with one long exhale. Presto! Everything was honky-dory.

Yeah, right. Bullshit.

He shook himself and cursed under his breath.

"Hey, Joe, you awake? Wanna share my dinner?" Apparently Blake's stress management consisted of four tacos, a pint of pinto beans and a liter of Dr. Pepper.

"God, that stuff smells awful. No wonder I couldn't get into my meditation."

Blake burst out laughing, almost spitting the messy meal onto the front of his white, short-sleeved shirt. "Your what?"

Hatch grunted. "Never mind."

He turned his face to the buildings across the street. He hated stakeouts. They were boring, tiring and rarely produced anything interesting. So far, nothing about this night led him to any other conclusion.

He looked over at the house they were watching. One of his informants assured him a gangbanger named Quintero had information on the murder for hire case he and Blake were working. So there he was, on a balmy Thursday night in mid-summer, stuck outside some boarded-up bungalow in the worse part of the East Los Angeles barrio. If that wasn't bad enough, he was trapped inside the car which was, thanks to Blake's dinner, slowly taking on the aroma of the surrounding neighborhood. He was ready to puke. Meditation be damned.

He grunted some response to Blake's dinner invitation and continued staring out the window.

Blake went back to devouring his tacos as silently as his wretchedly poor table manners would allow. Suddenly, Hatch sat up straight.

Blake responded immediately. "What's up, something going down?"

"Someone just sashayed around the corner. Looks like he's up to something. Shit! I think he's made us. He's walking right to us."

Hatch's right hand went to rest on the 9-millimeter Berretta which hung in a shoulder holster inside his jacket. The man, apparently familiar with dealing with police, raised open hands to the middle of his chest. As he got closer to the car, he called out in broken English, "Hatch ees me, Chavez. I'm comin' in. I'm clean."

"Chavez. What the hell are you doing here? First you send me on this fucking wild goose chase and now you show up and blow my cover. I've had it with you, you worthless piece of shit. I'm tired of you stringing me along. Now get the fuck out of my sight before I call a cop and have you arrested for loitering."

"Ha! Hatch, real funny. I come here to do you a favor. Don' wan' you wastin' more time sittin' 'round here while your fat ass gets bigger and bigger for nothin', mahn."

Hatch glanced over at Blake, who watched Chavez closely, while continuing to chew a mouthful of beans.

"What do you say, Blake? Should we pop this wiseass son of a bitch now or later?"

Blake answered with his mouth full. "Geez, Joe, not now. Can't you see I'm eating? You want me to get indigestion or something?"

Hatch turned back to Chavez. "Well, Chavez, this must be your lucky day. Saved by a taco. Something to tell your grandchildren about...if you live long enough to have any. Now what's so important you can't wait to talk to me through regular channels?"

"Quintero ain't here, mahn. I just heard he left for Chihuahua this morning to set up some big drug score. Should be goin' down sometime early next week. I'll let you know when and where."

"Sure. Sure. I bet you will. In the meantime, what do you have for me? Anything on Juarez? Jackson? What about Kingston? You heard from him lately?"

The Mexican was bent over, looking into the driver's side open window, only a few inches from Hatch's face. The booze on the man's breath overpowered Hatch. Red lines squiggled through his eyes. The junkie's eyes twitched and blinked nervously, shifting from Hatch to Blake. Always vigilant. Always looking out for trouble. A man on the run.

"No, mahn. Kingston's dropped out of the picture. I ain't seen him for eight, ten months. He used to be real tight with that Dills guy you was askin' about a while ago. I heard somethin' about him gettin' real sick, you know what I mean. Dun know if the dude is still breathin'. Dun know nothin' else, mahn."

The mention of Warren Dills piqued Hatch's interest. Maybe he could get more rope with which to hang that one.

"Who'd Dills hang with besides Kingston? Come on, Chavez. Give me something for my night's work. You owe me."

The Mexican scratched his head. "Geez, mahn, I, I dun know. Let me think. Yeah, yeah, you right. Dills had anotha homeboy. Little, Donny Little. That's right. He, Dills and Kingston used to party together. They was real tight."

Hatch glared at him. "How come you never mentioned his name before when I asked you about Dills?"

Chavez got visibly upset. "I dun know, mahn. I guess I just forgot. That's all. You know I don't hold out on you, Hatch. You me amigo, Sarg. You know that."

"Sure, bosom buddies, that's us. Now tell me, where can I find this guy Little? Or is he out of circulation now, too?"

"He lives with a black woman over on a hundred and twelfth and Hoover, the white house on the corner. He's one mean mother, Hatch. You won't tell him I fingered him, will you?"

Chavez's pleading eyes reminded Hatch of the scared rabbit he mistakenly caught in a rat trap last year.

"Now why would I do a thing like that? Aren't you my number one snitch, Chavez? Now get lost, and I'd better be hearing from you soon about Quintero."

Chavez smiled and backed slowly away from the car. "Adios, Hatch. I'll call you, mahn."

He took a few more steps backward, turned and headed down the street into the darkness.

Hatch reviewed the conversation in his head. At first something told him to just drop it, forget about Little. The Dills case was nearly closed, and Koosman assured him they had enough on Dills, what with his confession and all. Why take any chances on finding something that could jeopardize their case?

He caught himself. Where the fuck did that idea come from? Did he actually have a doubt about the authenticity of Dills' confession? Since when did he hold back on doing his job one hundred percent? His chest tightened. Fuck Griswold, anyway. No one was going to interfere with him doing his job his way.

He reached for the keys in the ignition and turned them. The car started and took off with such a jerk Blake's soda spilled down his shirt.

"Shit, Joe. What's your hurry? Look what you made me do." He gulped down another mouthful and then screwed the top back onto the bottle. "Where're we headed?"

"A hundred and twelfth and Hoover, and don't ever let me hear you say I don't take you to the best spots in town."

*   *   *

Twenty minutes later they pulled up in front of a small white stucco apartment house. Hatch had Blake run Little's name through their dashboard computer, and it spit out a rap sheet as long as a baseball bat. Little's list of credits ran from petty theft as a juvenile to armed robbery, no conviction, and five years' time served for possession and dealing controlled substances.

They got out of the car and headed to the apartment marked, "Manager." Hatch rang the bell. In a moment the door opened to a small, bald black man in jockey shorts, a dirty white tee shirt and bare feet.

Hatch and Blake flashed their badges. "Sorry to bother you at this hour, but we saw your light on. I'm Detective Sergeant Hatch. This is my partner, Detective Blake. We're looking for a man named Donny Little. I understand he lives here, possibly with a woman."

The manager eyed them warily. "What do you want with Little? He don't cause no trouble 'round here. Wish I could say the same for some of my other tenants."

"We just want to talk with him for a minute. You know which apartment is his?"

"O'course I know. I'm the manager, ain't I? He be in number six, down there on the left. I seed him come in a while ago."

"Thanks. Sorry to have bothered you."

Hatch and Blake turned and strolled down the cement walk, tense and alert to possible danger. Ah, Hatch sighed cynically, midnight in South Central Los Angeles. Glorious.

As they approached number six, he heard the sound of a television whose dim light appeared to be the only illumination in the apartment.

Hatch stood to one side of the front door, his hand on the Berretta under his jacket. Blake took the other side, ready to spring into action if needed. Hatch rapped his knuckles on the door and stood back.

A few minutes later, a man's voice called out, "What the fuck you want this time of night? Come back tomorrow."

"Donny Little? I'm Detective Sergeant Hatch, LAPD. I'm here with my partner, Detective Blake. We have a few questions to ask you, and unless you want your neighbors to know your business, I suggest you open up."

"You got a warrant, Hatch?"

"Don't need one. Just looking for some information. The sooner you open up, the sooner we'll be out of your hair."

It took a few moments for the man to make a decision. Then a light was turned on, and the door opened slowly. Donny Little was Caucasian, of medium build, in his mid-thirties. His face showed a few days' growth of whiskers. His hair was long and greasy, his eyes bloodshot. When the door was fully ajar, he stepped back and nodded his head for the two detectives to come in. He closed the door.

Hatch scanned the sparsely furnished living room. There was an old worn sofa, chair, small wooden table with three chairs, a floor lamp without a shade and a small screen television rested on top of an inverted milk crate. The floor was carpeted with stains running through it. Blake stood quietly with his back to the front door, watching the room. Hatch slowly walked about, peering down a hallway and into the small kitchenette off to the right side.

"Anyone else here with you, Little?"

"Just me and my woman. She's asleep in the bedroom. What the fuck do you want?"

He stood with his arms folded across his chest, feet spread apart, a centurion protecting his domain. Hatch didn't have to look into the man's eyes. Hostility oozed from him. It floated about the room like a heavy cloud of poisonous gas. He was silent, watching Hatch through slanted eyes.

"What do you know about Warren Dills?"

"I know he's in the tank looking at a murder rap. Guess he just happened to be in the wrong place at the wrong time. What's the matter, Hatch? You need a little more wood to add to the fire under that poor sucker?"

"When was the last time you saw him?"

"A few months before he started working for that judge."

"A few months? I heard you and he were pretty tight. What happened? A lover's quarrel?"

The man grunted. "We went our separate ways. The guy went soft on me, cleaned up and stopped hanging. Wasn't interested in the babes anymore, know what I mean? Suddenly got religion or something. Or maybe his old lady learned how to give good head. What the fuck do I know what happened? He just stopped coming around to the usual places. Dropped all his old pals. I'll tell you, Hatch, I don't have a lot of use for a guy like that. Serves him right you assholes nailed him. Kind of like cruel ass-backwards justice, if you know what I mean."

Hatch looked the man square in the eyes. "Humor me, Little. I'm just a dumb cop, remember? What do you mean?"

Little snickered, uncrossed his arms, walked over to the couch and sat down, his arms resting on the back of the sofa, his legs spread out wide in front of him. He leered up at Hatch. "I mean, all those years when Dills was doing real shit, you fucks were never able to pin anything much on him. Now you're going to fry him for something he didn't do. Personally, I find that kinda funny."

"What makes you think Dills didn't do the Griswold woman?"

Little became angry. "I already told you, man. He wasn't into the life anymore. Now I'm getting sick of answering dumb questions from lazy stupid pigs that get their jollies playing God with puissant whiney brats like Dills. Get the fuck out of my house before I call a real cop!"

Hatch nodded his head slowly. "Yes, sir. Dills is lucky to have a friend like you in his corner. Whatever happened to loyalty, brotherhood, homeboys?"

"Dills turned his back on us, man. I don't care if he rots in hell over this trumped-up case. Now get the hell out of here!"

Hatch turned and walked toward the front door. Blake stepped back and opened it. They left the apartment. They were silent on the way back to the car. Hatch was lost in his thoughts. Blake grumbled over the remains of his dinner still in the car. They slid into the front seat and pulled away from the house.

"Nice guy, Mr. Little. Can't say I blame Dills for not staying in touch. Well." Blake settled back into the seat. "This sure has been one wasted night. No news on Quintero and nothing to give Koosman on Dills."

As he drove back to the precinct, Hatch stared into the dark streets. There was that funny feeling in the pit of his stomach again. Happened every time he knew he was going to open his big mouth and stick his two cents in where they weren't wanted. Maybe even make some enemies.

He took a deep breath. Oh, hell, why should he change at this stage of his life? He'd rocked a few boats before, why not rock them again? What did he care? Just a few more years and then he'd be sunbathing in Tahiti for the rest of his life. Hah! Who the fuck was he kidding?

*   *   *

cHatch stared at the phone he'd just hung up. He'd spent a long sleepless night after his stakeout with Blake, and the call from Sara Bradley hadn't helped to alleviate the gnawing in the pit of his stomach. The Griswold case was really getting to him. In plain English, it stank worse than a burning tire. Confession or not, if he'd arrested the wrong man, then if anything happened to the kid, he'd never be able to live with himself. The more information he got about Dills, the more it looked like the murderer was still out there, and Carly Perez was in danger.

He decided to have another go at it with Koosman, and grabbed his car keys.

Koosman was on the phone when Hatch responded to his "come in". The D.D.A. appeared to be debating the finer points of California criminal law probably to some other legal beagle at the other end. Lawyers. They lived in a world all their own and breathed air so rarified it was amazing they managed to keep their feet planted on the ground. He pulled back a chair opposite the desk and slid into it, stretching his short, stocky legs out in front of him, his hands folded in his lap. Koosman waved to him absently while he completed his conversation.

Eventually, he hung up. "Joe. What's up? Anything new on the Mendoza case? My aides tell me we could use another eye witness. The last one you brought didn't do too well at the lineup, something about not actually having his glasses on the night of the robbery. Come to think of it, I doubt if he could tell the difference between a six-feet-tall woman with a shaved head and a Hare Krishna even if he had his glasses on. Geez, Joe. I hope you can do better than that."

Hatch smiled. "Just trying to keep you and the boys on your toes is all, Frank."

Koosman sat back in his chair with a big sigh. "I don't know. Sometimes it feels more like lead weights on my feet than penny loafers."

"For a more realistic picture, try tying those lead weights to your ass. I hear you boys spend more time in the chair than Perry Mason."

Frank grunted. "Now, what can I do for you? I'm busy."

Hatch wrinkled his forehead. "I'm here on the Griswold matter. I have a hunch we've got the wrong man. There's something too pat about his confession, his submissiveness. The word on the street says Dills is taking the rap for someone else. Besides, Sara told me she and the kid were almost run over in the zoo parking lot, and she's seen a man hanging around the school watching Carly. She's worried about her. In fact, she asked for a copy of Dills' mug shot so she could judge the kid's reaction."

"You refused, I hope."

"As a matter of fact, I gave it to her. I figured it might help the kid remember one way or the other."

Koosman appeared to be having a hard time holding in his temper. "And..."

"Sara said the kid showed no sign of anxiety, fear or aversion to Dills. She only recognized him as the man who takes care of the horses." Hatch raised his voice a notch. "What if we have the wrong man? What if the kid's at risk? I want to do some more digging, maybe tail Griswold, find out more about his alibi the night of the murder. You know, some good old-fashioned police work. I've run this past my bosses at LAPD, but they won't budge unless you give the word. Damn Griswold has every one tied up in knots."

Koosman slammed his fist on the desk and stood up. "I don't give a shit what the street says, and unless the kid verbally denies Dills was the man who hurt her mother and names someone else, I say we've got our man, confession and all, and I want it to stick. This is no time to be changing our story." He paused to take a breath. "We've already had one wrench thrown into this case with a change of attorney. Apparently, Mike Grey is trying to get Dills to change his plea and insist on a trial. We're late wrapping this thing up. If you want to play detective, get me more dirt on Dills, get me a statement from the kid implicating him and get me more substantiation on the motive. As it stands now, I've got a strong case against him. I'm waiting for his damned attorney to accept the plea we offered. So, don't come in here with theories. I need evidence, hard evidence."

Hatch shot forward in his chair and glared at Frank. "Then authorize some O.T. Give me a couple more undercover men. Let me prove the scuttlebutt wrong. Let me discredit any other possible suspect. Give me some loose reins here, Frank."

"You can have all the O.T. and additional men you want, Joe, but I want the investigation focused on nailing Dills' coffin, not locating another suspect. I'm under a lot of pressure with this one, and I can't afford to waste time."

Hatch squinted accusingly at his friend. Koosman wasn't going to budge. There was no sense banging his head against a stone wall anymore. He'd have to find another way around that obstacle if he wanted to sleep with a clear conscience. Wasn't the first time the D.A.'s office railroaded a suspect and, unfortunately, it probably wouldn't be the last.

"Sorry you feel that way, Frank. I'm damn glad I'm not in your shoes. As ugly as I am, at least I can look myself in the mirror in the morning without feeling sick to my stomach. How do you do it? After all these years, how do you keep it all together?" He tried to hide the rancor he felt.

Koosman sat down in his seat with a thud, a slick grin on his face. "Damn well, Joe. Damn well and don't you forget it. Now, get the hell out of here. I've got a department to run."

Hatch got up so quickly his chair toppled over, crashing onto the vinyl covered floor. He turned and stormed out of the office, slamming the door behind him.

*   *   *

Hatch finally saw him. He stood in the slowly moving line at the Asian buffet in the food court at the Children's Museum. The tall man appeared to be engrossed in his luncheon selection, his tray balanced in one hand, his other hand jammed into the pocket of his light gray pinstriped suit. He didn't seem to notice Hatch.

"I'd stay away from the egg rolls if I was you, Counselor. You never know what they put in them.

Me, personally, I like to see what I'm buying before I put my money out."

Michael turned abruptly, nodded a silent greeting. "Sounds like good advice before striking a deal with a hooker, but, me, personally," he mimicked Hatch with a slight smile forming on his lips, "I'm up for taking a big risk today. Feeling invincible."

Michael grabbed two egg rolls, a double order of vegetable lo Mein and slid his tray over to the cash register. After paying for his meal, he walked toward an empty table in a shady corner of the open courtyard. Hatch followed. They both sat down.

"Not hungry?" Michael took a fork full of hot, steaming noodles.

"Not brave enough." Hatch grimaced. "I've been looking for you all day. I hear you've taken over the Griswold defense. I must admit I was surprised. I couldn't help but wonder why a smart guy like you who must've had his fill of public service and its accompanying bureaucracy would want to get involved with this one."

He watched Michael closely, gauging his reaction.

"As a matter of fact, Joe, so have I. What can I do for you?"

"Actually, it's more like what I can do for you, or, more precisely, for your client."

Michael looked at him with more interest. He took a bite of an egg roll. "What's the matter? Prosecutor's office not giving you enough work these days, you have to moonlight for the defense?"

Hatch was tired of the game. He didn't like what he was about to do, and even though his conscience nagged him on, it was difficult to take responsibility for it.

His voice lowered. "I don't like what I see going on in the D.A.'s office. If I thought Dills was our man, I wouldn't be giving you the time of day."

"But you don't."

Hatch shifted in his seat, leaned forward and crossed his arms on the table in front of him. "I think he's been bought off, going down for someone."

"Based on..."

"My gut feelings, triggered by what I've been getting from my stooges and other people I've talked to about him. The only thing I can't get is why he'd do it. What's in it for him? I figure even if he's getting big bucks for it, when the fuck's he ever going to spend it where he's going? Frankly, I don't picture him as a sacrificing husband and father willing to give up his life for his family. He may not be a murderer, but he sure as hell isn't Pollyanna."

"Why are you telling me this? You're the detective. Detect. Give me some hard evidence to go with, and I'll listen. Until then, it's all gut feelings and grand theories. Nothing I can use in court."

Hatch slid back in his chair and stuffed his hands into his pockets. "You're forgetting who I work for. My hands are tied. I've been told to back off by my bosses and the D.D.A. So you and I never had this conversation, but if I was you, which by the way, I'm sure as shit glad I'm not right now, I'd give Griswold a closer look. Have him tailed. Check his alibi. I'm too close to this to do Dills any good."

He stood up, pushing the chair back a bit. "Hope I haven't spoiled your lunch, Counselor." He smiled. "Me, I think I'll head back to my office for an hour of stress reduction meditation. You ought to try it. Something tells me you're going to need it."

Hatch turned and walked away, his hands jammed in his pockets. He raised his head slightly, took a deep breath of LA air and let it out slowly. That was that. He'd done all he could. What was it Pontius Pilate said, "I wash my hands of this matter" or something like that?

Yes, it's done. He'd washed his hands. His conscience was clear.

SIXTEEN

Michael was having trouble following the movie. He sat against the soft cushions of Sara's sofa, his long legs stretched out over the coffee table, his arm snugly wrapped around her shoulders. His mind kept going over the conversation that afternoon with Joe Hatch. What was that all about? He'd known Joe for many years, knew him to be a good cop, fair and honest, no sucker for a sad story. There must be something to his gut feelings. That thought only added to Michael's sense there was something going on with this case that Dills' wasn't up to admitting.

He was surprised Dills agreed to the change of attorney. Yet, it was in line with the complacent resignation Michael saw when he first met the man at Wayside.

As soon as the case was officially his, he gave his investigator, Pete Neilson, the file and instructed him to follow up on some loose ends. Now, after listening to Joe, he thought of a few new leads to give Neilson.

Michael had visited Dills after getting the case. He was still sullen, uncommunicative and impatient to be rid of Michael and get back to his cell. His demeanor was definitely not the usual incarcerated criminal's approach to his defense. The man just wasn't interested in changing his plea and going to trial. Michael would have to find out what was going on, if he wanted to prove the man's innocence.

Occasionally, he wondered why he cared. If Dills wasn't interested in saving his own skin, why was he?

"Michael? Hello? Earth to Michael?"

The sudden pressure of her warm lips against his cheek brought him back to the present. "Sorry. Distracted." He returned her kiss with one on her forehead. "You were saying?"

She took a huge handful of freshly popped popcorn and tossed it in her mouth, snuggling closer against him.

"I offered my humble analysis as to why I love watching serial killer movies. Crazy, huh? You'd think given the work I do I'd be horrified by all the violence. But," her speech garbled while she chewed the popcorn, "I think that's precisely why I'm intrigued by this genre. I find it fascinating watching how the dysfunctional psychotic mind works."

He marveled at the fact he found everything she said and did utterly charming. Serial killer or not, an urgent need to make love to her suddenly rushed through him.

He grinned. "Can't say I share your fascination, but I'd fight to the death for your right to have your opinion."

She punched his chest playfully. "Spoken like a true attorney." She sighed and shut off the video. "Thank goodness. The criminal justice system wins once again."

She turned her attention to him and pulled him closer. Her hand rubbed against his shirt for a long moment before moving it and caressing his face.

"You look tired." She kissed his mouth.

He ran his fingers through her thick hair. "Busy day. This new case is demanding more time than I thought it would."

"I'm glad you found some time for us."

He shifted in his seat and drew her face to his. "You keep me sane, Sara. I hope I never get so involved with work I forget that."

He slid his lips across hers then moved and kissed her nose, her closed eyelids then her mouth again. His heart raced. Hers responded while he continued exploring her face and neck with his mouth. The more he saw her, felt her, the more he wanted her, and that night was no exception.

Suddenly, the phone rang.

"Leave it," she pleaded.

The ringing continued incessantly.

She pulled back, her breath shaky. "Damn. Sorry. Maybe it's a patient. I better answer it."

She reached for her cell phone in her jeans pocket but stayed as close to him as possible. "This is Dr. Bradley."

She immediately jerked up. "Dana? What's the matter? Are you hurt?"

Her expression changed. It no longer registered the passion they'd share seconds before. Instead, her forehead was lined with concern. Her voice sounded frightened.

"Have you called the police?" Pause. "Okay, okay. Just keep the door locked. They'll be right there. I'm on my way. Hold tight. You'll be fine." She jammed the phone back into her pocket and stood up.

"What is it?"

"That was Dana. Her ex-boyfriend showed up at the house tonight, drunk, trying to break in the door. He's been harassing her since she called off their relationship."

"Is she hurt?"

"No, but I have to go to her." She rushed to the door, grabbing her purse off the foyer table. Michael followed. "I'll drive. You're too upset."

"You don't have to come. Between the police and me, she'll be all right. I'll bring her back here."

"I'm going. I don't want you walking into a dangerous domestic disturbance by yourself. We'll take my car."

He put his arms around her and kissed her forehead. Before she could object again, he opened the door and with hand on her back, they hurried to his car.

*   *   *

They reached Dana's Hollywood Hills condo in less than twenty minutes. Two uniformed LAPD officers were leaving when Michael and Sara approached the front door. Sara ignored them, but out of the corner of her eye she saw Michael stop and talk with them. She rushed inside. Dana sat on the sofa, blowing her nose. As soon as Sara entered, Dana stood and fell into her arms.

"I'm sorry I called you. I guess I just panicked. I don't know why he spooked me. Must have been in a very vulnerable state or something."

"I'm glad you did. Are you sure you're all right?" Together they moved to the sofa and sat down.

"Yeah, just shaken up. I never expected him to get so violent. He was like a crazy man, shouting, banging on the door. He wouldn't stop, even when I threatened to call the police. He kept on screaming, cursing me, banging." She let loose a nervous giggle. "I think the noise got to me more than the words. I was more concerned about what the neighbors might be thinking. I told him I dialed nine-one-one, but still he didn't stop. It wasn't until the sirens were heard he finally left. After, of course, threatening to come back and finish the job, whatever that meant." She shook her head and blew her noise again. "God, Sara, he was a maniac. How did I ever let myself get involved with someone like him in the first place?"

Sara ran her hand along Dana's cheek. "You couldn't have known what he was like when you first started dating. We all put our best foot forward in the beginning of a relationship. But you did get a sense of who and what he really is, and that's why you ended it. So, don't blame yourself."

Just then Dana looked up. Sara turned. Michael stood by the sofa. "Dana, this is Michael Grey. We were just finishing a bowl of popcorn when you called."

Dana smiled weakly at him. "Sorry to disturb your evening, Michael, but it's good to meet you. Sara's told me a lot about you." She reached out her hand.

Michael leaned over and held it briefly. "Sorry we had to meet under these circumstances."

Sara said, "Have the cops left?"

"Yeah. They took their report and will follow up with background checks, see if Greg Liston has any outstanding warrants, et cetera. You'll need to go down to the Hollywood station tomorrow and fill out a request for a TRO. Otherwise, there's not too much else they can do."

Dana sighed. "I know. Maybe when he wakes up tomorrow with a splitting hangover, he'll realize what a fool he's been and leave me alone."

"There's always that," Michael said, "but in the meantime, make sure you have good strong locks on all the doors and windows. Keep a can of pepper spray handy when you're walking to and from your car and just be very vigilant."

"You're coming home with me." Sara added.

"No. No. I'm all right. There's no way he'll come back here tonight. Thank you both for coming over. I'm much calmer now. It's not like me to get so freaked out. All the tough stories I've investigated over the years never bothered me like this."

"That's because this is personal." Sara gave her a kiss on her cheek. "Are you sure you don't want to stay with me, at least for tonight?"

Dana stood. "No. No. You kids go on home and finish that popcorn." She gave them an impish grin. "Or whatever else I interrupted." She hugged Sara and led them to the door.

"I'll call you tomorrow and make sure you're feeling better. Why don't you take a day or two off from work? Go to the beach. Relax. Anything to put this behind you."

Dana's shaky laugh seemed a bit overdone to Sara. "Actually, I have a full day tomorrow, and in the evening, I'm hitting that club I told you about. There's nothing like a little fantasy to wash away stark reality."

Sara gave her a final hug. "Just be careful. That place sounds too weird. Talk to you tomorrow."

She and Michael left. When Sara turned for a last look, Dana stood at the door, a worried look now shadowing her pretty face.

SEVENTEEN

Sara sat on the floor in her office, Indian style. A blue and white striped stuffed alligator and a Barbie Doll lay on her lap. Carly sat across from her, her legs in the same position. She wore clean, white shorts and a yellow and pink flowered cotton top with short sleeves. White ankle socks and crisp, new sneakers covered her feet. Her long straight hair was parted in the middle and pulled into two neat ponytails, one on each side of her small oval face.

Sara checked her watch. They were twenty minutes into their session.

Carly colored on the large pad on her lap. She chattered about her new friend at school and the kitten Juana had brought home.

"Did you give the kitten a name yet?"

She shook her head. "No. I just can't think of a perfect name for her. She has big green eyes and her fur is all different colors, like some of the leaves that fall off the trees by my house...brown and yellow...but," she giggled, "no green. That would be silly. A green cat."

Sara smiled. "I think you're right. I've never seen a green cat before and probably never will. I'll bet she's very pretty. Maybe Juana will let you bring her to see me next time you come to the office."

She nodded enthusiastically, her ponytails bouncing in rhythm to the movement of her head. "Oh, yes. I'll ask Juana. I'll bet the kitten would like to ride in the car. Maybe by then I'll have a name for her."

"Do you want to give her a person's name or call her a thing, like Cupcake or Sneakers or something like that?"

The child was thoughtful for a moment. "I think a person's name, so she can be like another friend. Maybe I'll call her Kathy or Annie or Jenny."

"Any of those would be great names. Did you ever have a kitten before?"

Carly paused for a moment. A dark shadow fell across her face. "I think we had one a long time ago, before we moved to my house. I think Mommy had a kitten named Dusty when I was very little. She used to talk about it sometimes. She missed it. I don't know what happened to it. Maybe it died like Mommy. Do you think they're together in heaven?"

Sara smiled. "Probably."

"I hope so. Maybe Mommy won't miss me so much if the kitten is with her. Maybe she wouldn't feel so lonely."

Carly got up and walked around the room. Her little hand touched the soft upholstery of the couch, the nearby rocking chair and then the wooden desk on the other side of the room. She reached for one of the large cloth dolls which sat on a wooden shelf along with other toys. She grabbed the doll to her breast and hugged it tightly, while she continued walking about the room.

She became more withdrawn, clutching the doll tightly and staring off in front of her.

"I'll bet your mommy would be glad to know you have a kitten now, too. Someone you can love and take care of, just like she loved and took care of you."

Carly sat down in the rocking chair, still looking off somewhere far away, her large dark eyes wide open. What did they see? Perhaps they imagined the place where her mother might be now. Or maybe they saw her mother as she was that last horrible night months ago, beaten and bloodied. Or more frightening, perhaps they saw the face of the murderer as he struck her mother in an angry rage. Sara could only guess Carly's nightmares and thoughts, so far had the child gone into some dark mysterious place.

She stared at the vacant, haunting look in the child's eyes. Carly seemed to be in some dissociative, almost hypnotic state. She rocked back and forth in the chair. In an instant, Carly picked up one of the crayons and began hitting the doll. Again and again the crayon smashed into the doll, on its head, chest, arms and legs. No part of the doll was spared the vicious attack.

As Sara watched, she couldn't help but be shocked at the child's aggression. She was drawn into a macabre vacuum created by the motion of the moving chair and Carly's swinging arm.

Suddenly she saw herself as a child in another time and place mesmerized by similar motions. Her stomach clenched. The merciless pounding of her head brought her fully back to the present. The vision disappeared. She jerked to her feet.

The child turned her head slowly toward Sara and looked at her through unseeing eyes. After a moment, she blinked a few times and then smiled as though she hadn't missed a beat of their previous conversation.

"I think I'll draw you a picture of my new kitten. Then you can see how pretty she is."

She dropped the doll, moved over toward the coloring book and crayons and continued where she left off. Sara sat on a nearby chair. She inhaled a few deep breaths, trying to slow her shaky nerves.

Her chest was tight while she watched Carly color. There was something hypnotic in the way the crayon moved slowly across the page. Slowly, a tiny figure with four legs emerged.

"See." Carly looked at Sara. "I told you my kitten was pretty."

She drew another small stick person, put dark curly hair around the head and put a strange expression on its face.

"Who is that?"

"That's me, silly."

"Hmm. What kind of face do you have in that picture? Looks kind of scary to me."

Carly's voice was low when she spoke. "That's because I'm trying to scare my kitten away so she will go hide for a while until the bad things stop."

"What bad things, Carly?"

The child looked at Sara and that distant look appeared in her eyes again. Instead of answering, she dropped the crayon and stood up. "Where's Juana? I want to go home now."

Sara get go a deep sigh. She touched the child's shoulder and stood. "I think you're right. I'll bet Juana is outside waiting for you. Let's go check."

*   *   *

Later than evening, Sara paced up and down in Rose Goodman's living room, her arms clasped across her chest. Rage consumed her. Her voice trembled. Her words seethed with self-accusation and bitterness.

"I'm furious with myself. This has to stop. How can I concentrate on working with my patients when I keep getting piercing headaches and screaming nerves? I'm not one hundred percent present for them. I've always prided myself on being there for them, and now I feel like I'm failing them."

"Any patient in particular?"

"Yes, as a matter of fact. I'm working with a five-year old who may have witnessed a murder, and today I had a strong reaction to her. I blew the rest of the session by asking her a stupid question. Just when I thought she was ready to share what happened that night. I don't feel I can continue being her therapist."

"What was she doing that triggered you?"

"First, she was coloring. No problem. Then she took a doll and seemed to go into a dissociative state where she stabbed the doll again and again with a crayon. The anger and violence of the attack shocked me. I don't understand. Maybe I should take time off until I figure this all out. I don't want to jeopardize my patients by being emotionally unavailable to them if and when they need me."

Sara finally stopped pacing. She felt desperate and knew her frustration must show on her face. She looked to Rose to say the magic words to make it all go away so she could be the healer she knew herself to be.

"If you had a patient share this with you, how would you counsel them?"

Rose's rational words weren't what Sara wanted to hear. "What do you mean? If I had all the answers, I wouldn't be here. I don't know why this is happening to me."

"I'll repeat. What would you tell a patient?"

Sara was getting more and more frustrated. "I don't know!"

"Yes, you do. Your emotions are overriding your ability to think clearly. You're acting like a victim. I want you to think like the brilliant therapist you are."

Rose's words caused Sara to slam the door on her emotions and shift gears. She paused for a moment. "I, I'd probably tell her to stay with it, not run away. That something inside was begging to come out. To not be afraid, that I knew she could deal with whatever it was, and I'd be there for her."

Rose smiled. "Perfect. I trust you to be with your patients when they need you no matter what is going on with you at the moment. You know I'll be there for you, don't you?"

Sara's body relaxed. Tears filled her eyes. She took a long deep breath. "Yes, I do."

Rose patted the seat on the sofa next to her. "Come, sit."

Sara sat in the corner, her feet pulled up beneath her. Rose spoke in a smoothing mellow voice. "I understand your concern for your patients. You wouldn't be an effective therapist if you didn't constantly question your reactions, your emotions or be aware when patient transference was at play. It's because of your awareness I have every confidence in your ability to put yourself aside and be with your patients one hundred percent. What's troubling you may have been buried so deep in your subconscious it may take time to reveal itself." She paused. "Have you taken steps to retrieve your adoption records?"

"I asked Michael, and he seemed certain he could get them. I'm waiting to hear from him."

"Good. They might give you some insight as to why you react so strongly to this child. In the meantime, you must be patient with yourself."

Sara snickered. "Patience is one virtue I lack. I want to know everything right now. I want to be free to do my work and to be with Michael. I don't want anything to get in the way of our relationship."

Rose studied her. "Well, my impatient girl, there may be something we can do to shake it loose sooner, if you're really up to it."

Sara nodded. "I am. What do you have in mind?"

EIGHTEEN

Michael pulled his BMW into an open spot along the curb only a few car lengths away from the Dills' house. He sat for a moment, breathing in the ambiance of the neighborhood, recalling its ever-changing history. The small wooden box houses were built in a mad frenzy after World War II in an effort to encourage returning soldiers to remain in the area. However, the lure of cheap tract homes in the San Fernando Valley drew thousands of respectable shop owners and blue collar workers away from the inner city with the promise of paradise.

As those good citizens retreated, the area below the bustling downtown became overrun with drug dealers, substance abusers, prostitutes and hoodlums. Gangs sprung up everywhere and took over the streets. The remaining decent citizens found themselves terrorized daily, living in fear for their lives and the lives of their children. Property values plummeted until only the poor and disenfranchised were left to live the marginal existence that was South Central Los Angeles.

Shaking his head in resignation, Michael got out of the car, approached the front door and knocked. In a few moments, a young woman, possibly late twenties, wearing faded denim shorts and a white halter top that barely contained her large breasts, opened the door.

"Mrs. Dills? I'm Michael Grey, your husband's attorney. May I come in? I'd like to ask you a few questions." He handed her his business card.

She looked at the card briefly then up at him and frowned. "Sure. I guess so. Come on in."

Michael stepped into the small living room, and the woman closed the door behind him. She motioned for him to take a seat on an old worn sofa against the opposite wall. Children's toys were strewn about the room. She tossed some off the sofa and made space for them to sit.

"Sorry about the mess. You came at a good time, though. I just put both kids down for naps. You want coffee or anythin'?"

"No thanks. I have a few questions and then I'll be out of your way."

"No problem. Warren told me he changed attorneys. I really wasn't sure why. Mr. Weiss seemed to be a nice guy."

He was glad she was in a talkative mood. Maybe he could finally get some straight answers from one member of the Dills family.

"He was doing a good job. In fact, he asked me to take over the case because he felt he didn't have the time to put into your husband's case right now. He wanted to make sure Warren got every chance possible before sentencing. Have you heard from him lately?"

"As a matter of fact, he called collect this mornin'. You know, they have to make collect calls and with money being very tight now, he doesn't call too often."

"The last time I saw him he seemed a bit depressed."

"I, I guess he's all right, all things considered. He never did like bein' locked up. He says it makes him a little crazy. We've been together for four years. Got married when I got pregnant the first time and then Warren got picked up on some drug charges. He was usin' pretty heavy back then and kept gettin' into trouble. We spent a lot of time apart in the beginnin'. It was rough at first, you know, especially when the other kid came along."

She pushed a lock of long dark hair behind her left ear. "After a while, Warren seemed to change. He stayed out of trouble and things got better. He cleaned up, even went to meetings. I thought, well, looks like we might make it after all.

But now..." Her eyes filled with tears. "This is pretty bad, isn't it?"

"A murder charge is a serious matter. You said he got clean. What was he using?"

"Heroin. His arms are pretty scarred up. He was real sick for a long time before he finally stopped."

"Approximately how long ago did he detox?"

Lines appeared in her forehead when she looked up at the ceiling. "Let me see, it was just after the baby was born. I remember 'cause I had the both of them to take care of, and it was pretty bad for a while, maybe a year and a half ago. A few months later he got the job at the Griswold's."

Tears brimmed over onto her cheeks. "I remember how happy he was to be working a regular job. He was raised on a farm in Missouri and knew a lot about horses and such. He said his probation officer recommended him for it 'cause he'd been doin' so good, you know. He really thought Warren had it licked this time. So did I." More tears.

"I'm sure this is very hard on you, Mrs. Dills, alone with two children. How are you managing financially?"

"Please, call me Trudy. Well, I was getting' nervous about money and was goin' to apply for AFDC, welfare, you know, but Warren told me not to. Said he'd be getting' me some money real soon...to hold on a little longer. So, I've been makin' do with what we have in the bank and the food stamps. How much jail time do you think Warren will get, Mr. Grey?"

"Hard to tell, but I want you to know we're doing our best for him. Moving as fast as good judgment allows. One last thing, Trudy, and I hope you'll be honest with me. Do you think your husband killed Mrs. Griswold?"

"Mr. Grey, Warren's done a lot of bad things in his life, and he'd be the first to tell you, but he's never hurt anyone but himself all this time. I don't think he coulda killed that woman. I just can't understand it. I know he confessed and all, but he always talked good about her, like he respected her or something. Said she was a good person."

She took a deep breath. "I gotta be honest, though. He wasn't none too impressed with the judge. I could tell he didn't like him. But no, he wouldn't have hurt that woman. And he didn't have any need for stealing no more, what with his habit gone and all. We was doin' okay. I just don't understand any of it."

As she started to cry again, Michael pulled out a clean handkerchief and handed it to her.

She wiped her eyes.

"I'm very sorry for your troubles, ma'am. If there's anything I can do, or if you think of anything else that might help Warren, please call me." He got up and made his way toward the door.

She stopped crying and followed behind him.

He opened the door and turned to her, his hand outstretched. "Thanks, Trudy. I appreciate your honesty. I'll call if anything breaks." He turned and left the house.

No sooner had he slid behind the wheel of his car when his phone rang. He clicked his Bluetooth and started the engine.

His secretary's voice was stressed. "Mike? I know you didn't want to be bothered with calls while you were with Mrs. Dills, but Frank Koosman's been trying to reach you all afternoon. Says it's important. He wants you to meet him in his office before five."

He looked at his watch. "Damn. I don't feel like bucking rush hour traffic right now. Can't it wait?"

"I don't think so. He's called four times. How come you never gave him your cell phone number?"

He sighed. "For the very reason he can be a real pain in the ass when he wants something. Okay, call him back and tell him I'm on my way. Be there in thirty minutes."

*   *   *

When Michael opened the door to Koosman's office, he was seated behind the desk, shaking his head, listening to someone who seemed to be screaming at him through the telephone. His white shirt sleeves were rolled up past his elbows, indicative of the stuffiness of the office and lack of good air-conditioning. He waved Michael toward a chair opposite the desk. Koosman shook his head a few more times, rolled his eyes and stuck his middle finger into the air, indicating a definite disregard for the person on the other end of the phone.

"Yes, sir, I know, sir. As a matter of fact, Grey just now came into my office. Right, that's right. Of course, I'll call you later." He hung up the phone, dropping it quickly into its cradle as if it were a burning piece of hot iron and stood up.

"God damn son of a bitch. You were one smartass lawyer to get the hell out of government employment when you did, Mike. No monkeys on your back anymore. Where the hell have you been all afternoon? I've been trying to reach you for hours. Don't you tell that secretary of yours where you're going or is that too much of an infringement on your personal freedom?"

Michael laughed at the ridiculous expression on Koosman's face. He couldn't decide if it was pure anger or a mixture of jealously and desperation. "Now, now, Frank. Calm down. You'll be going into cardiac arrest pretty soon. What'll I tell your wife then? He croaked because he couldn't reach me on the phone?"

Frank snickered. "Looks like you've found your long lost sense of humor. But spare me, will you? I've had a rough day."

"So I gather. Well, I'm here now. What can I do for you?"

Koosman sat down in his chair in a huff, took a deep breath and looked at Michael calmly for the first time. "I was surprised you took over the Griswold case. I thought you only worked on sure things these days, nothing messy, nothing controversial."

"What can I say? Weiss hooked me. Actually, it was Dills who did it. I think you've got the wrong man."

"Spoken like a true defense attorney. Wrong man, my ass. We've got him placed at the scene, a solid motive..."

"What motive?"

"What do you mean what motive? The man's got a twenty year, two hundred dollars a week, heroin habit and a wife and kids to support. We've got a confession, for Christ sake. Dills is our man all right. I'll bet my life on it."

"I wouldn't be too quick to place that bet, Frank. The deeper my investigation goes, the more convinced I am he's going down for someone else. I just don't know who yet."

"Well, since you're an attorney and not a cop, I suggest you stop playing detective and have your patient sign the plea agreement we worked out with Weiss. We've already done him a favor by taking the death penalty off the table. Twenty-five to life without the possibility of parole. You don't want to know what I had to go through with my boss to get this deal. Griswold was in an uproar when he heard."

Michael laughed.

Koosman scowled at him. "What's so funny?"

"You're right. I'm so glad I'm not in your shoes, but you can be assured I'm not going to railroad a client just because it suits your office or Griswold. I don't believe Dills is guilty, and I'll fight for him as long as I can. If I'm forced by Judge Longmire to take a plea, you can bet your ass it won't be twenty-five to life."

If Koosman was a locomotive, steam would have come out of his ears. "What the hell are you trying to do, stop the wheels of justice just to prove a point? I've got my man, and you're wasting your time and energy trying to beat a dead horse. They'll be no more bargaining. What you have is all you're going to get, so go to your client and bring me back a signed agreement."

Michael leaned over and glared at him. "You can rant all you want, Frank, but I don't sell my clients down the river no matter whose wife was killed."

"Easy, Mike. I wouldn't want to see this case get between us. I called you in here in the hope we could settle this matter now. Griswold was madder than hell when you took over for Weiss, delaying his acceptance of the plea. He's concerned about his stepdaughter's privacy. Can't say I blame him. He doesn't want this to go to trial and force her to testify."

"What does this have to do with the child?"

Koosman seemed to weigh his words before he spoke. "This isn't for public knowledge. In fact, I'm surprised it hasn't leaked out already."

A warning light flashed in the distance. "What are you taking about, Frank?"

"Griswold's stepdaughter, Carly, was there the night of the murder."

"What?" He felt the blood drain from his face.

"We don't know if she saw anything, and if she did, what that might be. In other words, we may have a witness. However, she hasn't revealed anything yet."

Michael jerked up in his chair, as though he'd just gotten sucker-punched. "You've got to be kidding! This is nothing more than some bullshit desperate move on your part to get me to cave in and have the plea signed, and you know it. Your case is weak, but instead of trying to find out who really killed that woman, you're dragging a kid into it."

Koosman's face turned a dark shade of red. "I don't like being accused of using children to blackmail defense attorneys."

"Well, what would *you* call it, Frank?"

"A heads-up to a friend. I didn't have to call you in here and let you in on this. I could have let you go ahead with your pathetic quest for the so-called real killer, but I thought I'd do you a favor. You should thank me, not point the finger."

He reached down and handed Michael a copy of a report regarding Carly Perez.

Michael looked at Koosman through angry slanted eyes and then read the report. When he saw the name at the bottom of the report, his heart stopped beating.

He recovered as quickly as he could. "So you have a shrink who thinks the child may have witnessed the actual murder. What do you have beside the opinion of the shrink? You'll need some pretty solid testimony to sell me the idea Dills killed Mrs. Griswold. Otherwise, it's all circumstantial. Besides, you know kids make lousy witnesses."

"It's only a matter of time before we get a direct statement from her. Then you can kiss your plea change good-bye. There's no way a jury will ignore the statement of a direct witness, no matter how old she is. You can keep the report. Think about it. Talk to Dills and then get back to me. Soon, before I charge you with obstruction of justice." Koosman started shuffling around papers on his desk as a way of telling Michael the meeting was over.

Michael glared at Koosman. "How the hell do you sleep at night, knowing how much ass-licking you do all day?" He turned and left the room, slamming the door.

His mind reeled. It was as though he'd been hit by a steam roller. His chest was solid and heavy, he had trouble drawing a breath and a sick feeling began to gnaw at his stomach. The past just slapped him in the face again. The child might have witnessed her mother's murder, and the second bomb–the child was Sara's patient.

He cursed his own stupidity at having agreed to take the case. He should've trusted his first instincts and turned his back on it. Somehow he'd known it was going to turn ugly. Ugly couldn't begin to describe the scenes from the past that flashed through his mind, scenes he'd tried so desperately to forget, to wipe away. Now they've come back in a kaleidoscope of colors and faces.

He didn't remember how he got to his car, but once inside, he grabbed hold of the steering wheel as well as his spiraling emotions. His logical brain, which had kept him sane all these years, finally kicked in, and he pushed the past aside again. His heart stopped pounding. He thought about the case and his client. He had to see him, had to get the truth out of him once and for all. If he really did kill that woman and the child witnessed it, Michael didn't know how he'd stop from beating the shit out of Dills right then and there.

He drove onto the 5 Freeway heading toward Wayside, his jaw clenched, his angry eyes drilling the pavement while the car sped over it.

NINETEEN

An hour later, Michael stood with his hands stuffed deeply into the pants pockets of his light gray summer suit. The jacket was open and tucked behind his hands, his feet planted solidly on the floor. He stared out the window of the visitors' room of the super maximum security building at Wayside.

The surrounding countryside made little impression on him. The sun, continuing on its western path toward the horizon, cast a pinkish glow on the hillsides. The yellow straw grass and rusty brown shrubs swayed now and then as hot gentle breezes brushed over them.

His mind was fully immersed in the visions which Koosman's new charge brought to mind.

During the long drive to the prison, he'd struggled to keep his thoughts away from the ugly scenario which continued to flash pictures from the past. His attempts to stop them proved futile, so he'd surrendered to the memories.

Slowly he felt himself falling into the all-too-familiar despair which plagued most of his early life– his drunkard father, and the horror of his last day at the farm. Over the years, the walls came up and cement hardened his heart.

The door behind him opened, breaking his trance, intruding into his morbid thoughts. A deputy escorted Warren Dills into the small room. He sat Dills down, cuffed him to the table and left his prisoner lounging back in his seat. He appeared bored, indifferent, staring down into his lap, perhaps even a little put-off by the summons from his attorney so late in the day.

Michael leaned back against the wall and looked at Dills for a long time before speaking. The knot in his stomach was suddenly tighter. He was repulsed. He fought to push away nagging images of what the Griswold kid might have seen that night.

What if Dills had murdered the woman? What if the child was a witness? How could he in good conscience maintain objectivity and defend his patient to the best of his ability? He had to figure out the best way of conducting the interview and getting to the truth.

Dills looked at him. "What's up, Counselor? I hate being dragged away from *Wheel of Fortune*."

Michael ignored the wisecrack. "The D.D.A. called me in for a little chat a few hours ago. Looks like there was more going on that night at the Griswold's than you've been telling everyone. I don't like getting surprises, Dills. They really piss me off."

Dills moved around a bit in his seat. "I don't know what you're talkin' about, man. I've told you everything that happened that night, you and the other suit. I'm fuckin' sick and tired of repeating myself."

Michael ignored the intended insult. "Tell me, Dills. How's it been for you in lockup, the guys bothering you? Anyone make moves on you yet? I hear a lot of guys find it easier to do time paired up with a homeboy, insurance, you know what I mean?"

"Yeah, I know what you mean, but I ain't into that kind of thing. I don't need any protection. I mind my own business. I've done plenty of time, and I'll do it again."

When Michael didn't respond, Dills squinted and squirmed in his chair. "What the hell's buggin' you, man? You got a problem, spit it out. Stop bullshitting me."

"Got a problem with bullshit, do you? As a matter of fact, so do I. Tends to stick in my gut. Tell me again what happened that night at the Griswold's."

"No, man, I'm not going over that again. It's all down in writing. Read my confession. Like I told you before, that's all there is."

"Apparently, there's something you failed to tell the cops and Weiss and me. I just found out the D.D.A. may have a witness to the murder."

Dills jerked up in his seat. For the first time since Michael had known him, Dills looked confused and then scared, as though he didn't understand what Michael said.

"What the fuck you talkin' about?"

"You heard me. The kid saw you kill her mother."

"She did? She saw the mur...I, I mean. Yeah, okay. So what. Makes no difference to me." He squirmed in his chair.

Something in the conversation definitely upset Dills. Michael was having a hard time understanding what was going on with him, but he was determined to find out once and for all what it was. He decided to push Dills to see what he'd do.

"The problem is, now he has a witness, the D.D.A. might just decide to put the death penalty back on the table." The words sent rancid bile into his throat, momentarily choking him. His eyes bored into Dills. "You really did kill Mrs. Griswold, didn't you?"

"Yeah, I told you I did. Maybe now you'll believe me and leave me alone." Dills was back in his I-don't-give-a-shit mode. Yet Michael saw something else in the man's eyes. Was it worry, fear? "You know, Dills. I think you're full of shit. I still don't think you're a murderer. A career criminal maybe, an old junkie trying to change his lifestyle, but a murderer...I don't think so."

Dills drilled him. "Well then you got a problem, don't you? What is it they call it, a moral dilemma? You might just have to put away an innocent man. Probably won't be the first time, either." He snickered.

Michael lost it. He rushed to the table, leaned over, his face inches away from Dills', and smashed his closed fist on the tabletop, rattling the ashtray that rested on the other end.

"You fucking dirt bag! It's not my ass that's going to fry for murder. I think it's time you got your head out of your ass. You need to tell me the truth and fast, cause I'm the only chance you've got and you're blowing it!"

Dills yelled back at him, "Yeah, well maybe I don't give a shit."

"Did you ever think maybe your wife and kids do?"

They stared at each other like two bulls with steam billowing out of their nostrils.

"Come to think of it, you got a bigger problem now than you had before." Dills folded his arms across his chest and smirked.

Michael pulled back. What the hell was going on with his guy? "Yeah, like what?"

"Like if I didn't kill that woman the real bastard is out there, and the kid may not last very long once he finds out she saw him." He grinned. "But since it was me, and I'm in here, I guess your witness is pretty safe."

Michael's head hammered. He had to get away from this bastard before he grabbed him and threw him against the wall. He snatched his briefcase off the table. "Have it your way. Don't worry. I'll find a way to live with myself. If you're stupid enough to go down for someone else, there's nothing else I can do. My conscience is clear. I'll be back in a few days with the amended plea agreement, amended to include the death penalty. Sleep well."

TWENTY

"You look like hell. Anything I can do to help?"

Michael turned, startled by the interruption.

Alan stood in the doorway to his office.

"What're you doing here so late?"

"I have some last minute research to do on a case I'm presenting in court first thing tomorrow, and I forgot to bring the relevant law book home with me." Alan looked down at the pile of papers on Michael's desk. "The Griswold case?"

"This fucking thing gets more complicated every day."

Alan pulled back a chair facing the desk and sat down, resting a law book comfortably on his left knee. "Looks like you need a consultation. I promise my fee will be very reasonable. Maybe you could work it off babysitting when this case is over."

Alan's attempt at humor failed to put a dent in Michael's somber mood.

He looked at Alan for a moment, his forehead lined. Finally, he leaned over, grabbed a file and handed it to Alan. "This is the latest bomb. Koosman dropped it on me this afternoon. Apparently Griswold's stepdaughter may have witnessed the murder. They've been keeping this tidbit hidden to protect the child until they know for certain what, if anything, she saw."

Needing more light to read, Alan reached over and turned on the desk lamp. "I think a little light on the subject might help." When he was finished reading, he shook his head. "That had to be tough for the kid."

"That's one of the problems. Look who's been working with her."

Alan turned a few pages over until he apparently found the one he was looking for. "Shit!"

"I knew Sara was working with a five-year old, and I never mentioned the name of the new case I was working on. Neither of us put two and two together and realized we were working on the same case." He shook his head. "Sara'd probably hang some fancy psychological handle on that like denial, repression, who the fuck knows. All I know is, I'm more and more convinced this guy's covering up for someone, and now I have to withdraw from the case due to a conflict of interest. I was just putting my thoughts together."

"So, what's your plan?"

"I'm preparing a motion for continuance. I'll drop this bombshell on the presiding judge first thing Monday morning. I need time to find another attorney and brief him thoroughly. Koosman won't be happy with that, not with all the pressure on him to close the books with a nice long prison term for Dills. He'd like everyone to go home and forget it ever happened. Everyone except Warren Dills and Carly Perez, that is."

Alan shook his head. "Which of our illustrious dispensers of justice is handling the case?"

"Harry Longmire."

"Could've been worse, although I hear his term is up this fall and he's looking for a State Supreme Court spot. I doubt he's going to go along with a continuance at this stage of the game. I don't think you'll be able to get out of this so easy. Are you sure you want to?"

"Hell, I'm not sure of anything these days. Before today, I admit I was hoping for a change of plea and a good courtroom battle. With all the last minute surprises, as much as I hate to admit it, the case was looking like a real cliffhanger, and it's sure as hell's been a long time since I've had a good challenge. Does that sound familiar to you? Now it's turned into a God damn nightmare."

"Are you going to tell Sara?"

"After I hear from Longmire. If he accepts my motion and I'm off the case, my conversation with her can be held in the past tense. If he doesn't, better to hear about it from me now before we actually go to trial, if we do."

Alan nodded. "I see what you mean. So," he took a deep breath, "now that that's settled, how come I don't notice any great improvement in your mood?"

Michael was quiet for a moment, something else on his mind, weighing alternatives before responding. When he spoke, his voice was flat. "I've been thinking about the Yarrow case."

Alan nodded slowly.

Vivid pictures from the past floated to Michael's mind. He remembered the case well. Yarrow had been accused of viciously beating his nine-year-old son to death with a baseball bat in a drunken rage. The D.D.A. had a strong, clean case with two eye witnesses and a known history of violence in the family. As Yarrow's public defender, Michael's only job was to give his client the best defense possible. So, true to his commitment to the law, his keen mind discovered a loophole in the prosecution's case, a legal technicality. After much inner struggle, he presented this information to the court and the charges were dropped.

The D.D.A. was outraged and, rather than take responsibility for the mistake, he blamed Michael for getting the guilty man off. He taunted Michael mercilessly for a week, finally throwing a punch at him at the nearby happy hour hangout. Michael broke. He hammered the man's face until blood oozed out of every orifice before their colleagues pulled Michael off. He resigned from the PD office the next day. A month later he was in private practice with Alan.

"You never questioned me about it, never asked why I lost it with Brillman that night in the bar. All these years we've known each other you've never pressed me for any reasons and explanations for my lousy moods."

Alan's cheeks flushed. He shrugged. "You mentioned how it was with your old man once. A moron could understand why that particular case got to you. I figured if you wanted me to know more, you'd tell me."

Michael got up and walked over to the window, his hands jammed in his slacks pockets. "The bastard remarried when I was twelve. Left me alone pretty much after that. Life got better for me, but then..." He took a deep breath. "I didn't leave home because of anything the old man did to me. I left because I saw him beat my stepmother to death and nearly kill..." His hand automatically went to the scar on his cheek.

Alan let out a low whistle. "Jesus, Mike!"

"I was so scared I ran. I spent a few months on the streets of New York until I hooked up with a shelter for runaways. I was smart and big for my age, so they never asked too many questions."

As he stood at the window, the memories flooded back. He recalled the days he spent at the library, trying to keep up with his studies. Somehow he knew to survive on his own he needed an education. There was one particular volunteer at the center who took an interest in him. He found him a job off the books washing dishes at a restaurant and supported him in completing high school. By the time he graduated, he earned enough money as a waiter to pay for college, and later law school. So long ago, and yet as the memories few by, it seemed like only yesterday.

He turned back to face Alan. "Anyway, I never went back home. I have no idea what happened to...I should have stayed and seen how things played out. Not a day goes by I don't feel guilty about running away."

"You can't blame yourself for leaving, Mike. For God's sake, you were only a kid!"

"That's what I've told myself over the years, but it hasn't changed the way I feel, hasn't made the guilt go away." He shook his head slowly. "I can't push it away anymore. This case brings it all home to roost."

Alan was quiet for a moment. "Well, maybe you'll get lucky with Longmire. Let's hope he can get you off the hook. Do you need any help with the motion?"

Michael turned back to face him "Thanks, but it's done." He took another deep breath and smiled weakly. "Sorry to dump all of this on you, pal."

Alan squirmed a little in his seat. "No problem. I only wish there was something I could do to help. Tell you what. It's Friday night. Let's go down to

Sammy's and have a few. When was the last time we tied one on? I think you could use a break from reality right now."

Michael grunted. "May as well. My brain's pretty fried. I'm not good for anything else. Thanks, Alan." He put out his hand to his friend.

Alan grabbed it and held on before letting go.

Michael leaned over and shut off the computer. He stuffed some papers into his briefcase and looked around the room as if for the first time. "God, it's dark in here."

Alan laughed. "Welcome back to the real world, buddy-boy."

He stood and slapped Michael on the arm. They left the office, heading for the bar at the corner and a night of mindless recreation.

$$* \quad * \quad *$$

Michael entered Sara's apartment and checked his watch. Two a.m. The scent of newly baked pasta filled his nostrils. Another time the aroma would have watered his mouth, but now it only made his queasy stomach retch.

Closing the door behind him, he noticed a soft light coming from the kitchen, probably the small night-light above the stove. He was grateful for the muted darkness. It seemed to numb his pounding head. He wanted a hot cup of black coffee, but he knew if he drank some now, he'd never get to sleep, and sleep was what he needed most.

But sleep would be slow in coming. He was still too keyed up from the events of the day. He went into the living room, sat on the couch, pulled off his shoes, put his feet up on the coffee table and leaned back into the soft cushions.

He wanted to fight off the thoughts and feelings which swirled about in his Johnny Walker Red-soaked brain. But like a rag doll tossed around by careless hands, he was helpless to do so. The vicious hands of his father had never left him as battered and bruised as the day's events. He was unable to stop the pictures from flying across his mind like the tiny frames of some long-forgotten horror film. Failing, he stopped fighting and watched in silence.

His father would rant and rave around the house in an alcoholic stupor. He'd grab the leather horse reins and flailed them about until they struck Michael time and time again, leaving his arms, legs, back, even his face, covered with bloody cuts and gashes. His only reprieve came from his father's limited physical strength. Exhausted from the amount of energy needed to beat him, the man would collapse unconscious on the floor. Shame overwhelmed him at school each time he explained away the bruises and the black eyes.

That final day at the farm...no, he couldn't go there. All the alcohol in the world couldn't ease those memories. So he shut them off and willed himself to allow the dizziness to swirl around in his brain unencumbered.

Eventually, the kaleidoscope of memories had a mellowing effect. The tension slowly ebbed from his tired body. Maybe he could sleep after all, and maybe with the new day, things would seem clearer.

He felt her presence before he saw her. When he opened his eyes, she stood in the doorway, her arms folded under her breasts, a white silk negligee draped her long slender body. Light from a full moon filtered through the shutters, illuminating her silhouette, giving her the appearance of a ghostly apparition. He was drawn out of the darkness and into the comfort and warmth of the light around her. He took a deep breath, groaned, closed his eyes once again and rested his head back onto the cushions.

"You're lucky I'm not feeling up to snuff right now, or that nightgown would be on the floor, and you'd be in bed quicker than you could cry Rape." His words slurred in a mocking voice.

There was a smile in her voice. "And to what do I owe my reprieve from that fate worse than death?"

"About a half pint of scotch and three hours at Sammy's English Pub."

"Well, damn you for not including me in all the fun."

"Do I look like I've been having fun?"

"No, you look like shit."

He smiled. "Thanks. I needed that. A cold slap of reality to wash away the curse of demon rum."

She walked to him and sat down on the edge of the coffee table next to his legs. "Something tells me you've had a rough day. Do you want to talk about it?"

"Spoken like a true shrink. There's nothing I'd like better than to unburden myself, Doc. but I don't think my client would appreciate the breach of confidentiality. Low-life though he is, one must be true to the ethical codes of one's profession or what would there be left to trust?"

"Is this the case you've been putting all the time into lately?"

"The one and only. I hope the bastard is losing as much sleep over this as I am."

"I wonder what makes me think your emotional involvement with this case, and your need to numb yourself with alcohol, is not the usual way you prepare a case."

"Probably all that experience crawling inside people's heads with your little flashlight, dredging up their dark ugly secrets and playing patty cake with all their shit."

She laughed out loud. "What an incredibly unique and vivid description of my profession. Wait, let me write that down so I'll have it handy for the next APA convention." She made a move to get up, but he reached out quickly and grabbed her wrist.

"You leave me now, woman, and we're through."

They were silent for a few moments. Then she moved onto the couch and snuggled up against his chest. His arms went around her and held on tightly.

"I saw Rose again. I, I think I've got a long way to go before my nightmares are resolved. I want to tell you about it, but right now I don't know what there is to tell. I hope you can be patient with me for a while. I'm going to work very hard to get to the bottom of this, but it may take some time."

His arms tightened around her. He kissed her forehead. "I'll be there for you, Sara. I promise. I have to admit, though, some of my reasons may be purely selfish. I've let people down in the past, and it's important for me to know I won't let you down."

"Hard to believe you've ever let anyone down. I don't believe you're as selfish as you think."

"Tonight, for example, I should have gone home and not bothered you. I guess my coming here was the act of a desperate man."

"Beware, Michael Grey. One of these days I'll unearth all those dark secrets you've buried so deep. When I do, it'll be over for you. You won't be able to hide from me anymore. You'll be mine forever."

He took a deep breath. The soft scent of her fresh, clean skin and hair intoxicated him, washing away the cobwebs of the day's drama. His body relaxed with the feel of her, the closeness, and the childlike trust of her body against his.

His hand came up and caressed her hair, her cheek, her neck. He felt himself falling into her. At once, his emotional walls crumbled. He was vulnerable, raw, exposed.

He heard words slurred now with passion pour out of his mouth, words his mind had kept locked safely away these past few months, but which now his soul needed to say. "Sara, Sara," he whispered into her soft thick hair. "You're the most important thing in my life–your spirit, your strength, your courage. You light up a place inside of me that's been dark for so long. I *am* selfish. I take so much from you and give you nothing in return. I'm so afraid I'll lose you someday. I don't want that to happen. I want to spend the rest of my life with you. I need you to be in my life so it makes some sense."

As his words droned on, she relaxed deeply into him, her soft breath against his neck.

"My darling, all I want is for you to take from me all I have to give. This makes me complete, fulfilled. I want nothing more. I love you, Michael."

He pulled back for a moment to look into her eyes. Her tears, her flushed face, her full unconditional love and acceptance were evident. He groaned and brought his mouth gently onto hers. His hand caressed her cheek. She melded her body into his and once again he got lost inside her.

TWENTY-ONE

Hatch pulled the collar of his slicker closer to his neck. An early morning summer squall blew driving rain through the canyons of the Hollywood Hills. It left him extremely pissed off about the four a.m. call to a crime scene. He passed uniformed police, forensic techs and coroner staff. With Blake beside him, they worked their way to the open door of the first floor condo. In the living room, the body of a young woman lay on her side at his feet. Blake shook his head.

"Looks like a pretty girl. Young. Silk pjs. Nice place. What do you make of it, Sarg?"

Hatch pulled on vinyl gloves. "Has the Coroner been here yet?'

The uniformed officer who declared himself first responder nodded. "Yes, Sarg. He lives in the neighborhood and got here just before you."

"How did you get here?"

"The nine-one-one call came in from a neighbor who thought he heard screaming. Apparently it's a very quiet building with peaceful tenants. He was concerned with the noise."

"Did you touch anything?"

"No, sir. This is the way I found her. I called it in right away."

Hatch nodded and kneeled down. "Help me turn her, Blake."

Together they rolled the woman on her back. She had short curly hair and a small oval face. Hatched guessed her age to be mid to late twenties. Handprints ringed her neck. He sensed another man standing next to him and looked up at the county Coroner, Doctor Yee.

"Sorry to see you out so early in the morning, Doc. What can you tell me?"

"Looks like she was strangled. I may be able to get some prints off her neck." Hatch picked up the woman's hands and checked out the fingernails. "There's something under a few of the nails. Let's collect this and test it ASAP. What about time of death?"

"I'd say no more than an hour ago. Say between two-thirty and three-thirty. I'll know more when I get her back to the lab."

"Do we know who she is?"

"As soon as the forensic boys finished dusting for prints, the uniforms found her wallet in her purse." Yee, his hands also encased in vinyl gloves, handed the wallet to Hatch.

He opened it and removed her driver's license. "Dana Ingrahm. Twenty-seven." After a search through the wallet, he found something else. "Says here she's a reporter for the *Times*." A business card fell onto the floor. He picked it up and stared at it. Shit.

He stood up when the morgue techs came in. covered the body with a white sheet and placed it on a stretcher. They wheeled it out of the apartment. Hatch, Blake and Yee followed it outside and watched while the techs put the stretcher into the coroner's van and drove away. He turned to Yee. "How soon can you do the autopsy?"

"I'll get right on it. Hate to see the creep that did this have time to cover his tracks. I'll see you at the morgue later, Joe."

Hatch nodded and Yee took off in his car.

He turned to Blake. "As soon as it's light, I want the neighbors canvassed. I'll be in the office making phone calls. As soon as the canvas is complete, meet me back at the shop with any other evidence the apartment search gave up."

"Will do, Sarg."

Hatch left Blake standing there organizing the uniformed cops around the canvass. As soon as he got inside his car, he stared at the business card in his hand.

What was Sara Bradley's card doing in Dana Ingrahm's wallet? Was she a patient? If so, he knew it would difficult to get any substantial information from Sara because of confidentiality issues. Damn, why wasn't anything ever easy?

*   *   *

Promptly at ten, Hatch strolled into the Coroner's suite. God, he hated the place. The stark white walls, the frigid temperature, the stainless steel tables and trays with medical instruments of all kinds. The metallic smell of death and chemicals which shocked his senses every time he ventured there. He took a deep breath and walked to the examination table where the body of Dana Ingrahm lay. Her skin was gray and pasty-looking, her eyes closed. It was hard for him to imagine her alive and smiling, laughing, even angry, displaying any normal human emotion.

"Morning, Doc." Hatch slapped Doc Yee on the shoulder. A small Asian man, Yee had been with the County for as many years as Hatch could remember. He was extremely competent and very helpful with murder investigations. "So, what do we have here?"

"Nothing new to report from my first impression earlier this morning. Female, approximately five-five, a hundred and twenty pounds, between twenty-five and thirty years of age. COD strangulation. Small hands. I wasn't able to get any fingerprints. No indication of sexual trauma. TOD between two-thirty and three-thirty a.m."

"How soon before the lab tests come back?"

"Should be within the hour. DNA will take a few days. I did take her prints and sent them to the lab for ID confirmation."

"Okay. Let me know as soon as you get the test results."

"Will do."

Hatch left the morgue and headed back to his office. He hadn't heard from Blake. That wasn't a good sign. Probably meant he hadn't found anything useful from the canvass. Hatch couldn't get the face of the dead girl out of his mind. So young. What a waste. He decided to call Sara. Hopefully she could give a positive ID. Then he'd start with relatives and the woman's boss at the *Times*. He reached for the phone.

*   *   *

Sara wiggled out from under Michael's arm, hating to leave the warmth of his body, but the bedside phone persisted. She looked at the clock. God! She couldn't believe it was so late in the morning.

"Hello?"

"You still in bed? Damn, you lead a charmed life. Hope there's a hot and sweaty man next to you this time."

"Good morning to you, too, Joe. What's up?" Michael stirred and moved closer to her, still asleep. She smiled when his arm went around her again.

Hatch's voice hardened. "Sorry to spoil your weekend, but I caught another murder during the night. Someone you might know."

Sara stiffened, her attention fully glued to the phone. "Who is it?'

"The woman had your business card in her wallet. Name's Dana Ingrahm. Ring any bells?"

Sara gasped so loud it woke Michael. She sat up quickly, pulling the covers over her bare breasts. "Dana? Did you say Dana Ingrahm?"

"Yeah. Neighbors called in when they heard screaming. Was she a patient?"

Sara's heart pounded; her head was about to explode. Dana! God! Tears rolled down her cheeks.

"What is it, Sara?" Michael now sat up staring at her. The sheet had slipped to his waist. She put her free hand on his bare chest.

She latched onto his eyes in an attempt to steady herself. "It's Joe Hatch. Dana's been murdered!"

"Sara? You all right?"

She took a deep breath. "Sorry, Joe. No, Dana wasn't a patient. She's my best friend. What happened?" It was difficult to keep her voice steady.

"Don't know all the details. Sometime during the night, someone entered her apartment and strangled her."

Greg Liston's angry face flashed in her mind.

"Do you think you could meet me at the morgue and give me an ID? I can't move forward until her ID's confirmed. If you're up to it, I'd like to get a statement from you about her. Anything you know that might lead me in the direction of her killer."

She continued staring into Michael's concerned eyes. "Yes, of course, Joe. I'll be there within the hour."

"Thanks." Pause. "And, Sara, I'm sorry for your loss." He hung up.

She continued staring at Michael.

He took the phone from her.

"I can't believe, it. Dana. Dead. We…we have a softball game tomorrow. I just saw her for lunch the other day. Oh, Michael!" She threw herself into his arms and let her body dissolve in pain and loss. The tears flowed freely down her face, against his chest. One arm tightened around her, the other gently held the back of her head.

After a while, the tears stopped. She pulled away to look at him. "Do you think it was Greg? Could he really have been that obsessed?"

"I don't know, sweetheart, but I'm sure Joe'll find out who did it. He's a damn good cop."

She hurried into the bathroom. "I have to meet him at the morgue. He needs a positive ID. I have to get ready. I have to…"

He was right behind her, grabbing her arm and turning her around. "We'll go together. I don't want you doing this alone." He lifted her face and gently kissed her.

The strength and steadiness in his eyes calmed her. She returned the kiss. "Thanks. I can't trust myself to be very professional when I look at her. I'll feel better with you standing next to me."

"You don't have to be strong all the time, Sara." He kissed her again, this time the tenderness brought new tears to her eyes.

They dressed in silence and left her apartment in a hurry. Sara's mind played ugly scenes over and over. Who killed Dana? Had she suffered? What were her thoughts before she took her last breath?

She steeled herself against those painful questions and the knife-like feelings they brought. No matter what Michael said, she had to be strong. She would do everything in her power to find out who killed her friend. Only then would she be at peace.

*   *   *

She barely held it together. Only Michael's arm across her shoulders kept her from giving into her shaking legs and collapsing on the floor. She couldn't believe it was Dana lying there, so still, so white, so dead. It was nearly impossible for her to conjure up the vivacious, passionate, happy, committed woman Dana had been. The woman who could slam a softball out of the park. The woman who loved her job and thrived on the risks it sometimes entailed. Had one of those risks finally caught up with her?

After identifying Dana's body, she and Michael followed Hatch back to his office. Seated in a chair across from him, she forced herself to concentrate on Michael's hand which held hers. It kept her grounded.

"Are you sure you want to do this now, Sara? We can wait until tomorrow for your statement."

"No. I want to help anyway I can. You've got to find him, Joe. She didn't deserve to die like that."

"All right. Tell me about Dana Ingrahm. How long have you known her?"

"We met in college. She was a Journalism major. We were roommates. Since both of us were only children, we hit if off right away. We...we were very close." She took a shaky breath and let it out slowly.

Michael squeezed her hand.

"Tell me about this guy Greg Liston. I have a report here says the police were called to her apartment recently because he was drunk and threatening to break down the door."

"That's right. She called me, scared and crying, saying he was there insisting she take him back. By the time Michael and I got there, the police were leaving."

"What do you know about him?"

"Not much. I only met him once. Dana dated him for a couple of months. When she realized he had a violent streak, she broke it off. Apparently he couldn't handle 'no.' He called her constantly, left text messages, followed her, became very obsessive. I was worried about her, but she blew it off saying he'd never hurt her. Do you think it was him?"

"Don't know yet. We're looking for him. Hasn't shown up at his job for the last two days. When we find him, we'll bring him in and have a nice long chat."

Hatch looked at a file on his desk and then up at her. "She was an investigative reporter for the *LA Times*. What kind of stories did she write?"

"Exposés, different topics, things the average citizen might not be aware of. She loved being a detective and rooting out interesting places and people. Nothing too controversial."

"Do you know what she was working on?"

Sara thought for a moment. "She mentioned something about an underground nightclub. She found it interesting because everyone came in bizarre costumes. She told me she was planning on going in costume."

Hatch reached down and pulled up a box from under his desk, resting it on top. He opened it and grabbed what looked like black leather clothes. He showed them to Sara. "Do these look familiar?"

The outfit consisted of a black leather vest and very short skirt, both decorated with thin silver chains and buttons.

"I've never seen these before, but Dana said she wanted to go to the club as a dominatrix." Sara shook her head when tears slipped down her face again. "We both laughed. I couldn't imagine her dressed like that. Where did you find that outfit?"

"In her closet, along with a sexy pair of high black leather boots. "What do you know about this club?"

"Nothing. She didn't mention the name or the location, only that a source told her about it, and she wanted to do a story on it." She trembled. "Tell you the truth, the place sounded real creepy. I was concerned about her going there, but that was Dana. Never worried about taking risks. Always jumping into the next story, the next relationship. Dammit! I should have done something, said something, not made a joke out of it."

"We don't know if the club had anything to do with her death, Sara, so don't punish yourself." Michael looked at Hatch. "Anything else, Joe? I'd like to take Sara home now. She's had a rough morning."

They stood.

Hatch walked them to the door, patting her arm when she stepped into the hallway. "Go home and rest and don't worry. I'll catch the son of a bitch. I promise."

Sara kissed Hatch on the cheek. "Thanks, Joe. I know you will. Let me know if there's anything else I can do to help."

She and Michael were silent until they got to the car. Inside, she stared out the front window. "I can't believe she's gone. There's this huge emptiness inside me. It hurts so much."

He pulled her into his arms and held her as tight as he dared. She put her head on his shoulder and sobbed, her hand clutching his shirt, her body shaking.

*   *   *

Hatch stared at the back of his office door after they left. Interesting. Sara and Michael Grey. Wonder if they know they're both working on the Griswold case? That could be a problem, but then once the plea agreement was signed, Dills would be shipped to Folsom to spend the rest of his life, and the case would be closed for good. No harm, no foul.

He walked back to his desk. In the meantime, he had a new murder to solve and, thankfully, there'd be no son of a bitch judge to get in his way.

TWENTY-TWO

"Just what the hell is going on here, Counselor? First Weiss, then you, dragging your feet on accepting the D.D.A.'s plea bargain. Now you want a continuance so you can take yourself off the case. Surely, you jest."

Michael stood his ground when District Court Judge Harry Longmire exploded into his chambers, his black robe flowing behind. Longmire stormed over to his desk, holding the Blue Back Michael prepared...was it only two days before? So much had happened over the weekend. Dana's death. Sara's pain. He'd never felt so useless watching her cry and being unable to do anything to help her. Where were all those sappy words he'd told her about being there for her? When the shit hit the fan, he hadn't done a damn thing to make it better. He sucked in a frustrated breath.

He came back to the present with a jerk when Longmire waved the Blue Back in his face. He cleared his throat.

"Believe me, Your Honor, it's no joke. I've recently come upon information which makes it ethically impossible for me to continue as Warren Dills' attorney. I feel his civil rights would be jeopardized by my continuing on the case."

"It's my job to determine whether a suspect's civil rights have been violated, Counselor, or have you forgotten everything you learned in law school?"

"No, Your Honor. In fact, I believe that's where I first heard about legal ethics and moral responsibility."

Longmire snickered. "Don't get smart with me, Grey, or I'll make the next few weeks of your life miserable. What information have you recently discovered that's stirred up all this self-righteousness?"

"I found out yesterday the minor's psychologist is the same woman with whom I am personally involved."

Longmire looked closely at Michael through squinting eyes. "How long have you been practicing law, Grey, twelve, fifteen years? Most of it in the P.D.'s office, am I correct?"

"Yes, sir, but what has that got..."

"I don't know what your problem is, but I don't like being taken for a fool. Do you expect me to believe after all these years you don't know how to maintain confidentiality regarding your client...that you don't know how to keep your mouth shut and not discuss the case with your lady friend? Apparently this hasn't been a problem for either of you up to now, since you've only just found out about the possible conflict of interest. What makes you think you can't continue maintaining ethical boundaries?"

Michael remained silent. He realized Longmire wasn't expecting an answer, only making a point. Longmire sat down and looked at him, his eyes softening a little. "I'm going to dismiss your motion. As far as I'm concerned, you've exercised your ethical responsibility by calling this to my attention. You can be sure I'll watch for any problems in this regard until this case is closed. There'll be no more continuances. I don't have to tell you the pressure we're all under." His eyes drilled into Michael's. "If I don't get some closure on this matter before the end of the week, you'll find yourself with a big fat fine for obstruction and some jail time. Do I make myself clear?"

"Yes, Your Honor."

"Good. Now get the hell out of here and don't come back without a signed plea agreement in your hands." He began shifting through papers on the desk.

Michael stared at him, his chest tight with anger and frustration. So much for a reprieve. Looked like he was stuck on the roller coaster until the end of the ride. Damn Griswold and the power he wielded.

He decided to leave before Longmire started railing again, careful to contain his anger and not slam the door. He didn't want to antagonize an already hostile judge.

He left the Criminal Courts building and headed for his office. He felt trapped in a cage of someone else's making and every fiber of his being demanded he lash out at someone, something, to rid himself of the horrendous pressure building inside.

Yarrow's face flashed in front of him. He was the D.D.A. he'd fought with before leaving the P.D.'s office. The reminder hit him like bucket of ice water. His heart continued a steady beat, his breath came normally. The anger disappeared. He was left calm and in control once again, his rational mind taking over. No one forced him to take the case. For whatever insane reasons, he'd chosen to play God and rescue Dills from his own self-defeating choices. It was time to grow up and stop whining like a spoiled brat. He had a week left. He'd better make the most of it.

He ran down Temple Street and turned the corner toward his office, his head clear for the first time in the last forty-eight hours.

*   *   *

He closed the door of Sara's office behind him. She'd insisted on going right back to work. At least, she'd said, she knew she made a difference with her patients, even if she hadn't been able to save Dana.

The small waiting room seemed to invite people to relax and be comfortable. A gingham cover sofa, and a coffee table with magazines on top filled the room. A middle-aged woman dressed in a business suit sat in one of the matching armchairs, legs crossed, reading a *Psychology Today* magazine. She looked at Michael then continued scanning the magazine. He walked to the window and stared out. With his mind wrapped around the Griswold case, he barely took in the rocky hillside view.

After a few moments, a door opened. He turned.

Sara stood in the doorway, her attention focused on the woman who smiled and rose to meet her.

Then she noticed him standing near the window. She appeared surprised to see him. Her brow wrinkled. The woman walked past Sara and entered the inner office.

The corner of his mouth curved upward when his eyes met hers.

"Sorry to disturb you, Doc, but I was hoping you could fit me into your schedule this afternoon. I have an emergency I need to discuss with you."

She looked tired, but there was still a little sparkle in her eyes. "As a matter of fact, my last patient for the day cancelled. I can see you within the hour." She followed her patient, closing the door behind her.

He walked over to the sofa, sat down and made himself comfortable. He loosened his tie. He'd already discarded his suit jacket in the back seat of the BMW. He'd purposely left his briefcase in the trunk, needing to take a short break from work, but unfortunately he wasn't able to leave his thoughts as neatly locked away.

For the next fifty minutes, with his head leaning back against the sofa and his eyes closed, his mind raced over legal precedents in an attempt to piece together the puzzle that was the Griswold case.

He jerked back when the door opened to the inner suite.

Sara stood in the doorway, smiling. "Are you sure you want to see a therapist? I would think after last night you'd be more in need of a medical doctor. Besides, last I heard, Counselor, you had little interest in psycho-babble, I believe you called it. I wonder what's changed your mind."

His glance moved slowly down her beautiful face and along the length of her body, looking through the pale yellow linen dress and seeing only her nakedness with which he was so intimately familiar. "Actually, I'm not interest in the subject, only the practitioner. Or should I say." He smiled, "a certain female practitioner. She has of late blinded me to all rational thought and left me groping helplessly in the dark for something more tangible to hold onto."

She laughed. "So what brings you out of your cave so early in the day?"

Her words seemed to break the magical trance he fell under every time he saw her. He took a deep breath and stood, tension spreading through him. "I feel like shit bringing this to you now, after what went down this weekend, but I needed to talk to you as soon as possible. I didn't want to wait until tonight."

"Come in." She led the way down a short carpeted hallway and turned into a large, bright sunny office. After they stepped inside, she closed the door and walked to the desk, turned and sat on the edge facing him.

"What is it?"

He stuffed his hands into the pockets of his suit pants and looked into her dark eyes, watching for her response to his next statement. "I discovered we have a major ethical problem we have to deal with."

She wrinkled her eyebrows.

"We've been working on the same case these last few months."

"Which one?"

"Griswold."

"*What?*"

"I'm defending Warren Dills, the man who confessed to murdering the mother of the child you've been treating, Carly Perez."

"Are you serious? All this time...the big case you've been working on...the Griswold murder?" She shook her head. "I don't understand how neither of us ever put two and two together and figured this out."

"We're both too damn good at keeping secrets."

She got off the desk and went over to him. "We're professionals. We're morally and ethically mandated to maintain patient/client confidentiality."

He looked deeply into her eyes and relaxed.

"How did you find out? I thought Koosman was keeping that information under wraps."

"He gave me a copy of the report you wrote saying you believe the child witnessed the murder. I couldn't believe my eyes when I saw your name on the bottom. Then it all fell into place. Hell, I even remembered meeting her at the zoo that day. I went to the presiding judge this morning and asked to be released from the case, but he refused. Said he trusted our ability to handle this responsibly and wasn't about to grant me a postponement so I could brief another attorney."

He paused. "I'm sorry for putting you in this bind. If I'd realized you were treating the child, I never would've taken the case."

"I know." She took a deep breath. "So, what do we do now? I mean, where do I fit into your case?"

He was enormously relieved by her reaction, the way she heard the news and took it in stride, an action-oriented response rather than an emotional one. How much he admired and respected her.

"Koosman's pressuring me into leaving the confession stand uncontested. He wants my client to sign the plea agreement. He doesn't want me pursuing a not guilty plea and going to trial." He shook his head. "If I thought the man had killed Mrs. Griswold, I would've taken the case in the first place, but I'm convinced Dills had nothing to do with the murder. I can't, in good conscience, let his confession stand without a fight. What I can't understand is why he's so unwilling to stand up for himself." He took a breath. "My question to you is, has the child named Warren Dills as the man who murdered her mother?"

This was more difficult to talk about with her than he would've thought. For some reason he was very uncomfortable. He was tense. His chest was tight and his words were strained. He wasn't sure why.

Sara walked over to the desk and sat on the edge again.

He sensed her discomfort with the topic.

"Carly hasn't disclosed directly that she witnessed the murder. It was her recent behavior that had me write that report. I truly believe she saw something that was even more traumatic than finding her mother's body. She has a hard time staying focused for very long whenever I broach the subject. I believe the trauma of witnessing her mother's murder, if in fact she did, has made the possibility of a direct disclosure even more difficult. I'll make a statement to that effect if you want, but Koosman already knows this."

"I know. As I said, he wants me to back off and let Dills hang himself." His voice dropped a notch. "There's another problem. If Dills isn't the murderer then the real perp is still out there. If Carly was a witness, she could be in danger." He sighed. "This gets more sordid every day, doesn't it? I wish you weren't involved. I don't know why. I just have a vague feeling of doom when I think of you dealing with all this shit."

She got off the desk and walked over to him. "You don't have to protect me, but I love you for wanting to."

At that moment, his phone chirped. He pulled his eyes away from her long enough to grab it and read the text. He glanced back at her apologetically. "Sorry. I have to take this call."

She nodded and sat on the sofa, watching him closely.

"Hi, Katie, what's up?"

"I'm glad I caught you. Warren Dills' counselor at the jail has been trying to get in touch with you. He says it's an emergency. He wouldn't say what it was."

He cursed under his breath. "What's the number?" He grabbed a pen and pad from the desk and scribbled down a telephone number. "Thanks."

Immediately he dialed the prison and within moments was put through to Dills' counselor.

"Mr. Grey, glad you called. We've had a bit of a problem here. Warren Dills was just taken to Holy Cross Hospital in San Fernando with multiple chest injuries. I thought I'd better tell you. Doesn't look good."

"Christ! What happened?"

"We're not sure. Could have started out as a typical prison argument over telephone privileges and ended in a brawl between him and another inmate. He was unconscious before the deputies got to him."

"Terrific. Holy Cross, you say? I'll get right over there. Thanks for the call."

Michael punched the call closed. He turned around, his mood ugly. "I don't know what the fuck else could go wrong with this case. A shining example of Murphy's Law. Dills was involved in a jail fight, apparently over telephone rights. He's unconscious. I've got to get over there and see if he's able to come out of it long enough to make a statement."

She went to him, putting her arms around his neck. She looked deeply into his eyes. "Did I ever tell you how much I love you?" Her voice was barely a whisper.

Her question made him feel uncomfortable. He tried to make light of it. "I, uh, I believe you may have mentioned it while in the throes of passion."

She smiled and then kissed him softly. "Nonetheless true. Don't be too long. I feel another night of true confession coming on."

*   *   *

The distinct hospital ambiance of harsh disinfectant, antiseptics, drugs and glaring hall lights greeted Michael as soon as he entered the building. He was cleared both by police guards and hospital personnel and finally got into Dills' room. The lights were dim, the walls a pale shade of green. Before entering the room, the doctor had told him Dills was slipping in and out of consciousness. Several chest wounds from a prison-made shank barely missed his heart. He'd lost a lot of blood before the EMT's stabilized him.

He walked over to the bed. Dills lay there as white as the linen which covered him. Several tubes ran in and out of his nose and arms. Except for the heart monitor which beeped a steady rhythm, the room was silent.

Michael pulled a chair over to the side of the bed and leaned forward. "Warren, can you hear me? Warren, its Mike Grey."

Dills' eyeballs move around under their lids. He seemed to be struggling to grasp consciousness. He won the battle, for his eyes opened. They scanned the room and landed on Michael's face. "This sure don't look like hell. Guess I'm still breathin'." His voice was barely a whisper.

"Can you tell me what happened? Something tells me this was more than a fight over a telephone."

Dills moved his tongue slowly over his parched lips. "How about a drink?"

Michael reached for a nearby water container, poured some into a glass and carefully held it to Dills' mouth. Much of it spilled onto the man's chin and down his neck, but some of it made its way down his throat.

Michael replaced the glass on the table. "How much longer are you going to go down for someone else, Dills? Jail time is one thing, but damn it, we're talking about your fucking life! The doctor tells me half an inch more, and we wouldn't be having this conversation. Do you want the bastard you're protecting to go free and clear? Is that what you want? Help me, man. Help me save your life."

Dills licked his lips again. He must have sensed Michael's sincerity because tears formed at the corners of his eyes and slowly slid down his temples. "What's in it for you, another big win, fame and fortune?"

"What do you care what I'm getting out of this? Listen, you stupid fuck. I'm no boy scout, and you're no old lady needing to cross the street. You'd better open your mouth and start talking while you still can."

Dills closed his eyes. They remained closed. "I didn't kill Mrs. Griswold."

Michael leaned closer to hear him.

"I never went into the house that night. I'd never do a scumbag thing like that. Maybe he did. Maybe that's why..."

"Why what? Who are you talking about? Dills, Dills. God damn it."

He sat back, angry and frustrated. Dills had slipped into unconsciousness again. Michael stared at him. His mind raced with questions, hypotheses, names, faces. Twenty minutes passed. Dills didn't regained consciousness.

Michael left the room and walked over to the nurses' station. He caught the attention of the first nurse he found, pulled out his business card and handed it to her. "I'm Mr. Dills' attorney. I must speak with him the moment he regains consciousness. Please call me when he's able to talk."

"Of course. As long as the police have cleared you, there's no problem. I doubt it will be much before tomorrow, though. He was just given a large dosage of morphine before you arrived."

"Thanks." He walked out of the hospital, his hand jammed into the pockets of his slacks, but this time he walked briskly, lighter. Finally, Dills was ready to come clean. Now, if he only lasted the night...

*   *   *

"Where the hell've you been hiding, Liston?"

Hatch stared at the man seated across from him in the interview room at Hollywood Division. He was in his early thirties, short and slim, with brown hair and eyes. There was nothing particularly impressive about him. Except that apparently he'd been obsessed with Dana Ingrahm and hadn't been at his job as a car salesman since the murder.

He glared at Hatch. "Not that it's any of your business, but I was on a fishing trip up north with a buddy of mine."

"That buddy have a name?"

"Norm Yablonsky."

"He got a phone number, an address?"

"What's this all about? I get home from a great mini-vacation to find two cops at my apartment. Then they haul me in here. I'm not answering any more questions until you tell me what's going on?"

Hatch opened the file in front of him. "I see you like harassing women."

"What the fuck you talking about?"

"Says here a lady named Dana Ingrahm took out a restraining order against you. You do remember her, don't you? Ex-girlfriend. Gave your sorry ass the boot and apparently you didn't take it in stride like any decent guy would."

Liston squinted. "Yeah, I know her." He slinked back in his seat. "Bitch didn't know a good thing when she had it. Oh, well. Her loss. There are plenty other women who'd be real happy to have me hang around."

"When was the last time you saw Ms. Ingrahm?"

"Probably the night she filed that TRO, except I didn't even see her then. She never let me into her apartment before the cops came. What's the matter? She complaining about me again? I never went near her after that night. She's lying if she says I did."

Hatch stared at him. "Where were you last Friday?"

Liston paused. "On the road north. With Norm. What the hell's going on here? I know my rights. You can't keep harassing me like this."

"Dana Ingrahm was murdered Friday night. Actually, early Saturday morning. You wouldn't happen to know anything about that, would you?"

Liston's surprise seemed genuine. "Murdered? How? Who did it?"

"I was thinking maybe you went back to her place and had it out with her again. When she refused to take you back, you strangled her."

"Strangled her! Are you nuts? I may have been drunk that last time I was at her house, and I might have been pissed she dumped me, but I'd never hurt her, or any woman, for that matter. It wouldn't be worth my landing in jail. Like I said, there are plenty of other women out there."

Hatch was silent for a moment. Then he passed a pad and pencil toward Liston. "Write down the name, address and phone number of your buddy, Norm. We'll check out his story. Until then, you'd better stay close. If I have to send the dogs for you again, you won't be sitting here smiling at me."

After Liston wrote the information on the pad, Hatch nodded toward the door. Liston pushed back his chair in a huff, sending it flying backward. He slammed the door behind him.

Blake came in immediately after. Hatch handed him the pad. "Check out this guy's alibi ASAP. My gut tells me he was telling the truth. In the meantime, did you get anything on that story she was working on? Any information about the club?"

Blake took the pad. "Her editor at the paper said she tended to keep her stories to herself until she was ready to go print. He did give me a couple of people he thought might be her sources. I'll be checking them out next."

"Good. I want to close this one quick. I owe it to Sara, as well as the girl. Keep in touch. I'm going home before the wife divorces me and takes all my pension."

"Right, Sarg."

TWENTY-THREE

God, he was tired. After leaving the hospital the night before, Michael spent hours at the office preparing a motion informing the court, and the D. A.'s office, of Dills' medical condition. No sooner had he dropped the brief at Longmire's courtroom and Koosman's office than he heard his name called from down the hall of the criminal courts building.

"Grey! Wait up."

He turned. It was Pete Neilson, the investigator he'd hired right after his conversation with Hatch. Neilson, was medium height and muscular, with long crew-cut dark hair, probably fortyish. So much had happened since Michael put him on the case, he hadn't had a chance to update him.

"Pete, glad I ran into you. There's been a shift in the winds of this case. Dills was stabbed by some punk in the jail cafeteria yesterday. Must have given him a near-death experience because he's decided to come clean. What do you have for me?"

"I haven't bothered you before because I wanted to get it all together in a neat little package before I gave you this present. Guess the timing is right. You look like you could use a break."

Michael snickered. They continued walking down the long marble hallway. "What'd you find out?"

"I checked Dills' bank account like you asked, looking for a possible payoff. Nothing suspicious. Maybe someone was waiting for the case to close before paying. Besides, if money was involved, I couldn't figure out the motivation since he wasn't going to be around to take advantage of it. The only thing I came up with was he must've thought his life wasn't worth very much. But why? The story was he'd beaten the drug thing and gotten back with his wife. Everything looked rosy. Something must have happened to throw a big wrench into the works. I checked out a few things. Then, Bingo!"

He pulled out some papers from his jacket pocket and handed them to Michael. Both men stopped walking.

Michael's eyes scanned the fine print of a medical record from the office of Dr. Philip Somers. The name at the top read "Warren Dills."

Michael's eyes landed on a notation near the bottom of the last sheet. He let out a groan. "Bingo is right. I guess Dills decided he wasn't going to wait around for miracles. He's HIV positive. How'd you get his medical record? This is highly confidential information."

"Never ask a PI the source of his information, Counselor. You've been around long enough to know that."

Michael smiled. "You're right. I don't want to know. I assume you confirmed this by double checking with his jailhouse intake medical exam." Pete nodded. "Good work. We have motive for the confession. The next question is, if Dills didn't murder Mrs. Griswold, who did?"

"The bad news is I can't say for sure. The good news is I'm still checking on Griswold's alibi the night of the murder. Hatch was right. There are a few things that just don't jive. His service has him logged out at four-twenty p.m. the day of the murder and on his way supposedly to Santa Barbara for the weekend. I've checked every hotel and motel from here to Santa Barbara, and there's no record of him checking in anywhere. Nor does he own any property where he might have stayed. I'll let you know as soon as I have something solid."

Michael slipped the medical record into his pocket. "If I can get Dills to own up to his medical condition, we won't have to use this. Better if I can destroy it. In the meantime, keep me posted on Griswold." He shook his head. "Normally when a wife is murdered, the cops always look to the husband first.

Guess police procedures don't apply to bigwigs like the judge. I'd like nothing better than to nail him for this thing." He was thoughtful for a moment. "What do we know about Griswold? I mean beside the fact that he's a racist son of a bitch. What's his story?"

Neilson grinned. "I did some background checking as soon as my investigation led to questions about the guy. Seems he comes from a very wealthy family in Northern California. Apparently the source of their wealth comes from dubious dealings during the gold rush in the late eighteen hundreds. He was the only child left to fend for himself while his parents pursued wealth and power. I could feel sorry for him if I didn't know better."

"Save your tears. If the bastard killed his wife and set Dills up to take the fall, he deserves everything the legal system can throw at him. Anything else?"

"Nothing solid. Just rumors."

"Like?"

"Apparently the judge thinks he's a real ladies' man. Even after his marriage, he's known to go looking for it elsewhere. Then there's even a more-whispered rumor he likes to frequent a particular underground nightclub. Don't have the name of it yet, but as soon as I get it I'll be visiting the place myself."

"Good. I feel like we're finally moving in a positive direction. Let me know as soon as you have anything solid." Michael slapped Neilson on his shoulder.

"Right. Talk to you soon." Neilson turned and walked into a nearby elevator.

Michael looked after him. The pieces of the puzzle were beginning to fall into place. Dills is clear and maybe Griswold's their man. Why? What's his motive for killing his wife? What the hell was going on between them that was bad enough to push a man in Griswold's position to commit murder?

As he entered an elevator heading toward the ground floor, he shook his head. Longmire had given him a week to close the case. He hoped it was enough time to pull the loose ends together and press the D.D.A.'s nose in it.

*   *   *

He arrived back at his office a little after one that same afternoon. His body and mind cried out for sleep. He'd been up over thirty hours and the events of the past day and a half fell heavy on both him. Not just the case, but Dana Ingrahm's murder and its effect on Sara. She still wasn't her usual lighthearted, grounded self. Maybe he'd spare a few hours and leave early. The thought of soaking his tired body in a hot bath and taking a quick nap at Sara's before she got home appealed to him.

He took a deep breath. Beside the fatigue, he also felt a sense of relief and, yes, validation. He'd been right about Dills all along. It was gratifying to know his instincts were as sharp as ever.

Katie looked up from her computer. "Hi, Mike. Yikes! You look like you've been run over by a bus. Hate to do this to you, but..." She handed him a pile of mail and pink telephone message slips.

"Thanks for the sympathy. Hold my calls, will you, till I let you know."

He entered his office, closed the door, tossed his briefcase and jacket on a chair and moved behind his desk. Things were coming to a head with the case. He'd soon be free of it and the nagging memories it brought up. He looked forward to putting his energies into more pleasant endeavors. Maybe even make some changes, some commitments to living a more satisfying lifem.

Maybe he was ready to risk a full commitment to Sara. Damn it. Why did he always feel so fatalistic whenever he thought of the big "C" word? In truth, these past months with Sara had been the best he'd ever known.

He took a long drink of mineral water and absentmindedly scanned through his mail. A large, official-looking manila envelope from the State of New York grabbed his attention. He put the bottle of water down and opened the envelope. As he suspected, it was the response to his request for Sara's adoption records. He checked the contents of the envelope to make sure he had what he needed.

He glanced through several pages before coming to a dead stop. Three words leapt off the page and hit him full blast in the chest, searing him like a branding iron. He held his breath as he read the words over and over again until they forced their way through his defenses, into his brain and blasted his consciousness into blinding reality.

Edward William Young

Once again, in an instant, the past punched him in the gut. His chest tightened until his breathing became labored. He continued reading the documents, feeling sicker and weaker by the moment. My God! He read everything twice more, hoping each time the facts would change. He couldn't believe it. This couldn't be true. My God! No!

By the time he finished reading, he had to get out of the office fast. He needed time to digest everything, decide what to do. He also knew doing was a long way off. Right now feelings overwhelmed him.

He stuffed the documents back into the envelope, grabbed his jacket and briefcase and stormed out of the office.

His world collapsed around him. He was suffocating, trapped like a wounded animal escaping for his life. He drove the twenty-five miles to his apartment in the Marina like a man in a ghostly twilight zone, faces and scenes swimming past his vision.

He didn't know how he made it home without an accident. He was sorry he had, for death would've been preferable to the way he felt.

*　　*　　*

Three days later he opened the outer door of his office suite, his head and stomach still reeling from all the booze he'd consumed. He barely noticed the surprise on Alan's and Katie's faces when they looked up from the file they'd been discussing. They stared at him when he tossed a large manila envelope onto Katie's desk.

"Make sure this gets into the mail today." He walked into his office and slammed the door.

He sat in his chair thrashing around the files on his desk.

The door opened and Alan and Katie entered the room.

"Michael. We were worried about you. We haven't heard from you in days. Are you okay?" asked Katie.

"I'm fine." He answered shortly, in a deep, low voice. "Just leave the messages on the desk. I'll prioritize them, and we can get started returning calls. Anything from court I should know about?"

Alan answered. "When we couldn't locate you, Katie gave a couple of the immediate cases to me, and I made a few appearances for you. I think we're up to date."

"You can go now, Katie. I'll call when I've finished with the messages."

She seemed taken aback by his harsh tone. She looked at Alan, shook her head and left the room, closing the door behind her.

Michael ignored Alan and continued moving papers around. No one spoke for a long while. Finally, Michael looked up. "If you don't mind, I've got a lot of catching up to do."

"What the fuck's going on? You disappear without a trace, no phone calls, nothing for three days. Then you burst in here looking like shit. No word of 'thanks' to Katie for holding down the fort while you were off God knows where doing God knows what." He paused and took a breath. "I know you've been under a lot of pressure lately, but, Jesus, Mike. You've never let things get in the way of your work. This isn't the real Michael Grey I see. I don't know you anymore."

Michael glared at him. "The real Michael Grey." He snickered. "That's a linguistic contradiction if I've ever heard one. There is no real Michael Grey. I made him up twenty-five years ago. He's a creation, an illusion that has no basis in reality."

"It isn't an illusion I see in front of me."

"Yeah, well, what do you see? Tell me if you can. I'd sure as hell like to know."

"I see a man who's hurting right now, but who's trying to run away again. You can't keep doing this, Mike. You've got to stop running and face your ghosts, whatever they are, once and for all. Why don't you talk to Sara about it, or are you running away from her, too?"

Michael glared at him so intensely Alan took a step back.

"I think you'd better get out of here before I do or say something I may regret. And don't worry. You won't have to take over for me again. I'm back on the job."

Alan turned and stormed out the office, slamming the door behind him.

TWENTY-FOUR

Sara stared into the living room and absentmindedly sipped her morning coffee, barely noticing it had cooled to an almost undrinkable temperature. Her drifting thoughts finally came to rest upon Michael. Nearly a week had passed since she'd seen or heard from him. She guessed he was up to his eyeballs with work. He must've needed a break from her, too. Perhaps she was more of a distraction than he could handle right now.

She sighed. No matter what the reason for his absence, she missed seeing him, talking to him, breathing in the scent of his freshly showered body next to hers each night. She still ached with the loss of Dana. She'd been in touch with Hatch several times, but he had nothing new to report. Along with the hurt, the frustration was overwhelming.

Tears filled her eyes. She thought of Michael and how much she missed his gentle strength, his warm body, his love. There was a strong ache, a need to be with him, one she'd never felt before with any other man. It frightened her a little, but then she thought of him, breathed in and relaxed. She was struck by the fact that never before had she experienced the loss of a loved one, at least not consciously. She was protected from the loss of her biological parents, thanks to the total amnesia which blanketed the first few years of her life. But now what with Dana gone and out of her life forever and Michael...what was going on with him?

A sudden thought flashed in her mind. That must be what it felt like to lose a loving husband after many years of sharing a life. The need, the emptiness. Strange, though. She and Michael had only had a few months together. Still...

The ringing phone brought her back to reality. She reached for it. "Hello."

A heavily accented woman's voice broke through the silence. "Oh, Dr. Bradley, I so glad I find you!"

"Juana? What's the matter? You sound very upset."

"*Es la nina. Es muy loca* dis morning. She woke up crying, tearing at her bedcovers. Den at breakfast she trow her food on de floor, pushing de dishes off de table, jelling. She won' get ready for school. De judge go early to court. I don' know what to do with her."

"What's she doing now?"

"She ees in her room hiding in de closet. She won't open de door and jells at me if I try to open it. *Por favor*, Doctor, can you come? *Mi pobrecita!* She needs help."

Sara looked at her watch. She had several hours before her first patient. "I'll be there in twenty minutes. Just stay near her. Let her know you're there, and she's safe. I'll see you soon."

"*Gracias! Gracias! Hasta un momento.*"

Sara hung up the phone, put the coffee cup in the sink, grabbed her purse and left the apartment. This could be important. She hurried down to the garage. Perhaps the child was ready to deal with some of the rage she'd been withholding. As she pulled out of the garage toward the freeway, she was optimistic for the first time in months

Juana greeted her at the door, a worried expression on her face, her eyes strained from recently shed tears, her love and concern for the child very evident.

"*Gracias por Dios!* You are here! She ees still in her room. She did not go to school today. The doctor said to keep her in bed for a few days."

"The doctor? Has Carly been sick?"

"Oh, no, Doctor, didn't the judge tell you about the car accident?"

"What car accident?" Sara's heart pounded.

"Yesterday, on the way to the market, someone did not stop at the sign and ran into us. We were lucky he wasn't going very fast. They took us to the hospital to make sure we were okay. The doctor said Carly only had a mild concussion and just needs to stay calm." She shook her head, a worried look on her face. "But today, when I called her to breakfast, she was hiding in the closet. Come. You will see."

Sara followed Juana through the foyer, up the stairs and entered Carly's room.

Silence greeted her when she stepped inside. "Its okay, Juana. I'll take it from here." Juana closed the door and left.

The child wasn't visible, but she heard a slight movement in the far corner of the closet.

"Carly?" She called softly and walked to the closet door. "It's Sara, honey. Juana called me. She thought you may want to talk to me for a while. Carly? Can you hear me, sweetie?"

After a few moments, the door to the closet opened very slowly. Sara was able to see the child sitting in the corner, a bunch of toys in front of her. She was hugging a soft white lamb in her small arms. She wore pink floral pajamas, and her long hair was tangled from the night's sleep. Her eyes were wide with fear. Tears stained her cheeks.

"I've been a bad girl. Juana is very angry with me. She's going to yell at me if I come out."

Sara bent down and looked at her closely. "Juana's not angry with you. She knows you're feeling badly right now, and she's sad about that. Juana loves you very much."

Tears filled the child's eyes. "I'm a bad girl. That's why bad things happen."

Sara sat down on the floor at the door of the closet. "You're a good girl, Carly. You must remember that. What's happened to you is not your fault. You're a good girl. Juana and I both love you very much."

The child started to cry. Her little shoulders shook with great sobs.

"Come here, Carly. Let me hug you." Sara reached in, and Carly leaned forward. She pulled the sobbing child into her arms and held her tightly, caressing her head with one hand. They sat for a long time on the floor, rocking back and forth.

While she held the child tightly, Sara felt tears spill over her eyes and down her checks. Carly's frail body seemed to meld into Sara's. Somewhere inside Sara, the little child she'd once been was able to join with Carly. Together they grieved for all the loneliness they each felt, the sadness, the fear, the abandonment. This time, instead of feeling terrorized by the feelings the child evoked in her, relief washed over her and then bittersweet joy at her ability to grieve in a way she'd never done before.

After a long while, Carly stirred in her arms. Sara looked into the sad little face and smiled. She wiped the tears off the child's cheeks.

Carly looked at her. "You're crying, too."

"Yes. Thank you for letting me cry with you. It feels good sometimes to be sad with someone you love."

"My mommy used to cry sometimes when he would yell at her, but that didn't make me feel good."

"I would feel sad to see my mommy cry."

Carly's face suddenly turned mean and angry and her tiny voice filled with more rage than Sara had ever heard her express. "I hate him! I hate him! He hurt my mommy!"

"Who do you hate, Carly?"

"Him. You know. Him."

"Can you tell me his name, honey? Who hurt you and your mommy?"

Carly stared at her, as if taken aback by the direct question. Sara saw the emotion leave the child's face and the old stoic mask slide down over it.

She cursed herself for having pushed Carly too far. Damn! She was so close to getting at the truth. Now she lost her again. She took a deep breath. Well, this was a breakthrough, nonetheless. Next time, Carly would be strong enough to go further. She remembered that with this much trauma involved, she could only expect Carly to take small steps at a time. She had to be content with that.

Soon Carly and Juana were functioning normally again. The child was dressed and ready for school, and Juana was packing her lunch. Carly was singing while she finished a new picture she was coloring in her schoolbook. Sara kissed her on the forehead and walked to the front door.

She shook her head, puzzled. What went on in the house the night of the murder? What had the judge and his wife's relationship really been like? Did he have anything to do with Carly's trauma?

She wished she had all the answers to those questions, not only for the child's sake, but for her own. She longed for the peace which her instincts told her she'd find when the riddles were solved and the matter put to rest once and for all.

She walked toward her car but suddenly the sound of a baying horse caught her attention. She stopped and listened. The sounds were coming from the stables. Somewhere from within the building another animal made its presence known. At once, she sensed a familiar feeling, one she couldn't quite put her finger on. She didn't remember being around horses, yet the feeling which now gripped her suggested she had. The *déjà vu* continued, stronger with the next whinny.

Drawn by some unseen hand, she strode toward the barn. The distinct smell of fresh hay, grain and manure filled her senses and continued to draw her into the stable. Her chest rose and fell. Her heart beat faster. She breathed deeply. Something was going on inside her she didn't understand, but her curiosity drove her forward. She wasn't frightened. In fact, she had a deep sense of peace and quiet when she entered the stable.

In the distance, a black stallion, whose head hung over the door of his stall, shook it from side to side as he whinnied. Still in a semi-dream-like trance, she walked toward the huge animal, her hand outstretched until it touched the horse's head. Gently she rubbed her hand up and down, his warm hide velvety smooth, his cold nose wet. Slowly her hand traveled down the side of his head toward his shoulder. She continued to bask in the pleasant, warm, familiar feelings evoked by the motion of her hand sliding slowly along the horse's neck.

As her eyes traveled down the length of the horse, they came to rest upon a pile of fresh, clean hay in the back of the stall. Her hand stopped exploring the horse. Her eyes riveted on the pile of hay. Heart pounded, and it was difficult to breathe. Her chest tightened.

She stared at the hay, but she wasn't seeing it. A picture came into focus, one so clear and vivid she questioned whether it was only a mental picture. A woman lay on the hay, bloody, barely breathing and a huge man stood in front of her, his back to Sara. As in slow motion, she watched in horror when he bent down, picked up a heavy piece of wood and swung his arm over his head until the wood came crashing down on the woman's face. The child in the vision screamed when he turned toward her, his arm rising again over her.

The shrilling scream broke Sara out of the trance. At once she let out a short cry. Her hand went to her mouth in horror. She turned away from the stall and leaned against the wooden planks of the stable wall. She drew her other arm around her waist, holding her stomach. Her eyes closed and a wave of dizziness passed over her. She was sure she was going to faint.

She didn't. Instead, she managed to make her way out of the stable, leaning against the walls for support. She got to her car, yanked the door open and slid in before she collapsed. She drew both arms around her chest, rested her head back against the headrest and allowed the tears to flow. Great sobs shook her body and memories filled her heart.

*   *   *

Sara spent the rest of that day and the next in a daze, going about her work, trying to keep herself together until her appointment with Rose the following evening. When the envelope from New York State arrived, she couldn't open it. Not then. She couldn't do it alone.

She'd tried to reach Michael several times, leaving messages at his apartment as well as at work, but he hadn't returned her calls. That only added to her vulnerable emotional state. By the time she reached Rose Goodman's home, she felt like a walking zombie.

Rose opened the door and let her in. "Sara." The older woman's eyes opened in surprise. "Come in. What's wrong? Why didn't you call me sooner?"

"You know me, Rose. I tough things out by myself as long as I can." She managed a small smile "I don't feel as badly as I look." She pushed her long hair back from her face and walked into the study, clutching the large manila envelope under her arm.

"I reschedule a few of my patients, so I had a lot of time to be by myself and process what's been going on with me. Nevertheless, I'm still in a state of shock."

She sat down on the sofa. Rose joined her at the other end, turning sideways, looking straight at her.

Sara took a deep breath and spoke in a quiet, shaky voice. "God, I miss Dana."

"Your friend who was murdered. Have the police caught the murderer yet?"

"No. No leads. The detective investigating the case has ruled out Dana's ex-boyfriend. Apparently he has a very solid alibi for the night she died."

Rose patted her arm. "I'm sure they'll find the guilty party soon. Is that why you look so beat up?"

"That's a very good description of how I feel. But, no, the main reason I called and needed to see you was something that happened yesterday after a visit with my young patient. I've discovered why the child's had such an effect on me. I've even begun to make some sense out of the nightmares I've had. It's possible I...I..."

She stopped speaking as shame and embarrassment overwhelmed her.

Rose remained silent.

After a while she spoke in a barely audible whisper. "I...I think I saw someone kill my mother. My birth mother."

It was still hard to say the words without tears. She expected Rose to respond with shock and disgust, but no such response came. Instead, only gentle kindness and support showed in Rose's face, which caused the tears to start flowing down Sara's cheeks.

"Wow. This is so hard to talk about it. It's so unreal. I must have been two or three years old. I don't know who the man was. I don't remember anything else except being in a barn somewhere and him smashing her face with a huge piece of wood. I screamed when he came toward me with the wood in his hand. I don't remember anything else. Sometimes the scene feels like a dream, but other times it's so real I can't focus on it for very long before I have to push it away."

"What do you feel when you see this picture?"

"Nothing. I don't feel anything. I'm numb. I only know it was me, but there are no feelings attached to the picture." She laughed. "I've seen so many patients go through the process of trying to recall past memories. I never imaged I might have something so insidious in my past."

"You mentioned your dream. How does your realization explain the dream?"

"It only explains some of it---the barn, the hay, the pain I felt and the demonic being that swirled around and around. There was always someone else in my dream, a kinder being, a more benevolent person, but I don't know who that was. I've been wracking my brain trying to remember more but it's not coming. I'm so frustrated. I know something of what's been tormenting me recently, but I want to find out everything."

"Do you think you're ready to probe further? Are you up to trying hypnosis?"

She wiped her tears away with a tissue and looked at Rose, fear raging through her. "I don't know. What if something else even more terrifying happened? Maybe I should wait." She paced the room, wringing her hands and shaking her head. "No. I said I want to know. We should give it a try."

"It's not a matter of 'should.' You don't have to do anything extraordinary to remember. It appears you're on the right path. You can let nature take its course and continue to allow life to reveal its secrets to you gradually. That was why I suggested you locate your adoption records. I thought knowing some facts about yourself might trigger more memories."

Sara stopped pacing, sat back down on the sofa and reached for the manila envelope. "Oh, yes, I forgot. This came in the mail yesterday. I haven't opened it yet." Her brow wrinkled. "Apparently it went directly to Michael's office. He mailed it to me. He's been so tied up with a big case this past week I haven't seen or heard from him." Tears filled her eyes again. "I...I want to talk to him so much. I need his support right now, but he's been so busy. I feel a bit lost without him. My abandonment issues are slapping me in the face. I guess I've gotten used to him being there these past months."

When she started crying again, deep retching sobs shook her. Rose moved closer, put her arms around her and held her. Soon the sobs stopped. Sara pushed away and reached for another tissue.

She smiled through watery eyes. "God, I feel like such a needy baby. I'm so embarrassed."

"I understand why you feel that way. You, who've been so grownup for so long, always caring for others, never asking anything for herself."

"This vulnerability is a new muscle for me to exercise, being willing to feel needy once in a while. I hope Michael will be able to deal with this part of me. I'm afraid of what he'll think when he finds out."

"I guess we'll have to wait and see won't we? In the meantime, just keep trusting your relationship. If it's real enough, it'll see you both through this."

Sara leaned back against the sofa and closed her eyes. Trust. Yes. That was all she could do until she saw him, talked with him. When would that be?

Rose's voice interrupted her thoughts. "Are you ready to open the envelope?"

Sara sat up and looked at it for a moment. She wrinkled her forehead and took a deep breath. "I guess so."

*   *   *

At home later that evening, Sara lay under her down comforter, hugging it closely to her chest. She'd just come out of a long hot relaxing bubble bath. Rose had suggested she pamper herself, give into her every self-indulgent whim, allow herself time to relax and be at peace. Well, the bath had definitely helped because she felt pretty good at the moment, secure enough to allow her mind to ponder the information she'd learned about herself that evening.

Her real name was Sara Ann Quincy. She was born in Oneida County in upstate New York one year after her parents, Virginia Jane Marshall and Lawrence Henry Quincy, married. When she was a year old, her father died of pneumonia. A year later, Virginia met and married Edward William Young, a widower with a twelve-year-old son. Both Virginia and Edward died a year later. The cause of their deaths wasn't mentioned. Since no next of kin was found, Sara wound up in the state orphanage. Not long after, she was adopted by the Bradleys.

That was it. Case closed. Her life in a nutshell. Unfortunately, the records read like a soap opera drama made for T.V. She felt utterly hopeless. She'd held on to the hope her adoption records would somehow open the door to her past and trigger memories which would shed light on her current situation. Everything she read fell on blind eyes. Nothing blasted the thick wall which hid the first four years of her life from her memory. She could have been reading the biography of a total stranger. She was left without any sense of connection or identity with the two human beings who created her. As far as she was concerned, she'd been born in the orphanage at age four.

She was falling further and further down a dark tunnel of despair. Once again, it seemed life had robbed her of her heritage, of a sense of identity which everyone else on the planet took for granted. A wave of sadness swelled up inside and, though no tears came, she was immobilized by a heavy weight on her chest. She sighed. Well, she wouldn't wait any longer.

She'd made an appointment with Rose for the hypnosis. She hoped something meaningful would come of it.

She was jarred back to the present by the ringing of the telephone. She reached for it and answered in a low, monotone voice. "Hello?"

There was a long empty silence. She was about to hang up when Michael spoke.

"Sara? Is that you? Are you all right? You don't sound like yourself."

She focused on his voice. "Michael. Yes, I'm okay. You sound so far away. Where are you?"

"I'm at my place."

Her voice dropped several octaves. "Oh."

"I'm sorry for not getting back to you sooner. I've been tied up...this case...the rest of my clients have suffered...I've had to put in extra hours..."

"You don't have to explain. I understand. I've missed you, though. I have a lot to tell you, but it can wait until you have more time."

"I, uh, that's why I'm calling. I'm, I'm really burned out. When this case is settled one way or the other, I've decided to take some time for myself. Maybe go away for a while. I don't know. Not important. I... I wanted you to know. I didn't want to leave you hanging."

There was desperation in his voice. She ached to reach out and comfort him. "What's wrong? What's happened? You sound awful."

"I'm fine. Don't worry about me. I'm a survivor, remember? You take care of yourself, Sara. Promise me that."

Tears began to slide down her cheeks as fear struck her. "You're not going to do anything stupid are you?"

"No, I'm okay. Promise me."

She mustered up all her strength to control the sobs which threatened to overwhelm her. Her voice was barely a whisper. "I promise."

Silence.

"I have to go now." Silence again. "I love you, Sara." The phone went dead.

Her hand shook. She was barely able to set the receiver back. What was that all about? Why was this happening when she needed him so much? What was he trying to tell her? Was this the end? Would she ever see him again?

An overwhelming sense of abandonment washed over her, leaving her breathless. Dana's face popped up. Not another person she loved leaving her. It was too much. She sobbed so hard she collapsed on the bed and grabbed the bedcovers, wrapping them around her. This time not even the down comforter could warm the icy cold that sliced through her body.

TWENTY-FIVE

Detective Sergeant Joe Hatch burst into laughter.

"You're amazing, Nico. I can't believe you have the balls to sit here and tell me you know nothing about the Seven-Eleven armed robbery on Washington last week. If I didn't find it so hilarious, I'd be damned pissed off you actually think I'm stupid enough to believe you."

The suspect wiggled in his chair in the interrogation room, refusing eye contact with Hatch.

"I've got the weapon in my possession with your fingerprints on it, the sworn statements of three witnesses who picked you out of a lineup. Then there's that very photogenic tape of you marching in, .355 Magnum in hand, demanding cash from the store manager. You really are a piece of work, Nico."

"I want a lawyer. I ain't sayin' nothin' 'til you get me a lawyer."

"The only good a lawyer's gonna do you is to stand next to you when the judge throws the book at you. Correct me if I'm wrong, but I believe this is your third armed robbery arrest. By the time the D.A. gets through with you, I promise it'll be your last. What a relief for me. I'm getting damn sick and tired of casting you out on the street and fishing you back in again."

The man seemed to sweat when Hatch mentioned his priors.

There was a short pause. "Tell you what, Hatch. I'm willin' to make a deal with you, lawyer or no lawyer. What do you say? You wanna deal? Maybe I got somethin' for you."

"That'll be the day a two-bit punk like you comes up with anything interesting for me." He walked to the other side of the room.

"Well, you might just be surprised, Hatch. Even an old deadbeat like me can be useful for somethin'."

"Like what?"

"Oh, no, not until you promise me a deal. You'd better speak to the D.A. I want it in writing. Not that I don't trust you guys and all." He snickered.

Hatch whirled around and grabbed Nico by the shirt collar. "Listen, you mother fucker! That Seven-

Eleven manager is in County USC Medical Center with a hole in his chest because of you. I'm not too sure you've got anything that would make me want to even talk to you again, never mind make a deal with a shithead like you." He let go of the man's shirt and pushed him back into the chair.

Nico was visibly shaken but forged ahead. "Oh, yeah, how'd you like to know who killed the Griswold woman?"

"We've already got that scumbag locked up. Sorry, Charlie."

Nico laughed. "You guys always think you're so smart, got all the answers. Well, you've got the wrong man for that job, but I ain't saying nothin' else 'til you get me a written promise from the D.A. I won't do more'n three years."

Hatch looked hard at the man. Something told him the guy wasn't joking around. Damn. Why couldn't he put this Griswold thing to rest? It kept coming up like a bad burrito. He sat down across from Nico.

"If you really have something on the Griswold case, I don't have time to go to the D.A. for a written deal. I need to know right now what you've got. If the info is legit, you'll get a deal, but I can't say what it'll look like. That's it, pal. That's as far as I can go."

Nico stared thoughtfully at Hatch. "A guy I met in a bar one night, stoned out of his mind, was bragging how he knew who really did Griswold's wife, like it was a great thing or somethin'. Like he was somebody special 'cause he knew, the fat fag. Anyway, he kept talkin' about the murder and seemed to know things I didn't figure any outsider would know."

"What's this guy's name?"

"I don't know, but I know he runs a small sex shop on Santa Monica in West Hollywood. You know, real sleazy, the kind all those little boys hang around lookin' for Johns and easy bucks. *Joy Toys* I think it's called. You go there, talk to him. Then you come back with somethin' for me to sign. I'm countin' on you, Hatch."

Hatch pushed back his chair and motioned to the officer nearby. "Take this gentleman back to the tank. I'll be in touch, Nico. You'd better hope I don't come up short on this one or your ass is mine."

*   *   *

Night was falling by the time Hatch and Blake got to *Joy Toys*. At least Nico had been accurate in his description of the place. The building was small, with only a small window and beat-up door in front. At the nearby corner, several young male prostitutes scanned the drivers of passing cars, hoping to find a customer or two.

Hatch entered the shop and glanced around. The interior of the store wasn't much better than the outside. Only a few colored lights illuminated the front room. A man stood at the counter near the back of room, looking bored and tired.

Hatch and Blake approached him, looking around the place as they walked.

"Can I help you gentlemen?" The man appeared to be in his early twenties. His arms were tattooed from wrist to shoulder, his head shaved.

"I hope so. We're looking for the guy who runs this place, what's his name, Blake? God, my memory's going."

The man behind the counter volunteered. "You must mean Victor Ingles. Well, he isn't here right now. Went out for a bite to eat, if you know what I mean." His sneer suggested more than a garden salad. "Anything I can do for you gentlemen? My name's Zamir."

"Well, Zamir, I think we'd better wait for Mr. Ingles." Hatch presented his badge. "If you know what I mean."

Zamir looked at the shield and shrugged his shoulder. "Suit yourselves, boys. He shouldn't be too long."

About ten minutes later, a man entered the store, medium height, a little paunchy and bald. Zamir looked up from a *Screw* magazine he'd been reading. "You're back, Vic. These gentlemen have been waiting for you." His high-pitched, singsong voice scratched Hatch's ears drums.

Hatch walked over to the man and again presented his badge. Ingles was visibly shaken, looked back and forth from Hatch to Blake and, in a flash, turned and ran toward the front door. Hatch was on him in a minute, pulling him by his collar and slamming his face against the back of the door.

"Now that's not very friendly, Mr. Ingles. Makes me think you've got something to hide. That doesn't make me very happy. Spread 'em."

While Blake frisked Ingles, Hatch kept his hand on the gun in his shoulder holster and his eye on Zamir.

"I've got nothing to say to you guys! You got no right coming in here to my place of business and harassing me. I'm a legitimate businessman. You'll be hearing from my lawyer as soon as I can get to a phone. Zamir, quick. Call Rex. Tell him I need him right away."

"I take that to mean you want an escort to the station. I wanted to make this as painless as possible for you, but you just won't let me. Let's go."

Hatch pushed Ingles through the open door with Blake following.

*   *   *

Fifteen minutes later Ingles sat in an interrogation room across from Hatch. Blake stood with arms folded, leaning against a wall staring at Ingles. Hatch watched the man twist his hands together in his lap. His small dark eyes shifted back and forth between the two detectives. Sweat drops streaked down his round face. His voice shook. "Why'd you bring me here? I don't have nothin' to tell you. You're just wastin' the taxpayers' money. Just wait 'til my lawyer gets here."

Hatch raised his eyebrows. "You sure you want to wait for your lawyer? All he's going to do is tell you to keep your mouth shut, which you're doing anyway. Then he'll send you a bill for a thousand bucks. Seems to me a good businessman like you would see the benefit in talking to us now. Just answer a few questions, and you can go. Save your grand and get home faster."

Ingles' upper lip curled up on the side. "You don't fool me, Detective. I know my rights. As long as I don't say nothin', you can't hold me. So I'll just wait until he gets here." He turned his head toward the wall and stared.

"Suit yourself." Hatch stood and left the room. Blake stayed to watch Ingles. Before he got to his office, another detective called out to him. "Hatch, line two."

Once in his office, he grabbed the phone. "Detective Hatch."

The voice on the other ended sounded muffled, but clear enough for Hatch to understand. "I understand you been asking around about an underground club that murdered reporter was writin' about."

Hatch instantly focused his attention on the call. "That's right."

"Well, I was the one who turned her on to it."

"That so? Who am I speaking with?" Hatch signaled to a detective just outside his office to trace the call. He needed to keep the guy on the phone for a while for the trace to go through.

"Oh no. That reporter promised me she'd keep my name out of it, so I sure as shit ain't gonna tell you."

"Fine. Why are you calling?"

"I'm willin' to give you the same info I gave her."

"Why's that?"

"I feel bad she got herself killed. Wondered if it had anything to do with that place. Feel a little guilty, maybe, since I was the one sent her there." There was a cough and then the sound of a throat clearing.

"A man of conscience," Hatch said sarcastically. "So, what do you have for me?"

"There's this club, see, over on Tenth and Olympia. One of those empty warehouses. The guy who owns it runs a kinky little club for perverts and weirdoes. It opens at midnight seven days a week and closes at dawn. Very private. Invitation only. Folks who go there don't wanna be seen, so they dress up in all sorts of freaky outfits."

"How'd you find out about this place?"

"Let's just say I used to work the bar but then it got too creepy even for me, so I stopped. "

"Just like that, you stopped going?"

"Well, uh, I had a little trouble one night. Figured it was healthier to end my association, if you know what I mean."

"Actually, I don't. Why don't you spell it out?"

The voice got angry. "I ain't calling about me. You wanna know where this place is or not?"

"Sure." Hatch grabbed a piece of paper and pen from his desk. "Shoot."

"It's called by its address, Ten Eleven Hoover."

"What was it about this place you thought would interest a reporter?"

"Like I said, it's kinky. Lots of drugs, booze, sex, all anonymous. Expensive. The clientele are the cream of LA doctors, lawyers, real estate moguls, politicians, sports figures; anyone who's rich and famous and thrives on participatin' in unusual activities without being fingered."

"Can you name names?"

"Like I said, everyone is in costume. They make up names to fit the outfits they wear, like George Washington, Batman. There's a white knight, someone who thinks he's part animal...never could figure out what that costume was. Anyway, no real names."

"What makes you think someone from the club is responsible for the reporter's death?"

"If they found out she was doin' a story on the place, they'd be real pissed. I wouldn't put nothin' past some of those freaks. I, ah, I gotta go. You check out that place. See what I mean. That girl treated me square. I'm sorry she got herself killed." The call ended with a bang when the receiver slammed down.

"Did you get a trace?" Hatch called out.

"No, Sarg." One of the detectives yelled back. "Not enough time. I recorded it, though."

Hatch stood there for a moment, his mind hashing over everything the guy said. Sounded like a real freak show going on over there. Why the hell would a woman want to get involved with something that nasty? Just for a story and a byline? People were crazy, just plain nuts.

"Sarg, your collar's lawyer is here. Want I should let him in?"

Hatch pulled himself back to the present. "Nah. I'll get him." He continued staring at a wall for a moment.

He walked over to a tall, thin man in a suit, briefcase in hand. He handed Hatch a business card. "Detective Hatch, I'm told. You're holding my client, Victor Ingles?"

Hatch took the card and scanned it briefly. Rex Oswald, Attorney at Law. "Yeah. This way." Together they went into the room where Ingles and Blake waited, closing the door behind them.

Ingles stood up. "Rex. Thank God you're here. These detectives were giving me a hard time. I have no idea why they dragged me down here."

"Sit down," Hatch yelled at Ingles.

When everyone except Blake, who remained leaning against the wall, was seated, Oswald started in. "Detective, unless you have evidence that my client engaged in any illegal activities, you can't hold him. So why is he here?"

By this time, Hatch's head was spinning. The call regarding the Ingrahm case was still fresh in his mind. He had little patience left for the two assholes in front of him. "I'll get right to the point. We have reason to believe your client may be involved in a murder investigation I'm running. This involvement being, at the least, withholding evidence and, at the max, being an accessory to the murder. So unless you both want to spend all day and night here, I suggest you advise your client to come clean and answer some questions."

"Since I haven't had a chance to speak with Mr. Ingles, may I have a moment alone with him?"

Hatch took a deep breath to release some pent-up frustration. "Let's go, Blake, and give these two gentlemen a chance to get their stories straight."

Oswald gave Hatch a dirty look before they left the room and shut the door.

Hatch handed Blake the address of the club he'd just gotten. "While we were waiting for Oswald, I got a call from Dana Ingrahm's source. Wouldn't give his name but seemed to know a lot about the club and the story she was working on. Check out this address he gave me. See who owns the building, if any permits were ever given for a business or liquor license or anything you can think of. Check with our techies and see if they managed to get any information off Ingrahm's laptop that might be relevant. I'll be in here with these two. You can join us when you're finished."

"I'll get right on it, Sarg. Good luck with them. I think you're going to need it." Blake left to do the follow up.

Hatch went back into the interrogation room. "You guys finished bonding?" He took a seat. "I haven't got all day. Let's make something happen here."

Oswald said, "I've advised my client to be as truthful as possible without incriminating himself. That's the best I can do."

"Right." Hatch nearly choked on his own sarcasm. "Okay. As I mentioned before, I have a witness who claims he heard you in a bar bragging you had information on who killed Felicia Griswold."

"Felicia Griswold?" Ingles raised his eyebrows.

"Yeah, Judge Griswold's wife. You read the newspapers, Ingles?"

"Oh, that Felicia Griswold. Well, now, where would I get any information about that nasty murder. I didn't even know the woman or her husband."

"That's exactly what I want to know. Do you remember bragging about the murder?"

"I thought I made myself perfectly clear, Sergeant. I know nothing about the murder. Is that all you wanted to know? Can we leave now?"

"Not so fast." Hatch leafed through a file on the desk. "Says here you're on parole for solicitation, drug trafficking and several business violations. You looking to get sent back to Wayside?"

"Why would I? I've done nothing wrong."

"I'll bet you still have a few contacts there. You know a druggie named Warren Dills? He's currently vacationing there."

This question had Ingles squirm a little in his seat. "Can't say as I know the guy."

"Seems like he got shanked recently. Somebody wanted him dead. Maybe tried to shut him up or clean up some loose ends. Know anything about that?"

Again Ingles shifted nervously. "Nope."

"We've nailed the guy who shanked him. I'll be heading up there tomorrow to talk to him. He must've gotten his orders from someone. I wonder what he'll have to say about your involvement in this whole thing."

Ingles leaned over to confer quietly with Oswald. They whispered for a few moments then Oswald spoke. "What kind of a deal are you offering my client for information?"

Hatch smiled. Finally, a break. "I've been instructed by the D.D.A. to give the first guy who tells me what the hell is going on with the Griswold case full immunity. So what do you say, Victor? Do wanna beat your pal to the finish line, or what?"

TWENTY-SIX

Michael finally gained access to the hospital room. The partially closed window shades admitted little natural light into the stuffy room. The dank smell of chemicals was hard to ignore. Only the monotonous beeping of the heart monitor broke the heavy silence.

He stood beside the bed looking into Warren Dills' pale face, noting the tubes which ran from his nose and arms to nearby machines.

Dills must have felt Michael's presence, for the man's eyes fluttered open. He spoke in a gruff, barely audible voice. "Hey, Counselor, what's up?"

Michael pulled a chair over to the bed and sat down, leaning toward Dills so he could hear him better. "That's what I'm here to find out. The doctor tells me you're going to make it."

A slight smile flickered across Dills' face. "A temporary situation."

"Nevertheless, you'll be with us for a while. With that in mind, I think you're smart enough to know the game's up. I want the whole truth. No more bullshit. You've already admitted your confession was a lie. Now what I want to know is, who killed Mrs. Griswold and why? Who set you up?"

Dills closed his eyes for a moment and licked his dry lips. "I don't know what happened. I was working in the stable. I never went into the house."

"Did you see anyone else beside the neighbor, Ms. Kessler?"

"No."

"What prompted your so-called confession?"

"About a week after the murder, I met some guy in a bar. He said he had a deal for me and there was plenty of money involved. I thought about it for a minute and decided to hear him out."

"What bar?"

"Some joint in East LA. I don't remember the name."

"What was the guy's name?"

"He didn't say, and I didn't ask."

"Do you remember what he looked like?"

"Nothing special–fortyish, a little overweight, bald." He paused for a long moment. "He said the man who sent him was willing to pay a hundred big ones if I confessed to killing Mrs. Griswold. In turn, he promised I wouldn't do more than three years. Said the man had connections, high-powered connections, and he'd protect me."

"Why did you take his offer?"

Michael was curious to see just how straight the guy was going to play it.

Dills was quiet for a while. He closed his eyes. "How about some water."

After Michael helped him take a few sips of water, Dills continued. "You know what they say, Counselor, if you play, you gotta pay. Well, I found out earlier this year I was HIV positive. No one knows. Not even my wife. Ironic, isn't it? Those fucks just happened to find the right guy, someone who was ripe for the deal. Kinda makes you wonder about fate and all that shit."

Emotion crossed Dills' pale face. He was silent for a moment.

"So you figured you had nothing to lose and, in fact, something to gain for your wife and kids' future."

"Something like that. Bet you never figured me for a fucking humanitarian, huh, Counselor?"

"I also never figured you for a murderer."

"Yeah, there is that."

"When you found out about the possible eye witness, you got scared. My guess is you wanted to renege on the deal and someone tried to shut you up with a shank. Lucky for you the guy had bad aim."

"Maybe down the road I'll be wishing he hadn't missed. So, now what? Where do we go from here?"

"I'm going to speak to the D.D.A. There's a good chance he'll drop the charges right away. If not, I'll have my investigator find your contact man. If you can remember anything else that could be important, let me know. In the meantime, you just concentrate on getting well." He stood up. "Call me if you think of anything. I'll keep you posted from my end." He turned and walked toward the door. Dills' voice stopped him. "Counselor?"

Michael turned toward the bed again.

"Thanks." The man sounded worn out.

Michael nodded his head, turned and left the room.

After leaving the hospital, Michael maneuvered the Beemer onto the Five Freeway south, heading for his office. He drove like an automaton, not seeing where he was going, ignoring exit signs as they flew by. Neither did he hear the monotonous drone of the newscaster's voice on the radio. Instead, his mind mechanically checked off the things he had to do in the next day or so, including formulating the script for his upcoming conversation with Koosman. He had to prepare for this meeting as he would for an opening argument in court. He knew it was the approach he'd have to take to get Koosman to listen.

Occasionally, he noticed his attention drift toward forbidden thoughts which hung in the background of his mind like thick dark clouds. From time to time they stormed into his awareness, but he managed to push them away before they fully engulfed him. He shook his head to clear his mind and get back on safer ground. Stay on track, he kept chanting to himself in those moments of weakness. Stay on track. Don't think about the farm. Don't think about Sara. Not now.

His cell phone rang. He turned on the Bluetooth and spoke, grateful for the interruption from the direction his thoughts were heading. "Grey here."

He immediately recognized Pete Neilson's voice. "I've got some interesting information for you. Do you have time this afternoon?"

Michael checked his watch. "I should be in my office in twenty minutes. Can you meet me there?"

"Perfect. I'm on my way." Neilson hung up.

Michael exited the Five Freeway at the One Ten Freeway and headed downtown, wondering what the meeting with Neilson would produce. Would this new information assist him in convincing Koosman to drop the charges against Dills immediately? He'd be glad to be rid of this case. He had to admit, though, this past week he'd been grateful for the demands work had made on his time and energies. Those distractions were a thankful relief from the nagging reminders of his painful, personal agenda which, once the murder charge on Dills was dropped, he'd have to handle. If he'd learned anything recently, it was he could no longer run away from his past.

Ten minutes after Michael arrived at his office Neilson knocked on the door and walked in. He sat down in the chair in front of the desk. Michael turned off the recorder he was using and gave the investigator his full attention. "So, what do you have?"

"I've been putting in a lot of time tracking down Griswold's whereabouts on the day of the murder, just following up a little hunch I've had from the start. Then I got lucky. Without going into all the boring details, our eminent dispenser of justice didn't go to Santa Barbara that day after all. In fact, he was in town and seen by several persons a few hours before the murder at a restaurant in Studio City. I've got sworn statements from three witnesses who can put him there."

"So what we have now is a confessed killer who is innocent and admits to being bought off, and a possible suspect who lied about his alibi. I don't think it's enough for Koosman to drop the charges immediately, not with Griswold watching this case like a hawk. He'll need hard evidence indicating a connection between Griswold and the murder or with Griswold and Dills. You've got to keep digging."

He handed Neilson a piece of paper. "Dills gave me information on the man who approached him with the offer. See what you can find on him. Let's hope we get lucky again. Remember, we only have a few more days before Longmire hands me a ticket to Men's Central lockup."

"I'll get right on it." Neilson got up and left the office. A moment later, Michael looked up, surprised to see Alan standing in the door way with his hands stuffed in his pants pockets. There'd been a stony silence between them the last few days, but now, seeing rigid determination mask Alan's face, Michael knew he could no longer avoid the inevitable.

"You got a minute, Mike?"

"Not much more."

Alan closed the door and sat down in the chair recently vacated by Neilson. "I, uh, I want to apologize for the other day. I was out of line. You don't owe me an explanation for your disappearance. I was acting like an over-possessive father. It won't happen again."

Mike lowered his eyes, realizing the effort it took Alan to apologize. When he looked up, he knew his eyes had softened. He took a deep breath. "Forget it. You were right. I'm the one who owes you and Katie both an apology and a word of thanks for helping while I was gone. I'll talk to her later."

Alan seemed to wait for him to continue, but when Michael didn't, he spoke. "You've said before I never pry, and I'm not going to start now. I just want you to know if there's anything I can do to help, I'm here, anytime."

"I know, Alan. Thanks." Michael pulled his eyes off his friend, put his glasses on, grabbed a law book which sat at the corner of the desk and flipped through it. He was uncomfortable with the silence but couldn't bring himself to go further.

Alan apparently sensed the conversation was over, got up and left the room.

Michael was relieved the hostility was gone between them. Now maybe he'd be able to concentrate on his work. He continued paging through the book, searching for precedence he could use in his upcoming confrontation with Koosman.

TWENTY-SEVEN

Sara sat on the carpeted floor of Carly's room, watching the child color with thick crayons on a large white pad. She'd met with Carly regularly since the child was very close to disclosing more details about the night her mother was murdered.

It was fascinating for her, as a clinician, to have the opportunity to work so closely with the child these last few months. Sara was inspired watching the steps Carly's mind took on the path to recovery. First, she was traumatized so badly that communication was sparse. It had taken weeks of patience on Sara's part before Carly started to trust her.

Then Carly's behavior returned to the pre-murder mode, and she laughed and played with her friends and resumed her school and social activities.

Soon the acting out began. Sara observed the child's unconscious mind demand recognition through negative behaviors, the anger, the fighting. Then the week before, Carly came so close to naming the monster who killed her mother.

What a brave little girl. Sara's eyes filled. She related to the child on a very personal level. She was very much like Carly. Although traumatized as a child, she'd also bounced back and ultimately become a productive, positive person. In a flash of humility unfamiliar to herself, she recognized the resilient power of the human spirit, and how it had manifested itself in her. In a moment of spontaneous connection with the child, Sara leaned over and hugged her briefly.

"I love your picture, sweetie." She released her.

The child smiled, her eyes sparkling. "This is the best picture I ever drawed. I like coloring the mommy's dress pink. It's my favorite color. See. The little girl is sitting on the sofa with her mommy."

"Pink's a beautiful color. The mommy looks very sad. Is that a tear in her eye?"

"Uh huh. She is very sad because she knows she'll never see her little girl again."

"Hmm. The little girl doesn't look very happy. I wonder what she's feeling."

"Very sad. Very, very sad. And scared."

"I think you're right. She does look sad and scared. I wonder why she's scared."

Carly kept drawing. This time she picked up a red crayon and began filling in the face and body of the figure in the picture.

"She's scared because she knows what's going to happen."

Sara caught her breath and chose her words and intonation very carefully. "What's that?"

Carly started drawing a picture of a smaller person who seemed to be hiding behind a door of some kind. Slowly the picture materialized. Sara watched spellbound as the drawing took shape.

"The mommy and daddy will yell and scream at each other. See the little girl? She runs and hides in the closet, but she can still see and hear. The noise gets louder and louder. The little girl puts her hands over her ears. Then the daddy hits the mommy so hard she falls down. The little girl can hardly hear the mommy cry anymore. Then daddy kicks her again and again and then kneels down and hits her face so many times. The little girl can't hear the mommy anymore. She's very quiet."

Sara spoke in a whisper. "What did the daddy do next?"

"He ran out of the house."

"And the little girl?"

Carly shook her head sadly. "She stayed in the closet for a long time, just crying. When she heard a lady coming, she went and stood by the mommy. She wasn't pretty anymore. All red. Just lots of red."

The child continued drawing and humming.

Sara found it difficult to breath. A shock wave went through her. It was the judge! He killed his wife. She drew in long breaths to calm her racing heart. She didn't want to frighten Carly by overreacting.

Then it hit her. All this time Carly had been living alone with Griswold. She closed her eyes, shutting out the horrible pictures of what could've happened to Carly if he'd known she'd been in the closet watching everything. Carly had been at risk all this time. Sara cursed herself for not finding the truth sooner. Then cooler thoughts prevailed. She stopped blaming herself and thought about what to do. Thank God the judge was in court all day. She had time to protect Carly.

She struggled to take a deep breath before she spoke. "Why don't you draw me another picture, honey, while I go downstairs and talk to Juana? I'll be right back."

She got up on shaky legs and left the room, turning briefly at the door to look at Carly busily coloring. She turned and, once in the hallway outside of Carly's hearing, took out her cell phone and dialed the child abuse hotline.

Juana was washing a few dishes at the sink when Sara entered the kitchen. She looked up and smiled at Sara. "How ees de leetle angel, today, Doctor? She ees doing better, no?"

"Actually, she's doing much better, Juana. I'm afraid something very important has come up though. Come, sit down. I'll explain what's going to happen."

The older woman dried her hands on a dish towel. She and Sara sat at the kitchen table. Sara reached out and placed her hand over Juana's clasped hands.

"Carly finally told me what happened the night Mrs. Griswold died. I've just telephoned the child abuse hotline and given them the information. A social worker and the police will be here shortly. They'll talk to her and then the social worker will take her to a foster home to be safe."

Tears rolled down Juana's cheeks. "*Mi probrecita.* I have been so afraid for her, so worried. What happened? Why must you take her away?"

"I'm afraid I can't tell you anything except she will be much safer away from here. You can talk to the social worker when she or he comes and perhaps they will say more. You must believe me when I say she will be safer with them."

"Why can't she stay with me? I will take her to *mi casa.* She will be safe there. I would never let anyone hurt her."

"I know you wouldn't, Juana, but you're not a blood relative or a licensed foster parent. Trust me. It's best this way. I'm sure the social worker will allow you to visit her when she sees how much you care for each other. Our biggest concern right now is her safety."

She patted the woman's clenched hands. "I'm going to go upstairs and explain to her as best I can what's going to happen. Please tell me when the social worker and police arrive." She got up and headed for the stairs, leaving the housekeeper sobbing into her hanky.

Sara had one more call to make. He picked up after two rings.

"Joe? It's Sara."

"I was just thinking about you. How's it going with the Perez girl?"

"That's why I'm calling. I'm at the house now. She just disclosed it was Judge Griswold who killed his wife."

"No shit! Finally we're getting somewhere. I've been busy, too. I've a lot to tell you about Dana's murder. Listen. I've got an appointment to meet Koosman in his office in an hour. Why don't you meet me there, and we can tie up all the loose ends and put this sucker to bed once and for all. After, I'll catch you up on Dana's case."

"Have you found her killer?"

"We're very close."

"Good. As soon as the social worker gets here to take custody of Carly, I'll be free to leave. See you at Frank's office."

Sara stayed with Carly until the social worker arrived. She introduced her to Carly and promised the little girl she'd see her very soon. Carly clung to her briefly before heading off with the social worker. Sara released a heavy sigh.

She was glad she'd be meeting Hatch and Koosman. Even though the day had been emotionally draining, she was relieved. Her work with Carly had bared fruit. Not only could she justify the many hours she'd spent with the child, she now knew for certain Carly was safe.

Thirty minutes later she stood in front of Koosman's office, squared her shoulders and knocked. She entered when he called out.

He sat behind his desk writing when he looked up and greeted her with a smile. She looked around the room. Hatch wasn't there yet.

"Sara. What a surprise. Have a seat. I haven't seen you since the party. I've been so busy. How's our little witness doing? Anything new from her."

She sat down. "As a matter of fact, Frank, that's exactly why I'm here. I have some information I think you'll find very interesting."

He put down his pen and pulled off his glasses. "Shoot."

"I've just handed Carly Perez over to Children's Service to be placed in a temporary foster home. Earlier she indirectly indicated to me she saw Judge Griswold beat her mother to death."

While her words sank in, Koosman seemed to be stunned silent. She imagined his mind running through all the possibilities the disclosure would have, both on his present case against Michael's client and his future career with the department. He sat back in his chair.

At that moment, Hatch arrived. He closed the door behind him, nodded to Sara, sat in the chair next to her and spoke to Koosman. "What've I missed?"

"Sara just broke the news about Griswold." He shook his head, apparently still having trouble believing it. "This is ugly. Opens up a whole new can of worms, not to mention putting a real damper on the case we're been working on for months. Christ! Nothing's ever simple."

He stood up and walked to the window, his hands jammed in his trouser pockets. After a few moments of silence, he turned back to them.

"Okay, Joe. Your turn. You said you had information about the Dills situation."

Hatch proceeded to enlightened Sara and Koosman regarding his interview and subsequent arrest of Victor Ingles.

"It seems this freak Ingles frequents an underground club where the pick of LA's weirdoes go for a friendly night out with fellow perverts. They dress up in costumes. Very anonymous. Very safe. Lots of drinking, drugs and sex between males and males, females and females, and so as not to be biased, males and females. Very eclectic bunch."

He paused and took a deep breath. "Anyway, one evening some dude dressed as a White Knight introduced himself to Ingles and asked if he would like to earn five large by brokering a deal with a person of interest to this White Knight."

Koosman asked, "What kind of deal? With whom?"

"Slow down. I'm getting to it. Anyway, Ingles agrees. The White Knight tells him to go to a bar in

East LA where this person of interest hangs out and offer him one hundred thousand dollars to confess to the murder of Mrs. Griswold."

"What?"

"Exactly. Crazy, huh. Well, apparently Ingles didn't think anything about it except the five grand he was going to make. With a description of the mark Sir Knight gave him, he hung out in the bar until the guy strolled in one day."

"Don't tell me it was Warren Dills?"

"The one and only. At this point, I have no idea why Dills accepted the deal, but he did. Ergo, his call to me, the arrest, the jewelry, which, incidentally, Ingles stashed in Dills' house one day when the wife wasn't home."

"What asshole would make a deal like that?"

"Maybe Dills will tell us. Anyway, this gets even juicer. It seems when Dills was told about the kid witness, I'm assuming from his lawyer, he called Ingles to find out what was going on. Ingles called the Knight, whose identity he'd found out, and told him Dills was getting antsy. The Knight paid Ingles another five grand to arrange a prison fight where Dills would get shanked. Not only was the Knight's shill then out of the way, but he was one hundred grand richer."

All this time Sara sat listening, appalled by the lengths someone would go to cover his tracks. She felt sympathy for Dills. She could only imagine what was going on in his life to make him susceptible to such a crazy scheme.

Koosman's voice brought her back to the conversation. "Okay. So who's this White Knight and how did he know Ingles would be the perfect patsy to orchestrate for the plan?"

Hatch smiled sardonically. "It seems our Mr. Ingles once appeared in front of a judge who gave him a very light sentence in exchange for some muscle work the judge might have for him in the future."

"Muscle work?"

"This judge didn't take kindly when defense attorneys found loopholes in particularly nasty cases and the felons went scot free. The judge felt he needed to punish these guys since the system had failed to do so."

"And this jurist with the God complex is…"

"None other than Julius Griswold."

"Unbelievable!" The three of them sat in silence for a long moment. "This Ingles willing to spill the beans on a sitting judge?"

"Oh yeah. The man has several outstanding felony warrants under assumed names. He's very anxious to make a deal and hand over Griswold."

Koosman, who'd been sitting during Hatch's story, rose and went to the window. After a moment he turned back. "I want to make sure we have direct evidence to link Griswold to the murder. All we have now is the indirect statement of a five-year old and a felon who has a lot to gain by accusing the judge. Get a warrant for Griswold's house, car, everyplace you can think of where he might have that White Knight costume and any other hard evidence. We've got to make this case solid. I'm not willing to risk my career on a circumstantial case."

Sara said, "What about motive? Do we know why a man like Griswold with a reputation to protect would kill wife?"

Hatch tossed in a few possibilities. "Could be anything. Maybe our illustrious judge was having an affair. Maybe she found out about his secret life as a mediaeval character in some Disney flick. Maybe she threatened to expose him. Who knows? Let's hope we get the chance to ask him."

Koosman was interrupted when his office door swung open and banged against the wall. Michael Grey stormed in.

Surprise flashed on Sara's face, more so when she realized the dark mood he seemed to be harboring

His eyes went straight to Koosman. Frank looked up, surprised at the intrusion. Michael noticed Hatch and then focused on Sara. He seemed equally surprised to see her. Then his face hardened again. He turned and stared menacingly at Koosman.

"Grey, you must be psychic. We were just discussing your favorite case. Come in and join the party. You know Joe Hatch, of course, and Sara Bradley. If I remember correctly, the two of you went swimming together in my pool a while ago."

Michael   dismissed   Koosman's   friendly attitude and totally ignored Sara. She had a stab of pain at his cold hostile rejection. His eyes drilled Koosman.

"Have a seat, Mike. I'll bet you're here on the same pretext we all are. Looks like we've arrived at the same conclusion at the same time. Quite a coincidence. It seems you and I have some negotiating to do."

Michael remained standing. "Negotiating? Are you sure 'face-saving' isn't a more accurate description?"

Sara heard a snicker from Hatch.

"Now, now, Mike. You don't have to rub it in. We're all entitled to make mistakes once in a while. I'm sure you've had your share of bitter pills to swallow." He pushed back his chair and crossed his arms. "What do you have for me?"

Michael pulled his briefcase into his arms, opened it, pulled out a file and tossed it on Koosman's desk.

"My notes. If you insist on being a ball-breaker, I'll have a motion in court tomorrow. I want the case against my client dismissed immediately. I want the guard continued at the hospital to insure his safety. When he's released from the hospital, I want him and his family placed in the witness protection program until this case goes to trial, and he testifies for the prosecution."

Koosman's easygoing attitude melted with Michael's demanding words and brittle intensity. "As I said when you came in, we were just putting our heads together over the latest developments. Given the new information Hatch and Bradley have brought to my attention, I've decided to do precisely what you've suggested. We now have strong evidence suggesting Griswold, himself, is our perp. Joe's shifting the focus of his investigation to include these new leads. I'm confident within a few days I'll have enough to nail the honorable Judge Julius Griswold."

He cleared his throat. "In the meantime, I'll take care of the motion to dismiss the murder charge. However, there's still the false confession to deal with. I might be agreeable to offer time served. I'll let you know as soon as I've worked out the details. Then you can have the pleasure of telling your client."

Michael didn't seem willing to let it go. "That's very big of you, Frank. I'll let you know if we decide to file a wrongful imprisonment suit against the department."

Without so much as a by-your-leave nod to any of them, Michael turned and stormed out of the office, slamming the door behind him.

Sara's breath came in such short gulps, she had to get out of there before the others noticed her reaction. She made some lame excuse about a meeting with a patient. She left the office as quickly as she could, but not before saying she'd have her report on their desks first thing in the morning. She couldn't wait long enough to find out what news Hatch had about Dana's murder. Her head was spinning, her hands sweaty. She hoped she made it to the car before passing out.

Once inside the car, she sat back against the seat and let her mind wander. After taking several deep breaths, her nerves calmed, but she had trouble understanding what had happened in Koosman's office. She remembered discussing the new turn of events with Koosman and then Hatch. Then suddenly Michael barged in. Why hadn't he at least acknowledged her?

At first, she was happy to see him, but it only took a few moments for her to assess his cold, formal words. Feeling the hostility of his mood, her pleasure turned to rage.

All her pent-up emotions from the last few weeks boiled to the top, choking her, making it difficult to breathe. She was incredibly angry with him for not being in touch with her, for pushing her away, and mainly, for not being there when she needed him.

Eventually, she forced herself to focus on driving. She needed time to process what happened, to calm down and to find a rational explanation for Michael's behavior. If she wasn't able to do that, she'd confront Michael. This time she'd get answers from him, whether he liked it or not.

At home, she took a long hot shower. The steamy heat ran over her tense body and finally relaxed her enough to dry off and fall into bed. She needed to get some sleep. She'd agreed to have Rose hypnotize her the next evening and decided to go ahead as planned. The more she knew about herself the stronger she'd feel when she confronted Michael. Her last thoughts before sinking into a fitful sleep were of Michael. Why had he ignored her, rejected her in

Koosman's office? What if he never wanted to see her again? Would her bruised ego and broken heart ever recover from the loss of another person she loved?

*   *   *

When Hatch got back to his office, Blake was waiting for him. His face was flushed with excitement. Ah, the passions of youth. Hatch could hardly remember how it had been for him twenty years ago when he first made detective. He'd seen himself as the savior of LA, the warrior for justice, the one who could make a real difference for the citizens of his city. Now he was just happy to close a case and move onto the next one, all the time wishing he was home with his wife and family.

He couldn't help but crack a smile at Blake's enthusiasm. "You look like you hit the lottery or something."

Blake smiled. "You could say that."

"Okay, what'd you have?"

"First off, Ten Eleven Hoover is owned by some real estate conglomerate. When I tried tracking down the individual owners, I hit a snag. Some of the names were phony, and those people who did exist denied any knowledge of what went on in that warehouse after hours. There was no liquor license on file. Then I got lucky. The techies were able to get into Ingrahm's laptop. It seems she documented several visits to the club, including conversations with some patrons. She even had a picture of herself in that leather outfit we found in her apartment, a big crazy smile on her face. I'm guessing she took it for kicks. Anyway, get this. She managed to snag a couple of glasses the patrons left on the bar and had some contact in our lab check for fingerprints. You'll never guess whose prints she found."

Hatch's eyebrows knitted. He almost expected to hear a drum roll. "Shoot. I can't stand the suspense."

Blake's mouth curved into a full smile. "Our very own illustrious Judge Griswold."

Hatch was silent for a moment while he took it all in. Then he cracked a smile. "Well, I'll be God damned! I think this is the link Koosman's looking for. We can nail the good judge for Ingraham's murder. It looks like we might get him for his wife's."

Blake nodded. "Yeah. I'll bet the judge found out she was a reporter and decided he couldn't take a chance his nocturnal perversions would become public knowledge. I doubt his humongous ego could tolerate that type of publicity."

"I'll bet you're right, Son. Let's do a little more digging to pull all the pieces together, and then we can give Koosman a call. We'll get all the warrants we need to put two homicides to bed and get rid of that son of a bitch at the same time."

Hatch slapped Blake on the back. "This has turned out to be a great day, my lad, a great day for us and a great day for Los Angeles."

TWENTY-EIGHT

Sara's mind still clung to the painful events of the past few days when she entered Rose Goodman's office. What was going on with Michael? Why had he ignored her? She'd almost cancelled the appointment for hypnosis. She was anxious to find him and get some of her questions answered. She doubted she was a good candidate for such invasive therapy as hypnosis since her mind was clogged with so many thoughts and feelings. She decided to keep the appointment anyway. There was a chance she'd remember some of the events of her early childhood. Perhaps knowing those things would help her deal with whatever happened once she finally confronted Michael.

After a short greeting and very little extraneous conversation, she sat in a comfortable high-back leather chair, and Rose began the hypnosis process. Slowly Sara slipped into an altered state of consciousness while still aware of her physical surroundings.

"That's good, Sara. Just relax. You're doing great. You can close your eyes if you like. You do whatever you must to feel comfortable. I'll be here to keep you safe. You have nothing to fear. There's no one here to hurt you. That's it. Close your eyes."

Rose's mellow voice soothed whatever trepidations Sara had. She sensed she was floating in a dream-like trance. Warm summer air lightly brushed against her baby-soft skin.

"Where are you, Sara?"

Sara spoke with a smile in a childlike voice. "I'm three years old. I'm riding on top of a big black horse. I can see the tall grass whipping across his legs while we ride faster and faster through the fields. The sun is warm on the top of my head. Even though I'm so little, I'm not afraid to be racing so fast on the big horse." She felt her smile widen. She giggled with joy.

"Why aren't you afraid?"

"Because I'm not alone. He's there behind me, holding me tight. He'd never let anything happen to me."

"How do you feel?"

"So happy, free and safe. I cry out with joy. Sometimes I hear him laugh, too. He loves to ride with me. We love to feel the big animal beneath us as we race. I wish we could ride like this forever and ever."

"Who is riding with you?"

"It's Eddie. He's much older than me, but he likes to play with me and take me riding."

Sara's mood shifted. She scrunched up her mouth in a pout. "Oh dear, the ride is over. We have to bring the horse back to the barn. I don't want to get off, but Eddie reaches up and takes me under my arms and swings me down to the ground. I laugh again. We walk into the barn. Eddie is holding the reins in one hand and my hand in the other."

Suddenly Sara's heart beat faster and faster. "Oh, no! What's happening? I'm scared!"

"It's all right, dear. You're safe. It's okay to remember. What do you see?"

"Mommy is screaming! The big man just swung a big stick and hit her so hard she fell down. The man kicks and kicks her. Now I'm angry. I pull away real fast from Eddie and run over and start punching the man's legs with my fists. Eddie yells at me to stop, but I can't. I must help mommy!"

"I'm screaming. The man turns around and looks down at me. He is so mean and angry his face looks like a red devil with horns. He's going to hit me with the big stick. I keep screaming. Eddie pushes me down. I fall in the hay. He grabs the man's arm that has the stick and pulls it away from him. He hits the man again and again and again. The man tries to stop Eddie, but he is too angry to stop. Then the man grabs a brush we use to clean the horses and hits Eddie on his face. This still doesn't stop Eddie. It only makes him madder. All of a sudden he swings the stick so hard he knocks the man down. The man lets out a big scream."

Sara jerked awake with a sudden burst of fear. Her chest heaved, her heart pounded loudly. Sweat mixed with tears ran down her face. She sat up in the chair. Rose took her hands.

"It's all right, Sara. You're awake. You're safe now. You're here in my office. Look at me."

Sara stared at Rose. Her body relaxed. Her senses mellowed out.

Rose smiled at her. "You did great, honey. I'm so proud of you."

Sara shook her head. "I could see everything so clearly. It was so frightening. How could I have forgotten something as vivid as that?"

"That's exactly why you forgot. In order to protect you from the horror of what you saw, your mind forced you into a state of amnesia. I'm sure you've experienced this with some of your patients."

"Yes, of course. It's just so different when it's personal." She took a long deep sigh and sat back in the chair, exhausted. "I still don't know anything more than I did before I went under."

"What about the boy, Eddie? Do you recognize him?"

"No, I don't know anyone named Eddie. I'm still at a lost to understand what really happened. Was the woman I saw really my mother? What happened to the boy? How did I get into the orphanage? Who was the man? I still have so many unanswered questions."

"You must be patient. This is only the first step to reclaiming your childhood, and it's a big one. Something tells me the anxiety attacks and nightmares you've been experiencing will lessen and possibly disappear."

Sara grabbed a tissue from the box, wiped her eyes and blew her nose. "That would certainly be a relief. Something to be thankful for." She yawned. Hammered by the events of the past few days and the emotional stress she'd just gone through, she could barely keep her eyes open.

Rose smiled. "I think you've been through enough today. Go home and relax in a long hot bubble bath and rest." She got up and offered Sara her hand.

She was a little disoriented when she stood, but regained her equilibrium and moved into Rose's arms.

"Thank you, Rose. You've always been there for me when I needed you most. I love you."

"And I you, dear." She walked her to the office door. "Are you all right to drive home?"

Sara smiled. "Yes. I'm fine. Thank you again." She left the office feeling as though a thousand pounds of bricks had been lifted off her shoulders. When she stepped into the sunshine and walked to her car, she was at peace for the first time in a very long time.

*   *   *

Was she awake or asleep? She seemed to float in and out of consciousness, like twilight sleep, where pictures danced around and strong feelings lived. It wasn't a nightmare. Not this time. Instead, the peace and serenity she'd felt after leaving Rose's office remained, intensified, bringing pleasant memories forward.

She was riding the horse again, with the boy behind her. With each passing second, the sound of the racing hooves got louder and louder until it filled every corner of the dream-state. Soon the pounding of the hooves mimicked the beating of her heart so closely her eyes flew open.

After taking Rose's advice of a long hot bath, she'd laid down. She was so relaxed and peaceful it didn't take long for twilight sleep to overtake her. But now, fully awake, she was in her dark empty bedroom.

She lay there listening to the retreating sound of the hooves until she recognized the sound as her beating heart. Yet the tranquil feelings of the dream lingered...the beauty of the natural surroundings of the countryside...the powerful animal beneath them...but, mostly, the overwhelming sense of safety and trust she felt with the boy who held her securely in front of him in the saddle.

With her eyes still closed, her mind and body engaged in all the sensations which the dream triggered. A vague sense of *déjà vu* floated over her. She concentrated on trying to recall when she'd felt that way before. Suddenly she gasped out loud and jerked up in bed. Her eyes opened wide when the connection was made.

She sat there a long time trying to sort out her confusion. Her heart beat wildly. She became frustrated and demanded answers right away.

She got out of bed, found her adoption records on the dresser and looked them over for the hundredth time. Now everything looked different. Things were falling into place, amazing, exciting things. My God! She closed the file.

She had to know the truth. Rose's admonition to be patient flew out of her mind. She needed to find out once and for all who she was and what happened in those lost early years. Her excitement grew, for now she knew who she could ask.

Tossing the file on her bed, she pulled on jeans and a sweater, grabbed her purse and left her apartment, not caring that it was two-fifteen in the morning.

TWENTY-NINE

At first the ringing of the doorbell seemed to be part of a dream, but the shrill sound finally pierced through Michael's subconscious, bringing him fully awake. He turned over in bed and looked at the clock on the nightstand. Fuck! Who the hell was at the door at this hour? He was tempted to roll over and ignore it, but the incessant ringing was making him crazy, so he got up, pulled on pajama bottoms and strode into the living room.

Eerie shadows pointed the way to the front door. He turned the locks and yanked it wide open, angered by the unwelcomed intrusion.

He blinked his eyes a few times to focus them until he was sure it was Sara standing there. In a flashback, he recalled her last unexpected visit to his apartment.

He looked at her. His forehead wrinkled. He realized this time there was something different about her demeanor. She was calm, almost peaceful. Had his sudden awakening jolted his senses, or was that a faint smile on her face? Immediately, he was sucked into her mellow mood, momentarily forgetting his recent painful realization. However, in a flash, the walls came up and his defenses returned. He drew himself up and straightened his shoulders.

"I have to talk to you, Michael. I know it's late, but it can't wait."

He stepped aside, and she entered the apartment. He closed the door and leaned back against it. She walked into the dark, shadowy room. He folded his arms across his bare chest. His gaze followed her when she strolled behind the sofa, running her hand slowly along the top. She flipped a wall switch and dim lights came on. She reached the bookcase and walked in front of it, touching the books seductively as if taking in the feel, the scent of him through his belongings.

As he watched her glide through the living room, the tension in his body grew.

"Do you remember when we first met? There was an instant connection between us, something very strange and extraordinary. I'd never felt that with any other man. At first, it was very unsettling. When I was alone and thought about it, I got very confused. After a while, I stopped trying to figure it out and just appreciated it. I learned to relax into the pleasure I always felt whenever I was with you. I never realized until tonight why that feeling we shared...I know you felt it too...why it was so intense, so real, so undeniable."

He still stood against the door, his arms now at his sides. "Sara, please, you don't understand..."

She stopped and turned to face him. "That's just it, Michael. I'm beginning to understand, some of it, anyway. Today I found out the source of some of my nightmares, but I need you to fill in the blanks for me. I've waited so long to know who I am. I can't wait any longer." She pushed her hair away from her face and watched him.

He moved away from the door. He felt weak, defeated. He'd tried so hard to avoid this confrontation, but now it was here. He sat down on the sofa and looked up at her, years of pain and guilt heavy in his chest.

"I'm sorry, Sara. I didn't know until..."

She held up her hand in midair and then dropped it to her side. "Stop. Not yet." She drew a breath. "I saw Rose this afternoon and remembered things I'd forgotten, frightening things, horrible things. When I went home and lay down I had a dream. Not a nightmare this time, quite the contrary. Tonight I dreamed I rode in a beautiful country pasture on a big, powerful horse. I was only a few years old, but I wasn't afraid. In fact, I felt wonderful, very happy, free, but mostly safe. I knew I was safe because there was a boy riding with me who was a lot bigger and stronger, who I trusted completely.

"Don't, Sara."

"When I woke up, I realized that was the way I felt when I first saw you in court. Exactly the same, *déjà vu*, you know. I got out my adoption records and read everything over again. Then I realized just how connected you and I are." Her wide-open eyes seemed to reach into his very soul. "I used to call you Eddie."

He closed his eyes and took a deep, shaky breath. This was it, the end of the line, the final scene of an ugly drama which began more than twenty-five years before. Well, maybe it was for the best. Get it out in the open. Get it over with once and for all. Nothing could be as bad as the last few years, or could it? What if he lost her? When she found out what he'd done...

Finally he spoke in a very low voice. "I've tried so hard to forget it all. I've managed to erase a lot of that year from my mind. Your name, for example. It never registered with me."

Her eyes were warm and soft and seemed to be full of compassion for him.

She continued in a quiet voice. "I must have been about three. My mother and I had just come to live with you and your father on the farm upstate New York. You used to take me horseback riding every day that summer. You never complained when I bugged you to take me."

She squinted her eyes, as though trying to conjure up distant, vague memories. "I think you enjoyed riding, too. That's why you were so willing. You used to read to me, too, didn't you?"

"I don't know. Maybe. I guess. How much do you remember?"

"Bits and pieces. Feelings, but not everything. That's why I need you to help me remember."

"Don't ask me to do that. It's better if you remember in your own time, in your own way, when you're ready. Please, I don't want to hurt you anymore than I have."

"Hurt me? How have you hurt me, Michael? When? Certainly not when we were children. And I've never been as happy as I've been these past months with you. I admit I was upset because you hadn't called or come over lately, but I knew you were under a lot of pressure with work. In Koosman's office you were so cold...but now I understand."

She came over and knelt on the floor in front of him, her arms resting on his knees, "You read my adoption records, didn't you? That must have been an enormous shock. I understand now you needed time to work it all through, but I need your help now. I want to know everything."

Gently he pushed her aside and stood up; her nearness suffocated him. He walked over to the French doors which led to the patio and stood with his back to her, his arms at his sides, his jaw clenched.

She pressed him further. "You told me once you ran away from home when you were thirteen. That must have been not long after we came to live at the farm. Why did you leave? What happened?" She needed to hear him say the words that would put a stamp on reality which no dream could.

He remained silent.

"Please, Michael. You promised you'd be there when I needed you. Well, I need you now to fill in the blanks. What happened to make you run away?"

He took a deep shaky breath. No sense delaying the inevitable. "Not long after you and your mother came to the farm, I realized the old man was using her as a whipping block instead of me." The bitterness in his voice was palpable.

"Your father. It was your father."

"Yeah. He was a mean, vicious drunk. Oh, he could be charming to others, but once he was home, the evil came out." He snickered. "A real Jekyll and Hyde."

She went to him and stood behind him. "Why did you leave the farm?"

He spun around and faced her. "Damn it, Sara. Leave it alone. You don't want to know what happened. I don't want you to know."

"Why?"

"Because every time you look at me, you'll remember, and I couldn't bear to see that look on your face."

Sara wouldn't be put off. "What kind of a relationship can we have if we can't be one hundred percent honest with each other? You once told me you knew trust was a major part of a relationship. Whatever happened at the farm can only come between us if you refuse to open up and share it."

He knew she was right. The desperation in her voice made him no longer think about himself and his petty guilt. He needed to be there for her. It took every ounce of courage to speak. "We came into the barn after a ride. The old man was beating your mother." He reached out and gently touched her cheek. "You were so brave even then, always thinking about others. You ran over to protect your mother and started hitting him. He turned and would have killed you, but I pushed you down."

"And then?" she whispered.

He shook his head, walked away and paced the room. He couldn't look at her, feared the accusation he'd find in her eyes when she knew.

"Michael, please."

"I grabbed the piece of wood he used as a battering ram and began hitting him with it. He kept backing up and must have tripped over something, because the next thing I knew, he was on the floor of the barn and I was kicking him. You were crying, but I couldn't stop. Somehow he got hold of a currying brush and sat up and whipped it across my face." Without meaning to, he reached for the scar on his cheek.

"What then?"

"I knocked the brush out of his hand and picked up a pitch fork that was leaning against the barn wall and jabbed it into his belly as hard as I could. He fell back and lay there next to your mother. Neither of them moved."

He sat down on the sofa, leaned over and put his head in his hands.

"He killed my mother." She whispered.

"And I killed my father."

"You saved my life."

He shook his head. "At the moment, I was only thinking about myself and all the beatings I'd taken from him."

Her fingers combed through his hair. "No. You acted in self-defense. You're not responsible for what happened, not morally and not criminally. You, of all people, should know that."

He looked at her. Tears brimmed in her eyes. "I'm sorry about your mother."

"I know you are, but my ignorance kept me safe and protected from everything that happened that day. You've had to live with the memories your whole life." She touched his cheek and drew a finger down the ragged scar. He put his hand over hers then took it and kissed it. "We're a pair, aren't we?" He almost smiled.

She snuggled next to him, resting her head against his bare chest. His arm went around her, and he held her tight. There was a long silence.

"What happened next? What did we do?"

He took a deep breath and pulled her closer to him. "I picked you up and ran into the house. You were crying on my shoulder while I dialed nine-one-one. After a few minutes, you stopped crying. I put you down. I'll never forget the look in your eyes, like a little puppy trying to understand it all." He kissed her cheek. "I knew I couldn't stay there. The police would never have believed my story, and you were too little for them to take anything you said seriously. I went into my room and threw some clothes and things into a duffle bag. I grabbed some money I'd been saving for my eventual escape. You asked what I was doing. I knelt down in front of you and explained the police were coming, and I had to leave. You were to stay there and wait for them. They would take care of you. You started crying again." He choked back a sob. "It broke my heart. While I hugged you and said good-bye, the sirens came closer. I left out the back."

"Is that how I ended up in the orphanage?"

"I guess so. I don't know. I took the first bus out of town and headed for New York City. I had to get as far away as I could. All these years I've never gone back to the farm. I never found out what happened to you or our parents. For all I knew, they weren't dead, but it didn't matter. In my mind, they were."

He looked into her upturned face, the tears still falling down her cheeks. "I want you to know not a day's gone by I didn't wonder, didn't feel guilty for leaving you, prayed you were safe and with a good family. I'm sorry, sweetheart, so sorry for everything."

She reached up and gave him a long, tender kiss. Finally she pulled away. "There's nothing to forgive. You were a child. There was nothing you could have done to help me, even if you'd stayed."

He saw strength and determination in her eyes.

"I want you to hear what I'm going to say, Michael, and believe it. You and I were innocent children caught up in a horrible reality not our own making. I'm still emotionally detached from the story you've just told, but in time, all the feelings will surface. I want you to be there when they do, so I can feel safe like I did back then when I was with you. That was what I remembered the moment I saw you in court the first time, that sense of peace and serenity. Now I understand why."

Her hand reached out and touched his cheek. "I know I loved being with you as a child. I felt safe and happy then and nothing that's happened that day can ever take that away. Nothing you've done as a man has ever once made me distrust you, or question your commitment to yourself, your clients or me. Or doubt your integrity, or your love for me, even before you spoke it. I love you very much, Michael."

She reached up and put her arms around his neck. "I have a lot of work to do on myself." Her quiet voice muffled against his neck. "A lot of healing. We both do. I want to do it with you. I want us to share the rest of our lives together as we shared that short time in the beginning."

He broke, his defenses tumbling down like an avalanche of snow melted by the warm rays of the sun. He held her tightly. He was too overcome by emotion to speak so he let his hand silently caress her hair. He buried his face against her neck. She stayed snuggled against him for a long time, tears flowing freely against his cheek.

*   *   *

It was late evening by the time Hatch obtained the warrant and arrived at the Griswold place with Blake and two other officers in tow. He rang the bell. No answer. Rang again with the same response. Then suddenly he heard a gunshot from inside the house. His heart rate shot up. He pulled his weapon and braced to kick open the door. With one powerful kick, the door swung open. He and the others raced into the house.

"You two," he pointed to the officers, "check upstairs." He and Blake moved into each room on the ground floor, their guns in front of them, seeking the source of the shot. When they reached the study, they breathed in the smell of burned cordite. Hatch entered first, then Blake, their guns swinging from side to side.

The only light in the room, a small desk lamp, drew their attention. It was then they saw him.

Judge Julius Griswold's head lay face down in the middle of his desk, resting in a pool of blood. Hatch walked over to him and stared. A small caliber handgun lay on the floor. Blake stood next to him.

"Looks like the little coward couldn't face up to standing trial. Probably for the best. Saves the kid the trauma of dealing with all that legal bullshit." Hatch sighed. "Call it in."

* * *

Michael sat in a lounge chair on his patio, his legs outstretched, looking out over the ocean. Somewhere in the east the sun had just risen up over the horizon. There in the west, fingers of red and yellow light seemed to reach up from the Pacific and dilute the black of night into the gray of dawn. A cool breeze blew off the ocean. Although he wore only pajama bottoms, he wasn't cold. He was impervious to his external body. Instead, he was deeply aware of a vast emptiness inside.

It wasn't the desperate emptiness he was so familiar with but a boundless, infinite serenity. Sometime over the last two days and nights with Sara, all the ghosts and demons which haunted much of his life had disappeared. They exploded into oblivion by the joining of the two ends of the circle of his life, the past and the present. The resulting fallout left him blanketed by a deep intimacy, the powerful emptiness of nothing.

Thinking clearly for the first time in many years, he knew now he had the power to have the remainder of his life be about what he wanted it to be, filled with what he put in it, not garbage from the past. He knew his future would include Sara.

She lay asleep in his bed and thinking of her there warmed him enough to ward off any chill the morning breeze sent his way.

He got up and walked into the apartment toward the front door, planning what he would do with this, the beginning of his new life. The Griswold case was closed. Warren Dills was back with his family. Maybe he and Sara might take a vacation, go somewhere they could relax. They needed time together.

He unlocked the door, opened it and reached down to grab the morning edition of the *LA Times*. Once inside, he locked the door again, went into the kitchen and poured himself a glass of orange juice. As he took a drink, he absentmindedly glanced at the headlines.

He stopped drinking and stared at the glaring black letters that leaped off the page.

JUDGE COMMITS SUICIDE

Judge Julius Griswold's body was discovered late last night by LAPD detectives. He was slumped over his desk, a gun on the floor, a bullet hole in his temple. While there was no suicide note, the medical examiner, Doctor Yee, stated suicide was definitely the cause of death. It was then learned the Los Angeles District Attorney's office had been planning on bringing double murder charges against the judge for the murder of his wife and a LA Times Reporter. Apparently the judge chose not to face the shame and embarrassment of a public scandal and murder trial and took his own life instead.

The article went on describing the gruesome details of the deaths of Mrs. Griswold and Dana Ingrahm.

Michael put the paper down and strolled to the bedroom. For some strange reason, an old saying he'd first heard in law school suddenly popped into his head. What goes around comes around. It was a fitting period to the long paragraph his life had been. He climbed into bed beside the sleeping Sara, pulling her close, feeling her snuggle against him. He relaxed into a deep peace, knowing with every fiber of his being, things happened for a reason. The past, as horrific as it'd been for both of them, was now complete. The future now lay in his and Sara's hands and whatever choices they make, they'd make them together.

*   *   *

The sound of cascading water pulled Sara from a deep sleep. As consciousness returned, she realized what it was. Her arm reached over to find Michael, but he wasn't there. She touched the sheets still warm from his body and their lovemaking.

She closed her eyes and inhaled a deep, satisfying breath. She felt light, relaxed, sated. The whirlwind of the last few days was gone and with it the anger, frustration and confusion which consumed her. In its wake was only peace, peace which came from finally knowing who she was and what'd been the defining moments of her young life. Also the amazing miracle of finding Michael again, the boy of her past, the man of her present and future. Yes, they would have a future together, and this time they'd decide what would fill it. She smiled.

Slowly she pushed back the covers, stepping over her clothing strewn around the bedroom floor. The air gently caressed her naked body when she walked into the bathroom. Hot steam floated around her. She approached the shower and slid open the door just enough to step inside.

Michael turned, a surprised look on his face. At once he reached out and took her hand, drawing her to him. She slid the door closed and went into his arms

THE END

Welcome Readers!

I was eleven years old when I wrote my first little story. It was about a fish that was separated from its family. Who knows, it might have been the precursor to FINDING NEMO.

Since then, between raising three children, attending college at night and working full time, I managed to write several short stories. When I finished earning my MA in Counseling Psychology, I set to writing my first full-length novel over twenty years ago. It is entitled BOILING POINT and is finally in print. Five other novels have followed.

Over time, and with much support from writers and friends, I'm honing my craft. But most importantly, I have become comfortable with my style of writing. My love for writing and creating stories and characters that portray the same human emotions as the rest of us is very satisfying and mostly fun.

I would appreciate your feedback.

Thanks for your interest in my work!

51658353R00214

Made in the USA
Charleston, SC
29 January 2016